BRITSTOPIA

John Kinderton

JOHN KINDERTON

Copyright © 2020 John Kinderton
All rights reserved

The characters and events portrayed in this book are fictitious. Any similarity to real persons, living or dead, is coincidental and not intended by the author.

No part of this book may be reproduced, or stored in a retrieval system, or transmitted in any form or by any means, electronic, mechanical, photocopying, recording, or otherwise, without express written permission of the publisher. The moral rights of the author have been asserted.

ISBN: 979-8-6380-9140-8

Cover design by: Sick Puppy Design

Instagram/britstopia

BOOK 1
Bless This House

"It is very, very easy not to be offended by a book. You just have to shut it."

Salman Rushdie

1. I DON'T LIKE MONDAYS

"Shut it!" said Purity, shaking her phone over the card reader furiously. The barista had a smile like a coffee cup - plastic and empty.

"Sorry," he shrugged, somehow managing to combine sarcasm and disinterest in equal spoonfuls. "I only work here."

Purity St. George blinked at the contactless terminal, puzzled. There should be more than enough money on her student account for a Strawberry Latte and Espresso Grande, but there it was in black and white. Or African American and Caucasian. Or vegan and carnivore. Gay and straight.

PAYMENT DECLINED

The spiky pink-haired barista waved the

payment machine under Purity's nose like a hi-tech wand magically making money vanish from customers' accounts. He was typical *KostlyKoffee* staff - slack jawed, baby faced and dead behind the eyes.

Robotically, he asked, "Again?"

Again, Purity held her phone over the device.

Again, the warning buzzer buzzed.

Spiky the Barista slotted the reader back in its holder and located a well-worn, faded card pinned to the till. Reading aloud, he said, "Thank you for choosing Kostly. If you'd like to come through to the office, I can put you in touch with one of our legal representatives who have a range of repayment options available at very competitive interest rates. Together, we can find one that's right for your circumstance and budget."

Purity patted her coat pockets for money, though when was the last time anyone used cash?

"No, that, that won't be necessary. I..."

At the far end of the counter by the glass fronted pastry display emblazoned with HOT BUNS, a raised voice was attracting attention. A blonde girl in a long white trench coat gestured and shouted at staff animatedly, while customers sitting nearby showed their concern by pretending it wasn't happening. Seeing his colleagues in distress, Spiky turned his back on

Purity and moved down the counter towards the source of trouble.

Purity glanced around the coffeeshop - all eyes, and ears were on trenchcoat girl. Quietly, she scooped up the two drinks and edged backwards out of the café. Turning left onto the main road, market traders were setting up their stalls for the day; home grown fruit and veg, and cheap, tacky royal memorabilia seemed to be in big demand. Dodging the cracks in the pavement, she reached the next building where a scruffy figure sat huddled in the doorway of a boarded-up *Kim Jong Blend*.

Unlike the beans themselves, it seemed two coffee shops so close to one another were not sustainable.

The vagrant was wrapped in a combination of blankets and twines of body hair and didn't look up as Purity approached. He was known commonly as Toothless Tom, though his teeth appeared fine and his real name almost certainly wasn't Tom; most days he could be found here, and most days Purity would get him a drink. She sat down on the cold, concrete step beside him and held out the cardboard cup, waiting for the aroma to worm its way through his thick layers. The mass of hair raised up slightly, suspicious eyes relaxing.

"Expresso, two sweeteners," he coughed through a grateful smile. The cough was thick and wet and shook his large frame. He took the cup from her and sipped noisily.

They didn't speak, they rarely did, but sat together watching the hustle and bustle of the world go by - practising the 'art of being invisible', as Tom called it. Eco friendly double decker buses and black electric taxis gridlocked New Islington High Street while white vans sounded their horns angrily. Workers hustled to work, shoppers bustled to shops, all of them ignoring the pair.

And above everyone, the Monoliths.

In a bold move, the government had finally taken charge of the housing crisis. There was no more land left in London to build out, so instead they built up. 300 storeys of cheap, affordable housing - cutting edge tower blocks with their own shops and communal areas. Vertical towns within cities.

Purity squinted in the morning sun at the two hulking superstructures dominating the horizon, a third under construction. The high-tech, high-rise solution to the housing crisis. Modern, minimalist apartments with views to die for.

One day she would be living there, she had promised herself.

One day.

More shouting from the coffee shop caught her attention. The argument continued inside but now sounded desperate, more urgent.

It was definitely escalating.

At least I got two free coffees out of it, she thought.

Purity took a swig of the chemically enhanced synthetic fruit-flavoured beverage.

"Aren't you late for school?" asked Tom.

The windows of KostlyKoffee exploded outwards in a fireball of hot glass, consuming pedestrians and cyclists alike. Caught directly in the blast, a double decker bus lurched wildly across the lanes, ploughing headlong into a row of parked cars. Choking, black smoke poured from the gaping storefront and rolled into the sky in a dense, angry plume; panicking pigeons providing a chaotic escort. Strewn across the pavement, molten plastic chairs and burning tables were scattered in a sea of burning lids and cups while a flaming confetti of napkins drifted in the air. A shower of roasted apples rained down, bouncing noisily off scorched vehicle roofs and bonnets and as the blast echoed away, the roar was replaced by a mosaic of screams and car alarms. On both sides of the road, the people still standing were frozen in shock, hypnotised.

Purity stepped over smashed salt shakers, smouldering menus and half a poster suggesting she TRY OUR FIERY CHILI LATTES - THEY'RE HOT STUFF! A tiny shape limped mechanically through the debris - windup toy Queen, her crown smoking and sparking.

"...Not amused! We are not amused! We

are..." it crackled, and fell onto its side, melting plastic legs twitching.

Purity peered through the smoke into the charred, blistering shell of a shop; other than the flickering, dancing flames nothing moved inside. The fumes had a sweet, chocolatey bitterness and she quickly covered her nose, the feel-good aroma of coffee now wholly inappropriate. It was dark inside, but beyond the twisted metal and shredded, warped seating, the epicentre of the blast was quite obvious, even to Purity.

HOT BUNS.

A lock of pink hair caught her eye and she turned away quickly, stifling the gag in her throat. She didn't want to think about the fleshy clump the hair was still attached to.

Above the noise of alarms and approaching sirens, a familiar bell rang out across the playing field behind the coffee shop and Purity suddenly remembered Tom's question.

Aren't you late for school?

"I am now," she whispered.

2. BAGGY TROUSERS

"It's a poster," shrugged Purity. The headmaster's room was small and cramped and smelled of despair and crushed dreams. Shelves overflowed with yellowing papers, folders and books piled upon books. Tattered cardboard boxes with handwritten labels sat on the threadbare carpet worn from the dragging feet of thousands of weary students. A towering papier mache model of the Queen lurked by the door, it's lumpy, badly painted features watching over proceedings silently. A wheezing, strained whirr escaped from the ageing laptop on the desk, the tiny sound expanding to fill the heavy silence.

Today's gripping subject of conversation - a piece of paper - lay face up on the antique oak desk inhabiting the no man's land between teacher and student. Purity suspected there would be no ceasing of hostilities or festive truce here today.

"I know it's a poster," sighed Headmaster Grimsdale. "What can you tell me about it?"

The poster was a sheet of A4 paper and torn at the edges - the main feature a map of the British Isles with a garish multicoloured rainbow running through it. Across the bottom of the page ran the headline:

LGBTTQQIAAP LIVES MATTER

"I can tell you the kids in Product Design need to work harder. Or they need a better teacher."

"Very droll, Purity."

Mr Grimsdale planted a finger firmly on the headline, or rather the red marker scrawl that had amended it.

"This. What can you tell me about this?"

In thick red pen, LGBTTQQIAAP was struck out, replaced by another word in loose red capitals.

ALL LIVES MATTER.

"Maybe someone disagreed with the message," she said.

He opened his laptop lid, the fan inside suddenly rising in pitch and volume as a jet of warm air poured from its vents.

"Maybe someone disagreed with the message," he repeated wearily under his breath.

Gripping the machine with both hands, he rotated it to face Purity.

On the screen in blurred, washed out colours was a view of the main hallway - banks of bashed, rusting lockers separated by painted concrete pillars. Students clutching bags and books passed to and fro, pushing, shoving, and there, dead centre, sat the poster in sharp relief. As they watched, the mass of schoolchildren thinned out until soon the corridor was empty.

Purity slumped in her chair; she knew what was coming.

A figure appeared in the corner of the screen and walked decisively towards the poster - a female figure with a pierced nose, dyed blonde hair and braids, wearing a tartan jumpsuit and carrying a SuperWet bag. She raised a hand clutching what looked like a marker pen. Mr Grimsdale clicked the PAUSE icon and the scene froze.

"Still know nothing about this?" he asked.

"Could be anyone," she shrugged.

He squinted at the girl in the video then back at the girl sat opposite him. The girl sat opposite in her tartan jumpsuit, SuperWet bag, diamante nose piercing and dyed blonde hair tumbling over her shoulders in tight, culturally appropriated braids.

"Well, not anyone," he said.

Purity held her hands up. "Okay, you got

me. It's a fair cop."

Mr Grimsdale turned the laptop back around and closed the video window.

"Why Purity? Why do you do it? I can't understand it. I've met your parents they're good people, work hard. You're one of the better off families in the school."

Purity stared at the scratches on her side of the oak desk - years of fingernail chiselled erosion from nervous school children sat in this very chair.

"I already told you. I disagreed with the message."

The headteacher frowned, studying the poster, rainbow bands of colour smudging beneath his fingers.

"I don't understand. What is there to disagree with? It's a simple message of inclusivity."

"Inclusivity," repeated Purity.

"It's inclusive. It means everyone's equal."

"They're not though are they?"

"What do you mean?"

"Well... LGBTTQQIAAP. I don't even know what half of these mean but I'm pretty sure I'm not on there, that's not very inclusive is it? What about me? Their lives matter, so mine doesn't?"

Purity crossed her arms. "If anything, I made your stupid poster even more inclusive."

Sighing, the teacher put his hands behind his head and leaned back in the chair, the springs squealing under his weight. He could still remember a time when he came to school to actually be a teacher - not a therapist, bureaucrat, law enforcer or moral philosopher.

"I think you're viewing this through spectacles of norm privilege. Your view seems rather... myopic."

"Myopic?"

He rubbed his eyes, it had already been a particularly long day and it wasn't even 10am.

"Short sighted," he clarified.

"I'm not a complete bungle, I know what it means. You think it's myopic to treat everyone as individuals?"

"I think you're willfully choosing to miss the point, Purity."

She held up her hands, "What can I say? My dad taught me to question everything."

"And that's all well and good, but some things don't need questioning - like gravity or the speed of light."

You can tell he used to be a science teacher, she thought.

"Or just good old-fashioned treating people with respect," he added, holding up the poster. "It's about equality, Purity."

She wrinkled her nose, "Then I guess some people are just more equal than others."

"Now you know you're not allowed to say things like that."

Mr Grimsdale turned to his laptop and eyed it warily.

Man vs machine.

He typed slowly, methodically with his index finger as the fan inside the computer span up louder under the strain of existence.

"Now, the damage to school property carries an..."

"School property? It's a sheet of paper!"

"The damage to school property," he repeated slowly, "carries an automatic penalty of three demerits and a full day exclusion. Now, I'm willing to reduce that to half a day, because deep down you're a good kid, you just need a little... focus. Nothing wrong with questioning things, but sometimes you need to ask yourself why you're doing it."

Purity stared at the desk waiting for it to be over while the headmaster tapped the cursor key noisily.

"Your lateness this morning adds another demerit."

"Lateness?" erupted Purity. "A sodding bomb went off! I was caught in a terrorist incident!"

He dismissed her complaints with a flick of his wrist. "All part of living in the City, I'm afraid. It's no excuse."

He finished typing and hit ENTER triumphantly, as if winning his own personal battle.

Man: One. Machine: Nil.

"The other thing, however, I can't be so lenient on."

Purity raised an eyebrow. "Other thing?"

"Defacing the poster is one thing. The nature of the defacement, well... that's hate speech."

A spontaneous laugh escaped Purity's lips. "Hate speech? I wrote three letters on a poster, Mr Grimsdale."

"Three letters. Three words. Three paragraphs. It's all the same - you were actively posting negative or threatening comments against a minority in a manner designed to disrupt or cause offence. I am bound by law, I'm afraid, to report this to the Ministry of Inclusion."

Purity sat open mouthed.

"Your parents will be informed shortly. You should tell them to expect a visit from the authorities."

He placed his hand on the laptop lid, the tiny fan inside powering down, exhausted.

Literally exhausted.

Neville Grimsdale leaned forward on his squeaky chair, his face level with Purity's. This close she could see the veins in his nose and the whites of his eyes - not so much white, more a sickly yellow. He smelled of popcorn and smoke.

"Every action has an equal and opposite reaction - that's just nature," said Grimsdale the science teacher. "You commit a crime, you pay a price - that's just society. Nature, society...

they're not so different. It's all elements working together to coexist, to benefit each other. And if something comes along to disrupt that system?"

He slammed the laptop lid closed sharply.

"The system stamps it out. Now report straight to Mr Bronson on the first floor - half day exclusion starting now."

In the corridor outside the Headmaster's office, Purity hovered in a daze, not entirely sure what had just happened. She unlocked her phone and touched a small purple app with a stylised hand drawn letter *F*.

For anyone and everyone using social media, the *feed* was essential. Regardless of the platform, Facebook, Twitter, StalkR, Tinder... *all* social media converged in the feed. One place to post, one place to read. All media in one easy to use, instant, convenient place.

Her thumbs danced across the glass, typing rapidly. She still couldn't believe what she had just sat through, and if she had stopped to think about it, might struggle to put it into words.

But she didn't stop to think about and didn't struggle to put it into words.

Over the photo of her *adjusted* poster she posted #MOREEQUALTHANOTHERS #WORLDSGONEMAD #HATESPEECH?

And pressed SEND.

A tiny 'swoosh' indicated it had gone and she returned the phone to her pocket.

Opposite the door, a small red box with a glass front was affixed to the wall

IN CASE OF FIRE BREAK GLASS.

Upstairs Mr Bronson would be waiting, sat in his dreary room with his dreary face, promising a long and dreary day ahead. Purity glared defiantly at the security camera, sticking her tongue out and silently raising two fingers.

"Bollocks to that," she said.

And smashed the glass.

3. THIS CHARMING MAN

"It was the will of the land! It was the will of the people!" Prime Minister Terrence August smashed his fist against the hastily erected dais in emphasis and the gathered crowd clapped and cheered enthusiastically. The charred and blackened shell of KostlyKoffee still smouldered in the light drizzle but had been cordoned off for the Prime Minister to make an impromptu tour of the area, laying flowers, projecting concern and sharing his outrage. A makeshift platform had been constructed in front of the burnt-out store and now with the nation's phone and news cameras on him, August's spontaneous, carefully rehearsed speech was winning over hearts and minds. The grey man in the grey suit held his head up proudly and basked in the waves of applause washing over him.

Nearly 17 years ago, British party politics had buckled and strained under the controversial and divisive decision to leave Europa, or Europe as it was then known. The governing party pushed an ideal they never believed in, onto a people who believed in *them* even less, while the opposition put up a noisy fight, nipping at their heels like a puppy itching for a scrap.

Then came the virus.

Starting on the other side of the world, it was easy to ignore over the noise of political rhetoric - a far away problem for the far east to worry about. Then fell the middle east and asia - the disease, spreading west at the speed of air travel. Only when the first cases were reported in Europa did the government finally take notice. By then, of course, it was too late. Euvid-21 invaded the shores of Britannica, a silent, stealthy invasion taking the lives of the young and old with callous impunity. Trapped in a spiral of indecision and paralysis, the old guard withered and died, and a new party rose from its ashes.

A party promising action.

A party promising swift and decisive change.

A party that would fulfil the will of the people.

The Puritan Party.

They wasted no time, their first act to pour concrete into the Channel Tunnel and begin construction on the EuroWall - a 30-foot-high barrier stretching from Margate to Hastings. Funding to the health service quadrupled, with an extensive network of treatment facilities for victims of the disease. Immigration ceased immediately, going from 627 thousand to almost zero in the first weekend. Six months later, all non-registered immigrants had been deported. Six months after that, most non-UK nationals and their families had been 'incentivised' to leave, those that remained retreating to pockets of isolated communities. The countries of Cambria and Caledonia retreated, safe behind hard borders of their own. Re-joining Europa, Ireland was annexed completely becoming the independent nation Hibernia. Within a year, Britain, now known as Britannica, had closed its borders to the world literally and metaphorically, its splendid isolation complete.

But still some people weren't happy.

"Yesterday saw another atrocity," continued August, his voice sombre and measured. "Another cowardly bombing by these evildoers. Fine, upstanding citizens going about their daily business, planning their day, planning their lives. Murdered by a lone suicide bomber."

On a temporary screen behind him, time coded CCTV footage showed the woman in the white coat gesturing and arguing against a backdrop of pastries. Suddenly, clear over the hiss of the audio, she yelled, "In the name of the Father!"

The screen flashed white, a saturated blur that turned to static.

"These terrorists," he spat, his anger rising, "These so-called Christian Extremists. They hate us. They hate that we can just walk into a high street coffee shop and buy a Triple Choc Chopped Nut Latte. They hate our decaffeinated beverages. They hate our freedoms. They aim to bring harm to us and our own. They aim to change this country. To change who we are!"

August nodded at the rain-washed crowd and they nodded back in agreement. He took a step back, letting the message, and the rain, soak in. "I must stress, of course, these are the actions of the fringe - extremists twisting the words of their religion to support their twisted ideologies. The vast majority of Christians, of course, are decent law-abiding people, and I will be working with religious leaders and Archbishop Runcible to stamp out these pockets of hatred springing up in our communities."

He gripped both sides of the podium tightly, voice rising.

"Let me be clear. We will find the perpetrators of these despicable deeds. We will find them and bring them to justice. They will pay for their crimes."

Applause rippled through the gathering.

"They will pay for their crimes, live, in front of the nation, in front of you, the people. On Purity Day!"

On their first day in power, a new national holiday was created: Purity Day. An annual celebration every March 29th on the streets of each major town and city; a street party to end all street parties culminating in a parade and concert outside Buckingham Palace.

"This year's celebrations are set to be the biggest ever," he continued, "And we have so much to celebrate. We are on the verge of fulfilling our three core promises.

He ran a hand through his thinning grey hair.

"We have tackled the problem of rough sleeping, head on. No more beggars in doorways. No more shanty towns, no more box cities under bridges. We have rescued the homeless from the streets, taken them in. We have given them direction. We have given them purpose. We have given them hope."

The audience clapped politely.

"We have tackled the housing crisis, head on. After decades of failed programs and broken promises of previous governments, we have fixed our country's housing problems. With the completion of the third Monolith, we will not only have reached the target for cheap, affordable housing, but will have set the template for all our major cities. And I can tell you now, already plans for a fourth Monolith are underway! No longer will the good, honest working people of this great nation struggle for a home. The future of housing for us, our children and our grandchildren, is secure."

The crowd cheered, the applause lifting.

"And we have tackled this country's economic growth, head on. We make a promise not only of economic recovery, but of economic growth. We have already made great strides with our Russia and North Korea agreements but now put forward an ambitious program of trade deals with some of the greatest nations on the planet. We have fought hard and fought well, and if I promise you one thing, I promise you this. These deals will be the biggest, most far reaching trade deals ever seen here, or anywhere in the world!"

Cameras flashed and more cheering broke out.

"Britannica will flourish, Britannica will grow. Britannica will be the greatest nation on this planet!"

The crowd roared in applause and August stepped back from the plinth, arms raised - a thoroughly choreographed pose for the cameras. He nodded and waved for a moment before stepping down from the platform, vanishing behind the security barriers. As an aide draped his grey raincoat over his shoulders, his personal adviser was waiting for him, tapping on a large tablet device.

"That went well, don't you think?" he asked.

Hattie Simms had worked as the Prime Minister's assistant for less than a year, but she was already the longest serving assistant he'd ever had. Very early on she had abandoned any attempt at managing August, and instead resigned herself to the job of firefighter, navigating him from one fiery outburst to the next. Short and heavy set, she wore a black jacket and skirt and had her dyed blonde hair pinned back tightly. Live statistics in the form of colourful charts and graphs filled her tablet display.

"You're trending positive on the feeds, it was very well received," she said, swiping through pages of data. "You missed out the Health Camp piece though and did go a bit off piste on terrorism."

Off piste? He raised an eyebrow.

Hattie hastily clarified, "Suggesting we will have the terrorists caught by Purity Day?"

"Oh that," he shrugged. "What can I say… I got caught up in the moment. Anyway, we'll have caught *someone* by then. They don't need to know the fine details, do they?"

August walked back towards his waiting vehicle, Hattie picking up the pace alongside him.

"Chatter around the Monoliths isn't

trending as high as we'd hoped," she said. "There was a peak during the speech, but it was short lived, mostly flatlined now."

"Flatlined?"

"People are emotional beings, Mr. Prime Minister. They can't get excited by bricks and mortar, no matter how high we pile them. We need to connect with them, make it more... personal."

"Personal?"

"I don't know… run a competition on the feed or something," said Hattie, "Name that Monolith."

August mulled it over. Hattie knew it was impossible to predict his reaction and had long given up trying.

"Name that Monolith," he said. "Yes, I like it. Like John, Paul, George and… the other one."

"Or 'the Four Freedoms'."

"Whatever, I like it. And we can reveal the names on opening day. I've got a great feeling about this, it's going to be the biggest Purity Day ever!"

Just as they reached the government limousine a shrill voice caught their attention.

"Mr August! Mr Prime Minister!"

A woman pushed through the staff wielding a microphone like a dagger, while a young man in a beret trailed behind balancing a professional minicam on his shoulder.

"Roberta Preston, PBC News 24," she said,

thrusting the mic under August's nose. Preston was the political commentator for the PBC and was pale and skinny with greasy, slicked back hair and thick black rimmed spectacles.

"Roberta," he said, a well-practised smile masking his complete and utter surprise at this sudden intrusion - this was supposed to be a secure area. "How delightfully unexpected."

"That was a fine speech, Mr Prime Minister," she drawled.

"Why thank you, I..."

"But a bit thin on the detail. Can you clarify to our viewers *how* exactly you have tackled the homeless problem?"

"Miss Preston, I'd ask you to show some respect. Look around you - people have died here, this is not the time or the place for a discussion on government policy."

"Yet you somehow managed to fit in quite a lengthy, some might say *self-congratulatory* speech?"

August glared at her, his mask now having to conceal contempt and bubbling anger. Roberta knew she had riled him and pushed harder.

"The homeless, Mr Prime Minister?"

August cleared his throat. "As I said, this government is committed to reducing the number of rough sleepers and has put in place a number of extensive and far reaching initiatives which will benefit both those unfortunate enough to have found themselves in that situation, and society itself."

"Yes, but how do the initiatives actually work?"

"These initiatives go further than any government before us and promise a radical shake up of the homeless problem. For the first time, being homeless does not mean being written off, being thrown on the scrap heap. We are giving the people a chance to be part of society, to give back. We are giving them hope."

The reporter sighed. "Mr Prime Minister, you've not answered my question now in three different ways. Don't you think you owe it to the people who voted you in, who put you in power? Your people..."

August placed his hand over the microphone and moved his lips close to her ear. When he spoke it was softly, firmly, almost a whisper.

"The people?" he hissed. "Fuck the people. Stop playing games, Roberta, we both know I don't give a shit about them."

His breath was hot and uncomfortable on her cheek. "You don't get it, do you? I could commit murder on the steps of Buckingham Palace, and still be in power tomorrow. I really could."

August released his grip on the mic and stepped back, straightening his amber tie, the only flash of colour on the man.

"The press already enjoy a great many freedoms," he said. "I suggest breaking and entering isn't one of them. How *did* you get back here anyway?"

Hattie had seen enough. She moved between them, separating both parties and August climbed onto the back seat of the car. Hattie opened the passenger door and sat next to him. The driver secured the locks and the vehicle pulled away. Through tinted glass, August watched storm clouds gathering overhead. "I won't be ambushed by the press. Call the Director General of the PBC, Miss Simms. I want Preston and her camera monkey out of a job by the morning."

He turned to Hattie.

"If she's so fascinated by the homeless, she can bloody well experience it first-hand."

4. THE SAFETY DANCE

"Brian?"

"Brenda," said Brian. "It's Brenda now."

Balancing a hot mug in his hand, Joseph St. George closed the office door gently behind him with his elbow and double checked the etched lettering on the frosted pane.

> BRENDA RUMBOLD
> OFFICE MANAGER

"Yeah, I saw the sign," he said, pointing at the door. "Thought I had the wrong room."

The modern corner office was decorated in whites and chromes with a plush, grey carpet and grey filing cabinets. Known not-so-affectionately as *the fishbowl,* it featured two large glass walls that overlooked the call centre.

Brenda, in a purple jacket and white blouse sat behind a large, glass desk arranging documents into a neat line. Joe sat down, placing his mug on the glass surface. Brenda wrinkled their nose.

"Not a fan of tea?" asked Joe.

They rotated the mug with their immaculate neon red acrylic nails - on one side was a round cartoon bomb, on the other a DangerMole logo. "You know you really can't have stuff like this on public display."

The Animal Equality Act banned all speech and imagery that could be seen to cause offence or promote feelings of inadequacy to citizens of the animal kingdom, and cartoons of talking cats, dogs or vermin fell victim to the ban first.

The animals of Britannica were not to feel ashamed just because they didn't speak the language.

Joe ignored them, instead focusing on Brenda's beard.

"You're a woman?" he asked. "Because if you are, you might want to think about trimming that goatee down a bit."

Brenda's face hardened.

"I'm genderfluid, non-binary," they said firmly. "I'm going to be working Mondays, Wednesdays and Fridays as Brenda, the rest of the time as Brian."

Joseph nodded awkwardly. Gender who? Non-what?

He glanced at the papers on the desk but instead caught sight of Brenda's grey pencil skirt through the glass of the desk. Before he could stop himself, his mouth was moving and he heard himself ask, "So, which restroom are you using?"

"The Ladies, obviously."

"And how do the *full-time* women feel about that?"

Brenda bristled at his provocative use of 'full time' in his sentence but continued nonetheless. "Well there was some concern when the urinal was installed, but on the whole they're fine."

Joseph sipped a mouthful of tea. "Wow... you really are having your cake and eating it."

"I don't find that particularly funny."

"You used to have a sense of humour."

"My sense of humour is fine, but some things just aren't funny: cancer in children, terrorist bombings..."

"Brian, seriously... you're not telling me wearing a dress to work is comparable to dying children?"

Brenda lowered their voice. "Look, it's not been easy for me, you know," they confided. "Obviously I've had to take a pay cut for the hours I work as a woman doing the same job - it's only fair. On the plus side though, I've been nominated as one of the top 50 up-and-coming women in I.T."

"Because being on the list of top 50 men in I.T. wasn't enough?" frowned Joseph, "...and up-and-coming? You're 45!"

"Not any more, I've decided to identify as a 19 year old," they said, brushing strands of jet black hair over their ear. "I can see you're not going to take this seriously, but I didn't ask you here to talk about me."

Joe settled back into his chair. Or tried to - it had a glass back and hadn't been designed with comfort in mind.

"Yeah, about that. Why am I here?"

"It's about your daughter"

He sat upright - this was the last thing he expected.

"Purity? What about her?"

"She's well? Doing okay at school?" Brenda asked.

"She's a teenage girl, what can I say? What's this about?"

Brenda moved the papers around on the desk, scanning them as they talked.

"There's been some... chatter... on the feeds. Quite high profile. It appears she's been promoting... inequality"

High profile? Thought Joseph. *Inequality?*

"And as you know this company fosters a culture of equality and inclusiveness - it's one of our core values. So, you have to understand when one of our employees takes to social media in such an inflammatory way, it reflects badly on us."

"Your employees?" shouted Joseph. "It was my daughter!"

"You. Your family. It's all the same."

"It's not even remotely the same."

"The point is, it's out there. The hate speech is out there. We, as a company, need to limit our liability and control the damage... you know we have a reputation score to maintain. And after these posts the companies score dropped ten points this morning alone. You can see why people upstairs might be getting a little bit... antsy."

Antsy? Is that even a word?

Brenda opened the manila folder and held up a coloured slip.

"Look, I was hoping it wouldn't come to this, Joseph. I'm sorry, I really am."

The red docket. Instant termination of employment, pension dissolved, social status revoked. With a red docket against his name he would become unemployable. A pariah.

Joseph had never felt his blood run cold before, he thought it a stupid phrase. But right there, right then, he got it. He ran his hand through his hair and scratched his neck nervously.

"Brian, please... we've known each other for years. I was the Best Man at your wedding!"

"Person"

"What?"

"Person. You were my Best Person."

Joseph held his head in both hands, rocking. This was all too much.

"I was at Nell's christening," he whimpered.

"Neil... he identifies as a boy now."

Joe slowly lifted his head, open mouthed. "Identifies as a boy? She's four years old, for Christ's sake!"

Ignoring him, Brenda continued. "And it wasn't a Christening, it was a non-denominational blessing. Please don't try and link me with those fundamentalists."

"This is ridiculous!"

"So, I'm ridiculous now too?"

"What? No. This.... THIS... is ridiculous!"

"All you've done since you sat down is hurl sexist, sacrilegious, homophobic hate speech at me. I can see where Purity gets it from."

"Purity?"

"Poor thing, raised in such a bigoted, closed minded environment... she never had a chance. I almost feel sorry for her. Almost. The apple never falls far from the tree, and all that."

Joseph snatched the red paper from Brenda's grasp, knocking the mug over. Hot, insipid tea splashed across the desk and onto their blouse.

They howled in pain, "Motherfucker!"

He shook the docket in Brenda's face. "I'm not having this; do you hear me?"

"You're mad," they groaned, doubled over.

"I'm. Not. Having. This," he yelled.

He staggered backwards kicking the chair away and the glass back struck the corner of a cabinet, shattering instantly in a crystalline shower. The crash startled him and he suddenly focused. The chair lay on its side, surrounded by glass shards and a large puddle of tea covered the desk leaving a sickly, minty scent in the air.

Brenda eyed him warily. "I think you should leave."

He picked up the mug and nodded, blinking. He opened his mouth to speak, thought better of it, and left.

Brenda leaned over and held down a red button on the desk phone. There was a long unbroken dial tone, then the crackly hiss of a connection.

They spoke slowly. Two words.

"Security. Now."

Joe staggered along the white marble corridor, head buzzing.

A red docket. No coming back from that. And the house. Oh god, the house, he realised. The banks wouldn't allow the mortgage to be renewed, they'd have to sell up. Downsize.

"Not living in a fucking pod," he muttered.

He'd seen it before, of course. Months back, Trevor in Person Resources had gone all militant one afternoon, mouthing off about immigration or something. Next day he was gone. Sally in Marketing said she had seen him living in a box by the underpass with some others, but when Joseph had drove by there was nothing there. It was like he had never existed.

The end of the corridor opened out onto a balcony overlooking the noisy main call centre area three floors below - a huge space with dozens and dozens of identical cubicles with identical workers reading identical scripts sat inside. Some cubicles had photos or children's drawings, others pot plants - vain attempts to personalise the impersonal. The balcony floor had just been cleaned and a yellow board warned:

CAUTION - FLOOR CLEANING IN PROGRESS!

It's come to something when you have to be warned about the perils of decorating, he thought.

He gripped the chrome balcony rail, breathing heavily, fingers sweaty. A ping from a cubicle below caught his attention.

Then another. And another.

Joseph peered down at a worker's screen, squinting to read the display.

Ping! You have new mail, it announced.

They had, and so had everyone else.

On every monitor as far as he could see, Joseph's face filled the screen in all its blurry pixelated glory. In large blocky lettering it read:

SECURITY ALERT DO NOT APPROACH

"Seriously?" he whispered.

Joseph turned to run, but instead faced three security guards. Big, thickset apes in black suits, wireless earphones hanging off their ears. He made to move towards the spiral staircase and as one, they all raised their tasers.

"Shit. Shit. Shit," he repeated, the mantra of a madman.

"Put the weapon down!" shouted the largest guard.

"Weapon? I don't have a…"

Then he realised. The mug. He was still carrying his mug.

He was officially living in a world where an empty mug was a deadly weapon.

"Mad… World's gone bloody mad," he muttered.

Frantically he turned the cheap ceramic over in his hands revealing the crude black cartoon sphere with its comically burning fuse.

He smiled at them. "It's just a picture," he stammered. "A picture of a cartoon bomb!"

"Bomb!" shouted a guard, arming his taser. "He's got a bomb!"

The remaining guards all armed their weapons, the devices emitting a high-pitched whine. Panicking, Joseph stepped back.

"Drop the bomb, now!"

"You don't understand," he pleaded. "It's just a pic…"

His foot skidded on the wet floor, slipping out wildly. He sidestepped, overcompensating, and fell backwards hitting the guardrail hard. His legs shot up and for an impossibly long moment he balanced on the barrier, half on the balcony, half in space, limbs flailing pathetically.

They really should have cordoned off that wet floor, he thought.

Then he was gone.

Forever.

5. THE EDGE OF HEAVEN

"Mum, this is horrible," whispered Purity.

"It's supposed to be horrible, dear. It's a funeral."

"No, the music," she clarified. "What *is* this?"

Aerosmith belted out from the crematorium speakers as Steven Tyler attempted to convince the mourners that he really, really didn't want to miss a thing.

"It's a lovely song," said her mother. "It's romantic *and* dramatic."

Purity vaguely recalled some old movie with Bruce Willis saving the world from falling space rocks and shaky camerawork.

"Dad hated rock music," she scolded. "This is one of *your* favourites."

"Oh shush, child."

The crematorium was small but very modern with little in the way of decoration other than heavy hanging drapes and strategically placed orchids. Rows of cushioned seats separated by a wide aisle faced a lowered stage with a podium and a row of screens where an impossibly handsome priest with impossibly white teeth was preparing. A subtle scent of cut grass and daffodils drifted through the air. The centrepiece of the stage was a raised platform supporting a grey, featureless coffin.

Dad's coffin.

Purity looked away, not wanting to think about the contents of that box. She pulled at the elasticated fabric constricted around her neck. She wore a white dog collar and simple black gown with a grey suede jacket. Her hair, dyed black was tied up and her nose carried a stud in the form of a polished onyx teardrop.

Funeral chic.

Her eyes were drawn to the overhead screens. Looping footage of green fields, crashing waves and sunlight through trees played constantly. Generic soothing imagery designed to catch the eye and distract the mind.

It wasn't working.

Out of the corner of her eye, Purity noticed a slim, elegant lady sit down next to her mother.

"I'm so sorry for your loss," confided the

woman taking Rose's hand in hers. "He was a good person."

The woman wore a black skater dress with matching cardigan and balanced precariously on polished black stiletto heels.

"I'm sorry," stuttered Rose, "Do I know you?"

"It's Brenda, I worked with Joe? He never mentioned me?"

Rose was distracted by their beard - she did like a well-maintained beard and Brenda's was... immaculate.

"I don't... I don't know. I'm sure I would have remembered."

"Well, he was a good worker, talked about you all the time."

Brenda lifted a shoebox from beside them and placed it on the floor by Rose and Purity's feet.

"Joe's possessions," they said. "Things from his desk. We thought you might like them?"

Purity glanced at the contents of the box. A broken mug, a matchbox, three pens and a snapped ruler.

It was, by anyone's standards, a thoroughly depressing summary of a life.

Brenda shifted uncomfortably on the bench and lowered their voice even more. "I think I was probably one of the last people to see him. He seemed very... confused."

Rose was alarmed. "Confused?"

"Like he had... things... on his mind."

"Things? What things?"

"I don't know, there was just no talking to him, we tried, we really did. You know the company - we're one big happy family - the last thing we want is for our employees to... He just jumped."

Brenda pulled at a loose thread on their dress. "There's no easy way to say this, of course. But because it was, well, suicide... the company life insurance doesn't cover him. If it was up to me, I'd..."

Rose could see Brenda's mouth moving, but all she heard was the muffled pounding of her own heart. She had already had letters confirming Joe's pension had been dissolved, another letter warning the mortgage would be withdrawn, the bank had frozen his assets through the Proceeds of Crime act, and now this. No life insurance on top of everything else. Penniless and homeless in the space of a week.

What have you done to us, Joe? She thought to herself. *What have you done?*

"Let us pray," said the Priest, bowing his head. "Our Father. Or Mother. Who art in a non-denominational afterlife. Hallowed be thy name thy identifies thyself with. Thy kingdom come..."

Purity tuned the droning voice out and raised her head slightly, glancing around the room. There weren't many people, and of the ones present she didn't recognise any of them. There were no more family left on her side, the other people presumably work colleagues and old friends of her dads.

"...the power and the glory. Forever and ever. Amen. Or Women.

"And so, we say goodbye to Joseph Beckham St. George. Father to a loving daughter, Purity. Husband to a loving wife, Rosemary. He will be missed."

Rose nodded, dabbing her eyes with a monogrammed hankie.

"And in accordance with his wishes, he leaves us now to the joyous sounds of one of his favourite songs. A beautiful lament, Rosemary assures me, that always brought a smile to his face."

The priest pressed a button on the podium and the speakers hissed gently.

"Mum?" Purity asked, suddenly very concerned. "What did you pick?"

At the back of the stage the curtains parted, and the coffin slowly receded.

"I had to choose something. It... it was the only thing I could find in his record collection."

At top volume, a pounding synthesized electronic drum beat filled the auditorium. A rhythmic, inappropriate melody that Purity recognised instantly.

Thirteen weeks in the UK charts, peaking

at number five.
    Living in a box.

6. ONE BETTER DAY

"God bless you, child!" bellowed Toothless Tom at Purity. Gnarled fingers in tatty woollen gloves surrounded the hot cardboard cup, steam rising into his unkempt, matted beard.

"Espresso, two sweeteners. Just the way you like it."

"You're a credit to your ma and pa, you surely are."

Tom had relocated one shop down and was now sat wrapped in a pile of blankets on the doorstep of the ex-KostlyKoffee. Debris, rubble and dust surrounded him, charred and blackened cups and napkins drifting in the cool breeze.

A burnt-out shell of a man in a burnt-out shell of a business.

Yellow tape criss-crossed the wreckage declaring to the world that it was a CRIME SCENE DO NOT CROSS.

"Not seen you around much, past few days," said Purity.

The beggar peered down the street, eyeing the cars suspiciously.

"Keeping a low profile. Lot a homeless been 'moved on' lately," he murmured, emphasizing the words 'moved on' with two wagging fingers sticking out from his cup.

"Don't know where they're moving on to... but I ain't seen 'em again."

Purity frowned. She *had* noticed the numbers of homeless decreasing in the area, but not really put any thought into it.

"I'll keep an eye open," she said, now more conscious of the number of featureless black cars on the street. "Gotta look out for each other, haven't we?"

"Precious little of that going on, love," said Tom sipping the thick syrupy coffee.

He squinted up at her, suddenly noticing how she was dressed.

"Now what the hell is that you've got on, girl?"

Purity wore a cream full length skirt ending just above the ankle, on her feet a pair of unfussy white brogues. A cream single-breasted blazer covered a white long-sleeved blouse and a simple embroidered lace scarf covered the top of her head, draped down her shoulders. From beneath the scarf, short, spiky platinum blonde hair peeked out as if afraid of the light. A simple silver crucifix nose stud completed the outfit.

It was safe to say Purity had embraced the makeover.

"Got a job interview today," she chirped excitedly. "Got a good feeling about this."

"A job, you say? What the hell do you want one o' those for? You're just a kid!"

There was no point going into the details. Money was tight at home. The house was on the market for a fraction of its actual value, potential purchasers balking at its 'hate speech and suicide' connections. If that was the sort of thing going on in the house, who knew what else was happening in the area. If and when it did get sold they would have to downsize, though there weren't many places to downsize to any more. It was more and more likely that they'd end up renting a pod in one of the Monoliths.

Suddenly, pod life didn't seem quite so appealing.

"Things at home, they're not what they used to be," she said truthfully.

Tom swigged the last of the burning coffee down and belched with no hint of embarrassment. With a groan he climbed up onto a knee then stood up. Even without the layers of blankets, it was clear he was a big man.

"Least ya got a home, love," he said without accusation, turning to leave.

"You do what you need to keep it that way, Expresso."

7. SPECIAL BREW

"So, what first attracted you to the world of decaffeinated fast food products?" Purity sat on a beige moulded plastic chair facing two individuals not much older than herself, though the term 'individuals' may have been misleading. Both baby faced and clean cut and dressed in soft, muted conservative colours, they might as well have been clones.

Attack of the Conservative Clones, thought Purity remembering some terrible old sci-fi movie she had watched with her dad. She relaxed a little, realising her attire was almost identical to theirs - It seemed everything she had read on the KostlyKoffee's embrace of Neo-Puritanism was true.

One less thing to worry about, at least.

"Well, it's an area I've been interested in for a long time," she lied, smoothing out an imaginary crease on her skirt.

The interview was at KostlyKoffee Headquarters - a huge, glass spiral building on the banks of the Thames overlooking Tower Bridge. When the clones had introduced themselves in the foyer, Purity almost choked on her complementary Triple-Nut Nut-Free Nut-o-chino: Chief Flavour Imagineer and Head of Liquid Entertainment.

They were obviously very important.

"I frequent your establishments regularly and I've always admired the level of service and professionalism of your guys there."

Clone One raised an eyebrow and Purity realised 'guys' might get her in trouble in a company like this.

Neutral... keep it gender neutral, she thought.

And *Frequent your establishments...* where did that come from?

"It says here you're still at school?" said Clone Two

"Yes, yes, until September. That's why I only applied for the zero hours job."

They nodded in unison.

"Let me tell you a bit about the position," said Clone One. "It's part time, as you already know. Evenings and weekends with a standard shift rota. Five days on, two days off. You'll be fully trained by our expert team in all matters pertaining to the role, so you, and we, can be assured our customers always have a consistent and world leading level of service at all times."

"Well you've gotta be consistent," agreed Purity.

"Quite. Tell me, have you ever worked agile?"

Purity stared blankly. "Erm... no, I don't believe I have."

"What about lean? Waterfall?"

The clones could have been saying anything - Purity had no idea what they were talking about. She had only ever seen waterfalls on Instagram. Didn't that famous escapologist go over Niagara Falls in a barrel once? She was pretty sure that wasn't helpful right now.

"Because you'll need to embrace a fluid, adaptive methodology to fit in here. We expect everyone to..."

Clone Two paused mid-sentence. Purity's hand was up as if in class, except she'd never held her hand up in class.

Ever.

"I'm sorry," said Purity. "I thought the job was just serving coffee?"

The clones stiffened at the word 'just', and Purity suddenly felt like that man in the barrel. Claustrophobic.

Locked in.

Falling uncontrollably.

"We're a large company. We have standards," said Clone One, seriously.

Clone Two gestured at Purity's ankles, barely visible beneath the hemline.

"Take that skirt, for instance. Don't you think that's a little... revealing?"

Revealing? Purity thought. *There's barely an inch of flesh visible.*

"And your modesty headwear... what is that? Is that a scarf?"

"It's not really doing the job is it? Still plenty of hair on show. It's a bit of an afterthought. KostlyKoffee have a very strict dress code, we don't tolerate workers dressing in an overly sexualised manner. We serve children and pensioners you know."

Purity really had thought she had gone above and beyond to fit in - this wasn't going the right way.

Not at all.

A soft chime emitted from their tablets and they both looked down. Within seconds, their expressions went from consternation to surprise, to concern and back to surprise again before finally settling on horror. Clone One's eyes flicked between her screen and Purity.

"We have the ..aah... results of your... erm... background check. As is customary, we do a complete trawl of all candidates public and private history across all digital channels... websites, mail, apps."

And there it was. Purity knew exactly where this was going.

"And social media."

"Look," stuttered Purity. "I think this has all got way out of proportion."

"Out of proportion, you say?" asked Clone Two, or was it One. Did it even matter anymore?

The clone held up her tablet displaying the defaced rainbow coloured poster in all its glory. "You don't think promoting hate speech online is a big deal then?"

"That's not..."

"We have many, many LGBTTQQIAAP employees here at KostlyKoffee, some are very close friends of mine. We work very hard to ensure they are all treated equally, yet you seem to think that's not important?"

"I didn't say..."

"You defaced a poster promoting equal rights and posted it online with the messages #MOREEQUALTHANOTHERS and #HATESPEECH."

"'Hate speech' was a question, not a..."

"I'm afraid that's not compatible with our values. And to be quite frank, Miss St. George, that's not compatible with *any* right-minded persons values."

As mirror images, the clones closed the branded covers on their tablets and stood up. "Thank you for your time," they said together in eerie harmony.

It appeared that the world of decaffeinated fast food products, and possibly *any* products was not for her.

8. THE ONLY WAY IS UP

"Mum, I'm home!" shouted Purity, slamming the front door shut behind her. Piles of letters and envelopes lay pushed against the wall, unopened and ignored: Demands, threats, offers for half price double glazing. Purity peeled herself out of the stifling jacket and sighed. The day had started so optimistically, but now? Well, it was back to square one.

One step forward, two steps back and all that.

"Cup of tea, Mum?" she said, popping her head around the door of the lounge. The curtains were closed, and the room was lit by the sickly blue half-light of the television. Rose sat motionless in a huge marshmallow chair of faded overstuffed leather staring at the fuzzy shapes on the TV, although her eyes were wide open it was clear nothing was going in. On the screen was Britannica's most popular game show 'You've Been Maimed' where Chelsey, a nursery nurse from Norwich with bad hair extensions attempted to guess what happened next in a series of bloopers and outtakes from the previous weeks public hangings. Overly tense music ratcheted up the tension as Chelsey's hands hovered over a comically large red button and the audience whipped themselves into a pointless frenzy as she gambled her meagre winnings for the holiday of a lifetime.

Purity couldn't watch, much preferring the satirical game show 'Have I got Noose for you', and quietly moved away towards the kitchen. Her Mother had become more and more detached since the funeral, and now it looked like she had finally checked out altogether. She clicked the kettle on and lifted out two mugs from the cupboard. She paused, studying one of the mugs; the KostlyKoffee logo proudly emblazoned along the side.

"I don't think so," she said and dropped it in non-recyclables.

She felt around the back of the cupboard, finally removing a chipped and weathered mug. Her mother never liked it, so it had been long relegated to the deepest, darkest corners of the kitchen. Dark green, heavily tea-stained, with a photo of eighties pop star Howard Jones and the words "THINGS CAN ONLY GET BETTER" in faded yellow.

One of Dads.

The water hissed and bubbled, increasing in volume and Purity leaned against the worktop with both hands gazing through the narrow, grubby window. Outside, the FOR SALE banner swayed gently in the wind. Clumsy graffiti scrawled across it read 'Haterz owt'

Purity lifted the mug in a silent toast.

Say what you like about the education system, she thought. *At least Dad taught me how to spell.*

The house wouldn't be theirs for much longer, that much was clear. Pretty soon all their memories, good and bad, would be packed up into little boxes ready for the future. Whatever that was.

She frowned. There was something familiar in that thought. Something connected.

Little boxes.

Boxes within boxes.

A matchbox in a shoebox.

Dad's possessions.

In the chilly hallway, Purity pushed the coats on their pegs aside to get to the cupboard under the stairs. Inside, surrounded by old shoes and rusting tools, his shoebox of work possessions was still waiting. Dad had never smoked, never even vaped. So why did he keep a box of matches with him?

"Got you," she said under her breath, lifting the matchbox out, immediately noticing it was much heavier than it ought to be. On the face of the matchbox her dad had written the letters D.M. in thick marker pen.

D.M? She couldn't think of anyone with those initials.

Depeche Mode? Dr Martens?

She shook the box, and something rattled inside.

Carefully, she pushed the matchbox open and something small and metal fell into her palm.

A tiny bronze key.

She turned it over in her fingers - it was cold, dirty and slightly greasy.

The loft entrance was a small square panel recessed into the ceiling at the top of the stairs. In all the years they had lived there, Purity had never seen anyone go in or out of the attic. It was never talked about, never mentioned... it was just there. Invisible.

Hiding in plain sight.

The only time she could remember ever asking about the attic, her mother had simply said, "That old thing? Oh, your father lost the key years ago."

Even back then Purity could read the subtext: *he* broke it, *he* can fix it.

Dad lost the key years ago.

Lost the key? Or hid the key?

She squeezed her fist tight, the metal sharp against her skin. Downstairs, the audience cheered. It seemed Chelsey from Norwich was on a roll.

Purity dragged an antique wooden chair from her parents' bedroom, placing it directly under the hatch. Gripping the backrest, she climbed up onto the chair and steadied herself, the stairs downwards perilously close.

This would be a spectacularly stupid way to die, she thought.

The hatch was secured by an ageing, dirty, oily padlock.

If no-one goes up here, why is it oiled?

She slid the key in. There was no resistance and it turned immediately, springing free. The loft hatch swung down an inch or so, then stopped softly on some kind of pneumatic hinge. Purity gingerly tugged at the edge. Assisted by gravity, the door started to open revealing a set of aluminium ladders and she ducked. In sections the ladders expanded loudly.

CLANG. CLANG. CLANG.

Until they reached the carpeted floor with a thump.

Still balancing on the chair, Purity listened. Surely her mother had heard that? But it seemed not. The distant cheering suggesting the Norwich nursery nurse was going all the way. The metal creaked and groaned under her weight as Purity carefully climbed up into the musty darkness. She peered into the gloom trying to make sense of the shapes and silhouettes, before noticing a modern plastic switch by the hatch. She pressed it and a single low wattage energy saving bulb faded to life.

Wooden beams crossed the floor and arched up into the roof space. Pipes and wiring emerged from one wall only to vanish into another. A small confined area around the hatch had chipboard laid down over the insulation allowing a person to stand up and walk without fear of crashing through the ceiling. Cardboard boxes of old video and cassette tapes were heaped in messy piles around some old hardware. A record player? A radio? Was that a video recorder?

At the centre of the floored area was a television. It was old, really old and built into a solid teak cabinet covered in dust. A big old cathode ray tube of a TV that must have weighed a ton.

How did he get it up here?

On the front was a tuning dial like an old radio, a volume dial and an on/off switch. Wires ran from the back of the cabinet, so it looked like it had power, at least. Purity prodded the power switch.

Nothing happened.

But then a distant, almost subliminal

whine. So high pitched she imagined next doors dog tearing at the walls to get through. Ghost-like, an image appeared on the screen, grainy and indistinct. It grew brighter, and as it did, clearer. It was wooden beams, and flooring. This attic, but on its side. Purity tilted her head to orient herself. It was this attic alright, but a large pale smudge in the foreground blocked some of the view. She leaned in to get a closer look and the smudge moved.

It's a live picture, she realised. Its right here.

Shuffling back, she saw exactly what it was. An old camcorder lay flat by her knee. It was obviously switched on and indeed *she* was the smudge. As she lifted it the picture rotated and blurred. It was surprisingly heavy for such a small device and was covered in buttons, switches and sockets.

Printed on a panel it read "PANASONIC VHS-C"

She turned it over in her hands, realising there was a tape still inside it. On a bank of buttons at the back of the device, she saw a familiar triangle symbol in a rounded rectangle, just like the ones on her video apps.

Her finger hovered over the button for a moment.

And pressed PLAY.

9. DON'T YOU (FORGET ABOUT ME)

"If you're watching this, it means two momentous things have happened," said Purity's father from the television screen. "One, I'm dead. And two, my DangerMole has actually figured out how to use a video recorder."

Of course, she realised. *D.M.*

DangerMole.

Dad's pet name for her.

Joseph St. George faced her across time and space, an analogue ghost, a magnetic echo of the past playing out on videotape. He sat cross legged on the wooden floor of the attic wearing faded blue jeans and a baggy white t-shirt with bold black lettering shouting CHOOSE LIFE!

Both hands were wrapped around a mug of tea.

Seeing her father so alive and happy, so unaware of what was going to become of him, Purity's eyes filled.

"I hope it was a grand, noble death," he continued, "like pulling orphans from a burning house or stopping a plane crashing onto a school. Not something stupid like choking on a peanut."

"Oh Daddy," she whispered, wiping away tears with her sleeve.

"I don't know what happened to me, obviously, but let me get this out of the way at the start: I'm sorry. Sorry I had to leave you. Sorry if we had an argument. Sorry if I didn't say I love you."

Purity shook her head trying so, so hard to *not* break down - they never argued; he told her he loved her every single day. Purity couldn't remember the last time she had reciprocated.

"Remember, you're not alone - I'm sure your mother won't be taking it well, but you look after her, it's just the two of you now."

He lowered his voice. "I mean, losing one parent is a tragedy. Losing both... well that's just careless."

Joseph took a long mouthful of tea. The mug was black with the yellow logo DangerMole on one side and a shiny cartoon bomb on the other. He stared at the patterns of milk swirling in the drink. "Well, that's rather brought the mood in the room down somewhat. So, I think we need a bit of this."

He reached behind him to the big silver Binatone turntable. A vinyl LP was already spinning, and he flicked the tiny plastic lever, lowering the needle onto the record. An air raid siren wound up and down accompanied by a full orchestral score and Joseph tipped his head back, eyes closed, arms in the air, conducting an invisible ensemble. Swaying, he soaked in the introduction until a relentless, machine gun bass guitar riff broke him from his trance.

He reached into a square silver case on his other side and held up an album cover, face forward to the camera. "Frankie Goes to Hollywood. Two Tribes," he shouted over the music. "33 weeks in the chart, Nine weeks at number one. Sold nearly two million copies but now banned under the Purity Act. Banned for obscenity, scaremongering, politicised messaging and suggestive dancing. And that was just this track. You don't want to know about the rest of the album."

He gazed upwards at the rafters, his head nodding to the beat, focused on an old memory as Holly Johnson yeah-yeahed his way through the song. Finally remembering he was recording a message for his daughter, Joseph turned the volume dial down a few notches leaving the music playing in the background and pulled out a handful of albums from the case.

One by one, he held the covers up to Purity.

"Rolling stones - Sympathy for the devil," he said, throwing it down onto the chipboard floor. "Little Mix - Black magic. C'est La Vie - B*Witched. Banned, banned, banned. All banned, would you believe, for promoting Satanism?"

"First edition, this one," he said as The Beatles' Sgt Pepper's Lonely Hearts Club Band filled the screen. "Lucy in the sky with Diamonds. Banned, The Shaman - Ebeneezer Goode, Walking in The Air by Aled Jones. All banned for promotion of drug use."

"Crazy by Gnarls Barkley and I suppose anything by Madness: Banned for making light of mental health conditions."

He held the last LP in his hands reverently and turned it over. "The Sex Pistols. Never mind the…"

He smiled knowingly. "I guess that one never *really* stood a chance."

Joseph returned the albums to the case, rearranging their order as he spoke. In the background Frankie covered Springsteen's Born to Run, censored for the overly-specific crime of 'promoting dangerous driving.'

"Banned. All banned. Purged from the internet, physical copies burned. All these musical classics lost to history. And what do we have instead? Safe, middle of the road, processed, pre-packaged fluff that sounds nice, offends no-one and says nothing."

He moved a stack of old, faded VHS video cassettes into view. "And it's not just music. They massacred TV too."

The first video cassette was a sitcom from before Purity was born. The box showed a grinning Del Boy and Rodders and a three-wheeled yellow Reliant Regal on the cover. "Only Fools and Horses, 1981 to 1991. Banned for glamourising illegal business practises and promoting a criminal lifestyle."

He fanned three more cases at the camera. "Allo Allo. It Aint Half Hot Mum. Fawlty Towers, I think we watched a few of those together, didn't we?"

Purity nodded, smiling at the memory of that angry lanky man poking a waiter in the eye.

"If I recall correctly, these were all banned for their 'casual racism.'"

He showed another video box - Nicholas Lyndhurst in a trench coat.

"Goodnight Sweetheart: Promotion of infidelity."

Ronnie Barker with a comb over and comedy moustache.

"Open all hours: Mockery of physical impairment. Also, technical inaccuracy since viewers saw the shop *close* at the end of each episode."

Three old geezers on a grassy hill.

"Last of the Summer Wine: Promotion of alcoholism." Joseph shook his head. "I don't know, did they even watch it?"

He paused on the next one.

"Love Thy Neighbour?" He pondered. "Okay, maybe I'll give them that."

A hairy yellow model dog and a red-faced *thing* with a spring for legs filled the screen.

"And then there were the kids shows they banned. Magic Roundabout: Drug Use.

"Demon Headmaster, Rentaghost, Grotbags: Satanism, again.

"Fireman Sam, Postman Pat: Sexism.

"Not to mention the dark stuff like Cartoon Club or Jim'll Fix It."

He shrugged apologetically. "Hey, I didn't say it was all gold. My point is: the world's broken. No one can say anything for fear of outrage or offence - the right to be offended trumps free speech every time. Anything, anyone that might cause offence is persecuted, *erased* from history. They took our music, we said nothing. They took our sitcoms, we said nothing. They took away our right to offend and disguised it as liberty."

He held up a well-watched copy of The Best of Tiswas.

"We shouldn't cover these up, bury them. They should be held up high, studied in every school, analysed by historians. Accept what they are and learn from them. How are we going learn anything by running from it, by hiding from it?"

He slumped, shoulders falling.

"We've been the same throughout all of history. What we don't understand, we fear. What scares us, we persecute. And what we persecute, we destroy. When it turns out the thing we hated, the thing we destroyed, was the very thing that could have saved us in the first place."

He raised his arms, taking in the contents of the attic.

"So, it only turns to me now, to bestow upon you my entire collection of banned esoterica, instead of the sanitised nothings that settles for art or entertainment these days. Do with it what you will. Probably best not to tell you mother though," he winked, "she's not a fan."

He closed the box of LPs and went to turn off the record player just as the next track was starting.

How apt, he thought and instead turned the volume up.

Frankie Goes To Hollywood. The Power Of Love.

"Look after yourself, DangerMole," he said. "You might only be small, but you've got a big heart, and way more courage than I ever had. Follow your dreams and don't settle for second best. It's your world. If you don't like it, change it. Never give up, DangerMole. Fight to your very last breath.

"And look, you might think you can't change the world on your own, but if you can make a person think, you can change their mind. If you can change a mind, you can change a belief. If you can change a belief, you can change a culture. And if you can change a culture... well then, maybe, just maybe, you *can* save the world.

"Oh, and take your nose out of your phone once in a while," he smiled. "There's a big old world out there. And if you have to film everything, make sure you're doing it for a reason."

Joseph raised his mug in a salute.

"To you, my DangerMole," he said proudly. "I love you."

The grainy image paused, her father's geeky smile frozen under a jumping band of static noise and the tears Purity had fought so well to stave off, to suppress, finally burst through and consumed her.

10. SPIRITS IN THE MATERIAL WORLD

PURITY: hey

With a polite chime, the speech balloon floated up the screen of the feed messenger app and Purity watched a tiny animated thumb dancing below it as the recipient typed a reply.

WINGNUT: SUP P?

She had known Warren 'Wingnut' Wingford for her entire time at high school. Admittedly he was a bit of a loner but hey, so was she. This wasn't a social call however, Warren was well known for his love of all things digital.

PURITY: i need a favour

WINGNUT: LOL. U NO UR NT MY TIPE :)
PURITY: not like that warren

She lay on her bed with her dad's old laptop balanced on the pillow, the full sized mechanical keyboard feeling alien to fingers so used to handheld glass devices.

WINGNUT: WT FAVR?
PURITY: i want to delete an old post
WINGNUT: WT PST?
PURITY: from the feed.
WINGNUT: HAHAHAHAHAHAHAHAHAHAHAHAHAHAHHAHA
PURITY: thats not very helpful

She grabbed a box of chewing gum for her bedside table and tore open it's silver wrapping. *HeimLicks'* weren't a favourite, but they would have to do.

PURITY: you still there?
WINGNUT: U SERIUS?
PURITY: yes
WINGNUT: TH FEED IS 4EVER.
WINGNUT: U NO THT.
PURITY: there must be some way to delete a post.
WINGNUT: N

She frowned.

PURITY: i thought you were good at this?

PURITY: i thought you knew about this stuff?

There was another pause.

WINGNUT: GIV ME A MIN

She rolled onto her back with her hands behind her head and blew a bubble. It burst with the unmistakable scent of vanilla and quinoa. Nik Kershaw and Boy George gazed down at her from faded posters on the wall - musicians her dad had introduced her to from an early age. Ground-breaking, pioneering acts, not like the bland noise that passed for music these days. Amongst the posters were pictures of unicorns and dragons - childish things from a childish age that she had really grown out of - but they were tangible connections to her past and she had no intention of taking them down anytime soon.

The laptop chimed.

WINGNUT: LK I SED THE FEED IS 4EVER
WINGNUT: CANT DEL NOTHIN :(
WINGNUT: !!!BUT!!!
WINGNUT: !!!BUT!!!
WINGNUT: !!!BUT!!!
WINGNUT: MAY B CAN MASK UR POSTS
PURITY: mask?
PURITY: what does that mean?
WINGNUT: GOD UR SCH A BUNG :)
WINGNUT: WE CN COVR UR OLD POSTS WTH NEW ONES
PURITY: really?

PURITY will that work?
WINGNUT: NVR TRYD IT B4 TBH
WINGNUT: DNT C Y NOT THO
PURITY: what do I need to do?
WINGNUT: SNDG U LINK NOW

A popup slid in from the side of the screen entitled 'TOP SECRET' and Purity allowed herself the smallest of laughs. There was no message, just the longest web address she had ever seen. A seemingly random jumble of letters, numbers and special characters, the link ran for at least 8 lines.

WINGNUT: U ND 2 INSTAL A FYL

She clicked the link and the browser fired up, filling the screen.
Instantly, the window closed. Then reopened. Then closed. This repeated five or six times, finally settling on a black screen with blocky green text and a single input field.
Very old school.

REZ-R-XN 3.11
"And the people will be oppressed, Each one by another, and each one by his neighbor; The youth will storm against the elder, and the inferior against the honorable. Isaiah 3:5-8"
ENTER EMAIL ADDRESS

Wait... was this a Christian extremist site?

PURITY: this is illegal isnt it?

As if on cue a cartoon hen flapped across the screen clucking melodically.

WINGNUT: U CANT MAKE AN OMLET WITHOUT KILLNG A FEW CHIKKINS

Weren't sites like this supposed to be monitored? Still, they couldn't watch them all, could they? But she'd come this far - In for a penny, and all that.

PURITY: thanks warren x
WINGNUT: STAY SAFE P:)

She typed her email address into the input field and hovered over the ENTER key.
What's the worst that could happen?
"Sod it," she said.
And slapped ENTER.

The screen cleared but for a single blinking full stop. Moments passed, then a line of text appeared at the bottom. Then another. And another. It looked like web addresses, but like the original link, contained a lot of weird characters. The screen filled up with more and more information until the display started scrolling. In amongst the nonsense she could recognise a few words. Twitter. Instagram. Fragments of old conversations, of old emails. It appeared to be trawling the entire history of the feed, pulling out everything she had ever said or posted.
How was this even possible?

More and more data scrolled past. Facebook? When did she last use that? Tinder? Familiar snippets of phrases once buried in the feed, now unearthed. Resurrected. The green figures moved fast, a blur of data. Now it was medical terms. Was that Doctors records? School reports. Old library books.

How deep did this go?

Her national insurance number caught her eye. Was it trawling Government records? That couldn't be good. Suddenly the screen froze and Purity found she was looking at a photo of herself full screen. A photo taken right now. By the laptop.

No. Not good at all.

Purity hit the ENTER key. No response. She tapped the escape key, spacebar. Nothing. The tiny light over the screen was blinking. The webcam. How long had that been on?

She recoiled, realising that she was being watched. Horrified, Purity spat her gum into her hand and squeezed it hard over the laptop camera. As she closed the lid a logo appeared - an eye inside a fist inside a triangle.

The Constabulary.

And underneath:

> PLEASE REMAIN WHERE YOU ARE
> SPECIAL CONSTABLES ARE ON THEIR
> WAY TO ASSIST IN YOUR ARREST.

At the foot of the page amongst a list

of characters and dots was her house address. "Shit!"

She slammed the lid shut and leapt off the bed. "Shit. Shit. Shit."

On the way, it said. Government goons on the way. Fire appliances were supposed to get to you in nine minutes, ambulances in six. But the Constabulary?

Purity grabbed her smartphone and ran down the stairs, leaping the steps two at a time. "Mum! Mummmm!"

In the lounge, Rose sat unmoved. She stared vacantly at the TV and its seemingly endless parade of overenthusiastic underachievers.

"Mum. Come on! We have to leave!" shouted Purity, glancing out of the window. "Come on!"

She knelt down directly in front of her mother, deliberately blocking the television and clasped her hands. "We don't have time!" she pleaded desperately. "Mum!"

Rose stared unblinking at Purity.

Through Purity.

The lights were on but Rose was most definitely not home.

Purity bowed her head and sighed a long, tired breath.

"Oh Mum," she whispered.

The screech of tyres cut through the audience's shrieks and a long, black van mounted the kerb outside. The doors flew open with a dull thud and two figures in tailored black suits emerged. One, stood in the open car doorway talking into an earpiece, the other approached the gate.

Purity dropped her mother's hands and stood up, acutely aware she had lost one parent already.

Losing one parent is a tragedy. Losing two? Well that's just careless.

Rosemary St. George, locked in her own little world. A world with no husband or daughter, no money, no house. No hope. Just a stupid sodding gameshow. A world where strangers gambled on the snap of a noose and big money prizes waited.

Wiping a tear back, she mouthed, "I'm sorry."

And ran.

11. RUNNING IN THE FAMILY

Officer Ronette 'Roni' Lister really, really wanted to hurt someone. She and Ronald Stott approached the house. They had been working together at the constabulary for some years, chasing down perpetrators, collecting debts. It was fair to say they had seen it all before - they had caught rapists and murderers, broken up gangs, foiled terrorist plots - so today's simple smash-and-grab, collect a young girl for interrogation, would be a walk in the park.

Sadly for Roni, there would be no hurtings today.

The partners were well matched. Lister was small and weasley with a thin smile and an even thinner temperament while Stott was the muscle. They paused at the ageing wooden front door with its peeling red paint and greasy window, the number 52 hanging at a jaunty angle above the brass knocker. Roni had discovered years ago they you could glean everything you needed to know about a house and its occupants from its front door.

And this one was tired, neglected and suspiciously left wing.

She rapped the knocker three times and waited. Not that she expected anyone to answer the door, they never did. But it was procedure, all part of the game.

Through the front window she could see the television was on. A young man in a striped jumper was excitedly hammering a huge red button while a body twitched on a rope behind him.

You've Been Maimed. Damn, she loved that show.

A small plastic gnome sat by the doorstep guarding the door. It bent over cheekily exposing its gnome bottom, the flaking paint suggesting some incurable skin condition. It had seen better days.

Lister was convinced it was probably breaking some obscenity law and she would have been more than happy to stamp her boot down on its irritating little grin. But frankly, she could without the extra paperwork.

Sighing, she rapped the knocker another three times.

Still no movement.

She pulled a pair of black leather gloves from her pocket and squeezed them on, flexing her fingers.

"Can't say they weren't warned," she murmured to Ronald.

With a single blow, Stott kicked the door in. Wood shattered inwards, the door shearing from its hinges and disintegrating into rotted matchsticks.

Wordlessly, Roni span a finger in the air and Ronald headed towards the side of the house. It was not uncommon for a perpetrator to make a run from the back of the property when they saw constables arrive.

Lister marched into the house, wood and glass crunching under her boots.

"This is the constabulary. You are under arrest for cybercrimes against the nation."

From the hallway she could see directly into the lounge and the gameshow playing continuously. An older female sat before it. The child's mother, no doubt.

She scanned the room for exits or hiding places then continued down the hall. In the kitchen the kettle had just boiled, steam drifting lazily from the spout. A bottle of milk and two mugs sat on the worktop. Two mugs. Two people.

The fridge door was wide open.

The girl was still here somewhere.

Lister gently closed the fridge door when something in the fridge caught her eye. A white plate with cellophane hanging from it, spots of blood and grease around it, on the shelves, on the door. She was pondering the significance of it when her earpiece squawked. It was Ronald.

"Target sighted. Rear of property. She's here!"

From the top of the fence, Purity glanced back along the length of the garden. A big man in a black suit, dressed for a dinner party, emerged from the side of the house.

Quickly, Purity dropped down into the neighbour's garden clutching her shoulder bag.

But not quickly enough.

She was sure the man had seen her.

Wasting no time, she ran across the mossy, unkempt lawn around a large, moulding trampoline. It was covered in leaves and mould; the kids having no doubt moved on to flashier, shinier entertainment. This house sat in the perpetual shadow of the Monoliths, and the constant gloom meant nothing ever grew there. She hopped over a rusty, abandoned bicycle rapidly mapping the garden's layouts in her head. This garden belonged to the Ropers, a young couple with two children. Next door to the right - and the fence Purity was running at - was a professional couple. They always seemed nice enough, but she had no idea what their names were. The garden after that, Mr Rossiter, then, the main road.

It was a lower panelled fence this side, and Purity vaulted it easily. Landing on shining white gravel, she sprinted across a postcard-pretty landscaped garden lit by fairy lights, leaping over a water feature. She landed awkwardly on a cobble, her foot twisting as she fell and crashed headlong into a miniature Chinese bridge. The bridge, built for its aesthetic value, collapsed flat instantly as if crushed by a rampaging Godzilla.

Purity looked up at the house. Luckily no-one had noticed.

Voices grew louder behind her and she scrambled up, shaking tiny stones from her palms. She limped to the other fence, reaching into her shoulder bag as she ran.

The last house.

Rossiter's house.

Bill Rossiter had lived there longer than anyone and would probably outlast everyone. There was certainly no way more Monoliths would be built around here while there was breath left in his body. He was a well-known figure on the street, and while once kids may have taunted him, everyone now knew full well it was better for everyone if they just left him alone. So, while Bill had quite a reputation for unpleasantness, his dog was worse.

She reached the top of the fence, wedging herself against the concrete post to keep stable. The dog was by the house, curled up asleep by the bins. Some kind of bull mastiff, black, stocky wearing a comical bright red collar with silver spikes.

Purity gingerly slid her hand into her shoulder bag and pulled out the slab of bloody meat.

"Grub up," she whispered, and threw the steak as hard as she could.

It flew over the animal's head and hit the wall of the house, where it flopped to the paving stones with a disgusting slap.

The dog's head shot up and it studied the source of the noise. Sniffing the air, it approached the lump cautiously. Recognising it for what it was, it pounced on the wet meat, tearing and snarling.

Purity lowered herself into Rossiter's garden, landing silently on the scruffy grass. The back of the garden had a row of thick bushes, and behind them an old red brick wall faced onto the main road.

Almost there.

She tiptoed backwards into the bushes, eyes fixed on the feasting dog. It hadn't seen her, it seemed. Just over the wall and…

Suddenly the fence panels clattered and shook, and Purity quickly dropped to her knees in the bush. With no stealth or subtlety, the two constables landed squarely on the lawn hunting for the girl.

Purity stooped low in the bush, out of sight.

Alerted by this sudden intrusion, the dog span, growling. Then without thought, ran for the officers. Both constables stood their ground, seemingly unfazed, and adopted a low, combat position. As one, they each reached into their jackets and produced a short stick, not unlike a cigar. With a sharp gesture, they shook their arms out and the stick extended nearly a meter, a faint electric crackle emitted from the devices.

"Shoksticks," Purity said quietly. A primitive, barbaric glorified cattle prod, controversially used by the police for crowd control during the Brexit riots and subsequently banned.

Or so she thought.

The dog pounced. Lister's arm swung down, the shokstick hitting its neck hard with a distinctive blue flash. The creature yelped, and a smell of singed fur filled the garden.

No, no, no, thought Purity.

As much as the animal was terrifying she didn't want to see it getting hurt. And it was entirely her fault this was even happening.

Ronald jabbed his stick forward catching the dog's flank. Another blue flash and the beast retreated warily, growling, its head down. They raised their sticks and advanced on the cowering animal.

Officer Lister was going to hurt something today, it seemed.

Frantically, Purity patted her pockets searching for the familiar shape. There was no way she could take the two constables on, but she could make a difference. Her hand closed around her smartphone. She lifted it up swiping the camera on, her father's words echoing in her head.

If you're going to film everything, make sure you're doing it for a reason.

She hit the red RECORD button as Ronald and Roni laid into the dog. Arms swinging down repeatedly, the garden bathed in a stroboscopic blue glow as the animal's yelps grew louder. Purity wanted to look away but couldn't. This had to be filmed. Recorded. For as long as she could remember she had been terrified of Rossiter's dog, but this... this was inhuman. She had seen enough. Hastily her fingers tapped the keyboard.

#TRUSTTHEGOVERNMENT? #ANIMALCRUELTY

And sent it into the feed.

The phone chimed a confirmation and the two officers froze, sticks still mid-swing.

"Oh shit," said Purity through gritted teeth.

She scrambled backwards and hit the wall as they turned to face the bushes. It was an amateurish mistake, a schoolboy error as her dad would have said. Or schoolgirl error. Or schoolperson error. Just what was the phrase, these days?

The agents cautiously approached, their shoksticks still extended. Purity took a deep breath. There was only way out of this. Abruptly she stood up, throwing her shoulder bag at them. It bounced feebly off Ronald's chest. The two regarded the bag and looked at each other laughing at this pathetic stalling tactic.

Purity raised two fingers at them and shouted, "Up yours!"

She hauled herself up onto the wall, registering their surprised faces before tumbling backwards over the other side.

Purity hit the ground running. She was on Pigeon Street, a busy main road leading up to the high street. Though there were many cars she was the only pedestrian. If she could make it to the high street she might have a chance - there would be a lot of people, more opportunities to get lost in the crowd. Sprinting along the pavement she knew she would only have a few seconds before the men appeared. This road was too long, she had to get off it quickly. Judging the spaces between the cars she darted into the road, cutting in front of a truck. The horn blared loud in her ears but she kept running, across the second lane onto the far side of the road, then down a narrow alley between houses.

Pigeon Street backed onto the school playing fields, and Purity ran, faster than she had ever ran on a sport's day, that's for sure. Maybe Mr. Baxter her P.E. teacher was wrong, she *did* have a career in Olympic running after all. Crossing the cobbled playground, the school loomed large in front of her. At this time of day it would be deserted, at least. She afforded herself a glance over her shoulder. No sign of them. But that wasn't an excuse to slow down. Purity raced down the side of the main building and past the gym, between the assembly hall and canteen and out through the main gates onto the high street.

The high street was busy, but not as busy as she had hoped for. Cars and trucks whipped by, but disappointingly there were only a dozen or so pedestrians. Straightening her jacket, she pulled her collars up and put her head down then adjusted her speed to that of the other shoppers.

Nothing to see here. Move on.

After a minute or so, Purity started to relax. The street seemed normal enough, maybe she had shaken them off, after all. She drew alongside the remains of the KostlyKoffee store, still cordoned off. Did that really only happen two weeks ago? It already felt like ancient history.

Movement up ahead caught her eye. Two figures had run into the street stopping cars.

Two figures in black suits.

Pedestrians slowed or stopped, trying to figure out what was going on. Purity however, turned around and started walking back the way she had come, but then what was this?

A black van, featureless with blacked out windows emerged from Pigeon Street and parked directly across both lanes. Horns blared. Drivers shouted. Traffic was going nowhere, and neither it seemed was Purity.

"Oh, give me a break," she muttered.

At the other end of the street the two agents were slowly advancing, checking cars and people. A pincer movement. Closing in.

Purity stepped back, looking left and right. There was nowhere to go.

Nowhere.

The constables were closer now. One looked up and angled his head, had he seen her?

"Expresso!" came a voice from behind her. Gruff. Familiar. "C'mere will you!"

Toothless Tom sat in the rubble of Kostly.

Had he been there all along? Were the homeless really that invisible or had she been too preoccupied with her own safety?

Tom beckoned to her and she darted under the cordon into the dusty remains of the coffee shop. "You got the face of someone who needs to be somewhere else. Seen that enough times! Come 'ere."

"I don't..."

In the leftovers of the back office. Tom hooked his fingers into a thin groove in the flooring and lifted. A cloud of dust kicked up and rubble slid off the hatch. Underneath, a ladder led downwards.

A door in the floor? A secret tunnel? Really?

"What is this?"

"Now I know you're not stupid, girl," he chastised, "And I also know there ain't much time. Now get yourself gone... I'll take care o' these amateurs."

The officers hadn't reached them yet, but she knew he was right. She nodded.

Tom held her hand as she climbed into the shaft, "Take care, Expresso."

He lowered the hatch shut, kicking rubble back over it and shambled out.

At what used to be the entrance to KostlyKoffee, the two constables stood silhouetted in the daylight.

"We'd very much like you to help us with our enquiries," said Lister, raising her shokstick.

Officer Roni Lister was going to get her wish, after all.

12. GOING UNDERGROUND

At the bottom of the ladder, Purity dropped into what appeared to be an old service tunnel, the kind that ran between drains or underground tracks. Dim, dirty lamps strung together by loose wiring bathed the corridor in a sickly amber glow and the air was warm and thick.

Just when you think you're rock bottom, there's always somewhere a bit lower, she thought.

She took a last look upwards towards the ruins of the coffee shop and sighed.

No going back now.

Here, below the surface, away from the street, it was eerily quiet - the silence broken only by the distant rumble of underground trains passing nearby. The corridor ran for a hundred metres or so before splitting in two directions. Only one was lit however, the other plunging into darkness almost instantly. She followed the trail of flickering lights, noticing as she went other unlit passages branching off into the dark recesses of nowhere.

"Where have you sent me, Tom?" she whispered.

The lights ran to the end of the corridor and stopped, excess wire trailing loosely on the ground.

Purity stood in front of a large iron door, all rivets and rust with a round wheel at its centre. It was the sort of door she would expect to see on a submarine or naval ship. She raised a fist to knock but felt a little ridiculous and lowered it just as fast. Instead, she pressed her ear against the cool metal.

Nothing. Just the sound of her own breathing in this increasingly confining space.

"Sod it," she said, grabbing the wheel with both hands and turning it as hard as she could.

Surprisingly, it didn't need much pressure at all and span freely. The wheel reached the end of its rotation with a loud clang, the sound chasing its own echoes away down the passages as a sliver of light peeked out from the frame. Although it was a sturdy looking door, again it moved easily, and Purity pulled it open bathing herself and the corridor in a mild, artificial light.

The doorway opened into a tall circular white room with balconies, alcoves and a domed ceiling. In contrast to the oppressive, grimy corridors this was bright, clean and modern. The first thing Purity noticed, indeed the first thing anyone would notice, was a giant marble crucifix dominating the far wall. It was tinged with a flickering blue glow from a large bank of monitors showing various video feeds. To the right lay a scattering of boxes of different sizes. Purity could see one box was opened and inside, was that guns? At the centre of the room lay a wide desk with what appeared to be maps and blueprints spread across it, pencils and mugs scattered randomly across them. Standing behind the desk and staring at Purity were two figures.

Tentatively, Purity stepped into the room. "Hello?"

A knife, cold and sharp, pressed suddenly against her throat and a voice, deep with a northern twang spoke in her ear.

"You lost, Goldilocks?"

She froze, not even attempting to turn but barked defiantly, "Goldilocks… Really?"

The voice moved closer still and the knife pushed harder. "You got a real zippy mouth, little 'un," he said.

A girl dressed in black jeans and a vest stepped forward. Her blonde hair was tied back in a harsh ponytail and expensive looking red-rimmed spectacles balanced on her sharp nose.

"My people have been lost sheep," she recited from memory. "Their shepherds have led them astray, turning them away on the mountains. From mountain to hill they have gone. They have forgotten their fold."

She seemed amused by Purity's confusion.

"We'll stick with the classics, then," she said, nodding at her colleagues. "We're the bears. You're Goldilocks. And it seems you've just broken into our house."

She pushed the glasses up her nose. "Samson, keep her away from my porridge, please."

A woman, tall and muscular - extremely tall, extremely muscular - emerged from behind the table and walked towards Purity. At over 6 feet tall wearing a poppy red skater dress and Dr Martens boots, Samson cut an imposing figure.

"Nice dress," said Purity.

"Why thanks, hun," smiled Samson in a voice so smooth and husky it would not be out of place on late night radio. Her huge, well-manicured hand gripped Purity by the throat and lifted her into the air.

The owner of the threatening voice behind her ear moved into view. His hair was slicked back, and he wore a black jacket with combat pants and brandished a wickedly long blade. Perched on his face was ridiculously bushy moustache waxed into a handlebar. He was either an older man trying to look young or a young man trying to look old, she couldn't tell.

"I'm sure you can appreciate, this place,

our home, it's not exactly signposted," he said. "We like to keep a low profile, if that's not bleeding obvious enough. So, tell me Goldilocks, how did you find us?"

Purity's legs kicked and thrashed in mid-air, her hands scrabbling uselessly against Samson's arm.

"...ommm..." she gasped, her windpipe tightening. "...hommmm..."

"You're gonna have to speak up, I'm not getting it."

Heart pounding in her ears and vision blurring, Purity tried again but she could barely inhale, let alone speak. Her limbs slackened.

"...ommm..."

"That'll do," barked Spectacles.

Samson released her grip instantly and Purity fell to the ground on her hands and knees, coughing and retching.

"If Tom trusts her, it's good enough for me."

The moustache nodded thoughtfully, folding away his knife.

The giant in the skater dress reached out her hand to Purity, "Hell, Tom don't trust no-one, girl. You must be real special."

Samson gently pulled her up. "Sorry about that, should heal fast enough though. You understand we had to be sure you were telling the truth."

On the bank of screens, Purity now realised what she was seeing. Every tunnel was under surveillance, every corridor, right up to the ladder. They had watched her travel the whole way. One screen showed the bombed-out interior of Kosta and Toothless Tom being carried away by a group of constables.

"...Taking... him..." she rasped. "They're taking him."

Spectacles nodded thoughtfully. "Yeah, we were just discussing what to do about that when you arrived."

Purity rubbed her throat, taking in the contents of the chamber. "Do? What is this place? Who are you?"

She stood up, steadier now. All the pieces were falling into place. Secret meeting place. Guns. Drugs. Bombs.

"My God, you're the terrorists, aren't you?"

They regarded her in silence.

Purity pointed at the hulking tower of a woman. "So, you're the muscle," she said.

She pointed at the man with the dodgy moustache. "The fists."

And finally, at the blonde girl with the big glasses. "I dunno... the big mouth?"

Purity stepped back, arms outstretched.

"So, tell me, where are the brains?"

Footsteps on the stairs caught her attention and she turned sharply to see a young man with a shock of ginger hair and big ears.

"Hello Purity," said Warren Wingford.

13. DOG EAT DOG

"Wingnut?" cried Purity in disbelief. Warren smiled his wide crooked smile and threw his arms around her, hugging her tightly.

"P! You made it!"

The team exchanged quizzical glances.

"Okay," yelled Spectacles, "Shows over. Stand down."

"You're a... a terrorist?" stammered Purity.

Warren shrugged. "I prefer the term 'Freedom Fighter' myself."

He put his arm over her shoulder and maneuvered her towards the team.

"Terrorists," she repeated.

He cleared his throat. "Folks, this is Purity."

"Oh, we know who she is," sneered The Moustache.

"The girl who broke the feeds," added Spectacles, tapping on her tablet.

The images on the screens blinked out in sequence, replaced by copies of Purity's recent posts and photos.

"I find this one particularly interesting," added Spectacles.

The centre screen showed shaky footage of two government agents beating some poor dog in the garden of a residential property.

"Hashtag Trust the government, indeed," she chuckled.

Overlaying the clip were the figures:

VIEWED 16.25million   SHARED 12.1million

"You've got quite the following, girl," said the giant, holding out her hand - the hand previously used to strangle Purity. She sensed Purity's hesitation. "Look, it was just for show. Theatre. It had to look like we meant business."

"I'm sorry," she added gently.

Purity studied her closely. Immaculately dressed with long, tightly curled hair, high cheekbones and piercing green eyes, she was quite possibly the most beautiful woman she had ever seen.

And built like the Hulk's girlfriend.

For reasons she couldn't fathom, Purity blushed. "Okay.... it's okay," she stuttered.

The Hulk's girlfriend smiled and spoke in that impossibly silky, soft tone. "The names Samson, you can call me Sammy. Or Sam. Up to you, honey. I'm easy."

The Moustache nodded at her.

"This is Gabriel," said Warren. "He's our... how would you describe it exactly, Gabe?"

Gabriel was cutting his fingernails with the switchblade, like a man peeling an apple. He didn't look up. "I do the stuff no one else will."

Purity whispered in Warren's ear. "Is he always that approachable?"

"Don't mind him," he replied. "I don't think he likes anyone."

There was only one other person in the room and Purity hadn't even noticed her until now. A small, pale girl sat alone in an alcove above them, scrolling through her mobile phone. Warren waved at her and she responded with an upturned thumb.

"That's Ariel. Doesn't talk much."

Spectacles was poring over a set of blueprints on the table.

"Apparently, I'm the big mouth," she said, sarcasm dripping from every syllable.

"Yeah, sorry about that," said Purity sheepishly.

"Oh, I don't know, I quite like it. Though I think I'll stick with Delphi for the time being."

Delphi's smile was thin and wide with dimples in her cheeks. A light scattering of freckles ran in a strip across her impish nose and her eyes, behind those oversized neon rimmed receptionist glasses, were sharp and clear.

"Like the oracle," said Purity.

Delphi smirked, "Most people don't usually get that. I can see you and I are going to get on."

"My dad taught me the value of reading."

"Well, he was a very wise man."

Samson shouted across the room. "Del, you'd better see this."

The screens were now showing a live news broadcast - PBC ONE news. The footage they had watched earlier was being shown in slow motion, but the voiceover told a different story.

"...clusive footage showing two brave government officials fighting off a rabid dog. The animal is believed to have been smuggled in by illegal immigrants through weaknesses in the Channel Tunnel and has since been destroyed..."

Purity shook her head. "Unbelievable," she tutted.

Delphi had seen it all before. "But not unsurprising."

She ran her finger along the map on the table. It was a full colour print of central London. "Samson. Gabe. Plot a few route options for a protest march. Maximum disruption. Warren, we really need those schematics."

They all nodded.

"Any questions?" she asked.

Samson raised her hand, "just the one."

She looked at Warren, her perfect, pencil thin eyebrows raised.

"Wingnut?"

14. EVERYBODY WANTS TO RULE THE WORLD

"What do you see?"

Purity frowned. It was a big question. Delphi had taken her from the catacombs of St Albion's Church where they had caught the tube south of the river. Now, they sat on a high grassy slope in Greenwich park surrounded by poplar and oak, the smell of pollen and freshly cut grass tickling the back of Purity's nose. Blackbirds danced overhead, and the hoot of woodpigeons echoed through the trees as the sun slowly crept down over Camberwell painting the scene in muted pinks and yellows. It was early Spring, and the sense of rebirth and new life was almost palpable.

"It's beautiful," said Purity, and she meant

it. It never ceased to amaze her that these tiny pockets of paradise still existed in such a densely populated area.

"It is, "Delphi smiled. "But I meant out there."

She spread her arm in a wide arc, gesturing at the horizon. From this vantage point they were afforded spectacular views of the City. Canary Wharf with it's crazy mix of architecture, the Shard and further out, Big Ben; on a clear day you could even see Buckingham Palace. Delphi ticked off the districts of the City laid out before them. "Mayfair, Westminster, Kensington. And over there…"

She pointed at the three hulking giants looming over the City.

"The Monoliths," finished Delphi. "The top 1% *literally* living in the shadow of the bottom 1%. Doesn't it bother you?"

Purity shook her head. "It's not a crime to have money."

"Not a crime to have money," Delphi repeated under her breath. "What about the bankers, making money off people's misery? And Jesus entered the temple and drove out all those who were buying and selling in the temple and overturned the tables of the money changers and the seats of those who were selling doves."

"Maybe they're simply providing a service."

"The Monarchy then? Inherited wealth. It's just money breeding money. The rich and the poor. The haves and the have nots. There's an inequality there don't you think?"

Purity shrugged. It wasn't something she had spent a lot of thought on.

Delphi frowned. "I thought you of all people would understand."

"What does that mean?" asked Purity in confusion.

"We're all equal," Delphi quoted. "Just some people are more equal than others."

Purity hesitated. That was the hashtag she had used with the mess about that poster.

Delphi adjusted her legs on the grass and gestured at the giant towers silhouetted on the horizon. "The Monoliths, look at them. People crammed together like battery hens. Its barbaric."

"Yes, but people have got to live somewhere."

"That's not living, that's just existing."

Purity wasn't entirely sure where she was going with this. "What's your point?" she asked.

Delphi buried her fingers between the blades of grass and plucked a fragile daisy free. "They're a symbol, a bloody huge symbol of oppression and they want to build more."

She held the daisy close to her eyes, studying its pale petals. "And I'm ending them."

Purity's eyes widened.

"Metaphorically, I mean," she added. "If these are seen as a success, every council in the country will start throwing them up in the brownfields and greenbelts. Keep the poor contained, keep them in one place so they're easy to find when they need someone to blame. In no time at all, every city will have their own monuments to poverty and the government will tell us they've saved us."

Purity turned to her, trying to gauge her expression. "So, what are you going to do?"

Delphi twisted the daisy in her slim fingers. "Yeah, this is where it gets… tricky." One by one, she began pulling petals from the flower. "These buildings, these towers… everyone knows councils have no money. So, a big project like this, it only stands to reason that they'll have cut corners during the build just to get them finished."

"Cheap materials."

Pluck.

"Poor fire safety."

Pluck.

"Cheap wiring."

Pluck.

Purity went pale as the realisation sunk in. She spoke slowly, in a whisper. "You're going to burn them down."

She nodded, crushing the stalk in her fist.

"Wait a minute!" panicked Purity. "The people… what about the people?"

"Hey calm down. Calm. We're not like the other cells, we're no killers. We're just forcing change."

Purity eyed her warily, "*Good terrorists*, then."

"Tower three's still under construction, but tower two is practically finished, no one's living there. We're going to use that one."

Purity thought for a moment before shaking her head. "No-one will believe it was wiring."

Delphi stood up and stretched her legs. "Two words, Purity: Reasonable Doubt. No one will question a local authorities inefficiency. Once the media get hold of the story and whip the people into a frenzy, there'll be marches and demonstrations. The people will want answers.

"And when the Prime Minister arrives for his 30 second sound bite in the shadow of the towers while all the world watches, we'll be waiting."

Purity raised an eyebrow in a silent question.

"To ask the really difficult questions."

Delphi helped Purity up and they stood together, the setting sun warm on their faces.

"Sounds like you've got it all worked out," said Purity.

"I've spent a lot of thought on this. Are you with us?"

Purity watched the families and children in the park closing their deckchairs and folding blankets - packing up for the day, getting ready to go home.

Quietly she said, "I don't want people to die."

Delphi opened her fist, her palm now a grubby wet smudge of green.

"Trust me, the last thing I want is a mess."

15. EVERYTHING MUST CHANGE

"You can stay here tonight."

They stood at the entrance to Monolith One - three hundred floors of concrete, 200 Pods per floor, 60,000 dwellings in one place. A sprawling shopping mall covered the ground floor and extensive communal areas and parks and recreation spaces were spaced every other 50 floors. An endless repetition of concrete and windows punching angrily through the clouds - a vertical town within a city. Purity held her phone up and craned her neck, leaning backwards squinting to see to the top.

"It's huge," she said.

Nearing completion, Monolith Two stood alongside, both structures joined together by narrow skybridges. In a state of early construction, the third Monolith skulked behind them, an embarrassed cousin.

"We have a few spare pods here, for special cases such as this."

Purity raised her eyebrow. "So, I'm a special case now?"

Delphi reached into her trouser pocket and produced a key with a small round blinking fob. "That's to be decided," she replied with a wry smile. "Either way, you're being hunted, and I wouldn't fancy anyone's chances of finding someone in this place.

"Anyway," she said, holding up the key, "Your state of the art, palatial pod awaits."

Purity had dreamed about pod life for as long as she could remember, now it was right in front of her she didn't feel so sure.

A hand squeezed her shoulder. "Hey P."

Purity didn't need to look around, she'd know Warren's voice anywhere.

"Warren will help you settle in," said Delphi, placing the key in Purity's palm and closed her hand around it. "You good?"

Purity exhaled slowly. Friendly faces, somewhere to sleep. Yes, she was good - she was, in fact better than she had been for a long time.

Purity nodded.

An annoying sound of a cat howled from Delphi's phone and she read the screen. "It's Arial, I have to take this. We'll catch up tomorrow, yeah?"

Delphi turned to leave. "Look after her, Warren," she said. "I've got high hopes for this one."

Purity flicked to selfie mode, framing herself and Warren on screen. Over their shoulders, shaded in sunset purples and reds, the Monolith squatted impassively.

"Everyone say 'loser,'" she said.

"What?" spluttered Warren as the phone flashed.

Purity giggled, an easy laugh but Warren just shook his head.

"God, you're such a bungle," he said.

The reception area of Monolith One opened out into a huge open communal space. At its centre was a recreational park of symmetrical undulating hills with fake trees, plastic grass and worn paths leading around damaged playgrounds covered in multi coloured graffiti. On the swings sat a few teenagers staring silently at their cell phones, hoods drawn tightly over their heads, plumes of raspberry scented smoke over their heads. Above them, dangling from a tangled array of wire cables, a large plastic sun bathed the interior in a sickly, artificial glow. Around the perimeter of the park were shops, cafés and stalls; a mini town centre to provide for the denizens above. Burger Queenz, Novichock Noodles, Kim's Plucky Fried Chicken - all the big names were there, and they were all boarded up apart from the ever-popular Korean fried chicken store.

Which was strange because whatever the meat was, it certainly wasn't chicken.

"The government, they bug everything. Emails, texts, phone calls, messages... it's all monitored 24 hours a day. They're always listening."

Warren had the back off Purity's phone and a thin cable ran from the guts of the device to his own phone. The software he had written ran quickly and her phone buzzed twice, a photo of Mr NoseyBonk appearing on the lock screen.

"That should keep the snoopers out."

He clipped the cover back on the phone and handed it back.

"What do you make of her?" asked Purity.

"Delphi, you mean?"

Warren chuckled lightly. "She's... driven. Very vocal, not one to hide at the back of the class or let something go. She sees something broken, she just wants to jump in and fix it. If anyone's going to change the world, reckon it'll be her."

Purity stepped through a scattering of rubbish - broken bottles, polystyrene containers, mouldy food - debris from a public bin that appeared to have been danced on. Vigorously.

"Change the world," she said with a sneer, kicking a rusted can. "Is that why she's *here*?"

"She's here because society is broken, she intends to fix it. You should try and give her a chance - she's one of the good ones. They all are in fact."

He paused in thought before adding, "Well, maybe not Gabe. I'm still not sure about him."

They arrived at the bank of elevators and Warren pushed the glowing arrow beside the doors.

"So how long have you been a terrorist, Warren?"

Wide eyed, Warren threw a nervous glance around the mall. "Keep your voice down, will you?"

He didn't relax until they were in the elevator and the doors had firmly closed behind them. "Guess you can blame my Grandma," he said. "She pushed for me to do extra Religious Studies, sent me to Sunday School. That's when I met these guys."

"Are you saying you were indoctrinated?"

"No, no, not at all. They showed me there was another way of getting stuff done - of actually making a change."

"By blowing people up?" she provoked.

"Blowing *stuff* up," he corrected.

Purity raised an eyebrow, remembering the words he had used in the messaging app. "You can't make an omelette without killing a few chickens?"

He shook his head. "We're not murderers."

"Yeah, I keep forgetting. You're the 'good' terrorists."

He lifted his phone, tapping an app with his thumb.

"Look, let's face it," he said, holding *The Whole E-Bible* to her. "If reading a few words in *this* is going to turn someone into a murderer, they were a murderer already."

With the abolition of the Human Rights Act and introduction of the Living Space Bill, the definition of a home was re-classified. Houses became rooms, and rooms were reduced to ultra-compact habitation units. Or pods.

They stopped at a featureless pod, in a sea of featureless pods. He tapped the key on the tiny chrome plaque 74-344.

"This is you, kiddo," he said, handing her the key. "You'll be safe here; these things are tough." He rapped on the hatch feeling the metal reverberate deep inside. "Genuine Americana steel, built for redneck survivalists waiting on a nuclear war."

Warren gestured down the corridor. "If you need anything I'm in 312, down there. Toilet block is around the corner, about half way along but I wouldn't go in there alone, especially at night."

She slid the key in and turned. The hatch popped open with a hiss and rolled haltingly to one side, a wave of lemon bleach and mould assaulting her nostrils.

The pod was about 3 metres long and a little over a metre high. Big enough to lie down and sit up, but little else. A thin mattress covered the entire floor area with a hard pillow at the end. The cream, metal walls curved around like a tube and had a number of sliding compartments and shelves for storage. She crawled in on her hands and knees and rolled onto her back. Overhead, a monitor was built into the ceiling, angled so it could be watched while lying down. It was currently showing reruns of the weekly hangings and Purity quickly turned the channel over - she was not a fan of *Noosenight*. She punched a large red button on the wall and the hatch shuddered to a close with a pneumatic hiss.

Purity closed her eyes, feeling the strength drain from her body as she finally relaxed.

"Living the dream, Purity," she murmured to herself. "Living the dream."

16. TOWER OF STRENGTH

"What in buggery blue bollocks is this?" cried the Prime Minister. On the tablet, he watched two constables laying into a defenceless dog with primed shoksticks, cobalt electric blurs sparking and arcing fiercely in the shade of a garden. August's face grew visibly redder as he watched.

He stood up behind his oak desk and waved the tablet at Hattie. "You know when they say, '*all* PR is *good* PR'?"

He hurled it as hard as he could. It span past her head, end over end, embedding itself in the plastered wall. It wasn't the only dent there. "Bloody animal rights will have a field day with this! How on earth is it trending?"

Hattie composed herself. As used as she was to his outbursts they were still challenging.

"Sometimes things break through the noise of the feed, sometimes it's hard to predict what'll go viral."

But live acts of government violence? Animal cruelty? Sometimes it's not that hard to predict, she thought.

"For some reason, this obviously struck a chord with the people," she shrugged.

"Struck a chord! Struck a chord?! Well bloody unstrike it then!"

"It's already out there, we can't delete anything from the feed. But I have traced the clip back to the source. The original post was from a Miss St. George on the run from two arresting constables. There's already a warrant out on her. Hate speech. Resisting Arrest."

August sank back in his leather chair and stared at the ceiling.

"You know what? I don't care. Just deal with it, will you? Just get rid of her."

August rubbed his temple, it throbbed angrily.

"Make her go away, please."

Hattie tapped the glass surface and began typing a short message to the Chief Constable.

"Tell me, Miss Simms, do you have any good news? Anything at all? How's that poll coming on?"

Name That Monolith - the poll to soften the imposing perception of the two and a half, ultimately four, huge superstructures squatting over the City. Hattie read from her tablet. "There's been a big uptake on the feeds, lot of people getting involved. Let me just sort these."

She swiped across the glass, arranging the results into some semblance of order. "So, as you know, the name 'Monolith' is scoring high on 'recognition' but very low on 'likeability'. We set up a poll on the feeds, open to everyone, for naming suggestions - something to humanise them, make them more approachable."

She cleared the lowest results and listed the favourites in a stack.

"So currently in third place," she said, "We have the suggestion: Rainbow Towers, naming the towers Geoffrey, Zippy, George and Bungle."

"I don't get it."

"In second place, Not The Nine O'Clock Mews, with the towers named Mel, Griff, Rowan and Pamela."

"I still don't get it."

"And in the lead, by quite a wide margin I must say, we have…"

"Yes?"

"It's probably not what you were hoping for."

"What do you mean?"

"I think we should maybe rethink…"

"Spit it out, woman. What is it?"

She took a deep breath.

Here goes another tablet, she thought.

"Skyscrape McScrapeFace."

August bristled, his already radish red face reddening like a beetroot as his complexion worked its way through the spectrum of root vegetables.

They were going to need to order more tablets.

The door opened, and a tall man entered. Frail, effeminate and slight of build, he wore long golden robes over an ornate white frock, a thick heavy pectoral cross hanging from his neck. He carried a long staff with a jewelled crooked top which he used as a walking stick. His hair, long and silver, was tied into a braid which ran over his shoulder.

"Terrence, great speech the other day," he said warmly.

Archbishop Randall Runcible approached the Prime Minister with his arm outstretched, a huge gold ring glistening obscenely on his finger. They shook hands energetically.

"Randy," said August with fake humility, "You're very kind."

The Archbishop lowered his hand. "I am a Christian, you know. It's my job."

The days broadsheets and tabloids, were spread across the Prime Minister's desk. The KostlyKoffee bombing was still headline news.

"Terrible business with that terrorist," said Runcible, smoothing an unkempt bushy eyebrow, "Shocking, just shocking. We have publicly denounced these so-called Christian extremists, obviously and you have my deepest assurances the Church is conducting a full and frank investigation into its membership."

Runcible shook his head. "We have to, it's bad for business."

"Keeps the masses occupied though," replied August, "Takes their gaze away from the government, at least. How *are* things on that front?"

"No different. Worse, if anything. I think the Defence Secretary and Deputy PM Ramona are up to something."

August had held suspicions about some of his party members for some time. Quiet conversations in side corridors, secret meetings, funny looks. He knew more than anyone that politicians weren't to be trusted, but this felt a little too close to home.

"Something?"

"Gut feeling is a coup of some kind. Suspect they'll leverage the bombings against me, use it to force me out."

"There's no proof of that," chipped in Hattie.

"I know, I know, but I don't trust them," said August. "It's what I'd do if I were them."

The Archbishop stood in the window and looked out over St. James' Park.

"You can't run a government looking over your shoulder all the time," he said.

"I know, I know. But what they're doing..."

"If they're doing anything at all," added Hattie.

"Yes, if they're doing anything at all. What they're doing is perfectly legal."

Archbishop Runcible breathed on the ornate gold ring and polished it against his frock, his brow heavy with concentration. "All things are lawful. But not all things are helpful. Corinthians 10:23."

He fixed the Prime Minister a steady glare.

"Maybe you should change the law.

17. HOUNDS OF LOVE

"Where are we going?"

Purity's forehead rested on the bus window and she watched the early morning streets of London blur past. They had just left Little Poland and were passing through the narrow streets of Pocket Pyongyang, the chimneys of Battersea looming in the distance. In a city of over 10,000 buses, another bright red double-decker bus was the perfect disguise.

Hiding in plain sight.

Delphi sat in the driver's seat and manoeuvred the vehicle confidently through the traffic. In the back of the bus Purity and Warren sat on a long, padded vinyl bench while Gabriel and Samson faced each other over a flimsy fold down table. Gabriel had laid out a couple of straws and was carefully unfolding a crumpled white envelope as the bus rocked and bounced. From tinny speakers, the band UB40 sang 'Red Red Wine' off an underground compilation tape of banned classics - this one removed from circulation for its blatant cultural appropriation and overt promotion of alcohol.

"You sleep alright, hun?" asked Samson.

Purity thought for a moment.

"Yeah, actually," she said, surprising herself. With the pod door closed, the only sound was the constant rumble of the air conditioning and the occasional distant bang of hatches closing. They were impressively soundproofed, and Purity had quickly fallen into the deepest of sleeps.

Purity watched fascinated as Gabriel emptied the contents of the envelope onto the table. It was a tiny amount, maybe half a teaspoon of powder.

White powder.

He offered a straw to Samson and she took it smiling.

"Is that what I think it is?" asked Purity.

Gabriel arranged the powder into a line, singularly focused on the task. "Drop of the white stuff? Just a little something to focus the mind, get the blood pumping?"

Samson offered her pink striped straw, "Want to try some, hun? It's *fantabulous!*"

Warren raised his hand. "That won't be necessary," he said. "We don't do sugar."

"Don't say I didn't ask," giggled Samson leaning forward, sucking up the pale granules.

Sugar. Before the Puritan Act it was everywhere. Soft drinks, sweets, cereals, sauces, ready meals. It was quickly decided that children had been taught to crave it from an early age with adverts aimed squarely at toddlers and infants with gaudy playful characters. The adverts were the first to go, swiftly followed by the products themselves. Within months all sugar products were banned, belonging in the same category as all addictive substances. Drugs, alcohol, tobacco and now sugar. Purity had never even seen pure sugar before - the powder sold on the high street was some weird low fat chemical approximation - yet here it was, taken openly in front of her. What kind of people had she fallen in with?

"It's Sunday," said Purity. "There won't even be anybody there, will there?"

Delphi glanced up at the rear-view mirror. "Always get the biggest crowds on a Sunday. Weekend Warriors."

They reached the brow of the hill and slowed down, the demonstration ahead now in full panorama. As far as the eye could see, from Covent Garden Market to the railway, people were shouting and chanting, fists in the air. The square was heaving with protesters and a rhythmic barrage of yelling, singing and steel drums filled the air. Some wore face paint, some masks, but all had been brought together under a common goal in the shadow of the power station. Dozens of banners shook angrily, hastily painted in a bedsit or lovingly constructed by the whole family.

ITS NOT FUR

A PET IS FOR LIFE NOT JUST FOR X-PERIMENTS

And one message Purity noticed more than a few times. She pointed her phone out the window, taking a picture and uploading to the feed instantaneously. It was a still. A photo from her feed of the goons beating the dog. In large yellow letters it read:

MORE EQUAL THAN OTHERS

Purity shrunk in her seat. There were a lot of people here.

A lot.

Meaning the Police would be here soon in some number, riot gear, maybe water cannons. Nothing good could come of this.

"Why are we here?" she said, rubbing her eyes. "Adding five more people to this protest won't change anything."

Delphi swung the steering wheel hard and the bus veered off onto a side street.

"Told you she was bright," she said.

"That's why we're not going to it."

The bus bumped and shook down a cobbled avenue lines with parked cars.

"This place will be swarming in filth within an hour," said Purity.

"We're counting on it. If the police are dealing with a few thousand angry dog huggers," said Delphi pulling over to the kerb, "Then they won't be looking over here."

Across the road was a squat, single storey, red brick building. There was no signage to speak of and what windows there were, were dark and frosted. It was a building going out of its way to be inconspicuous. It was only when you looked closer, really looked, that you would start to see the electrified fences, the electronic passes, the micro-surveillance cams.

"Animal experiments... that's what goes on here. It was bad enough in the old days when they'd torture rabbits for the sake of a lipstick or eyeshadow. But this... You're familiar with gender reassignment?"

Purity nodded, she's known a few kids at her school that had 'swapped', never really thought anything of it.

"This is the next big thing: Animal Gender Reassignment, where pet owners with depressed dogs or cats and animal psychologists decide they're sad because they're trapped in the wrong body."

"So, Lassie becomes Laddie," mused Samson.

"The Battersea Towers are the public face of government research. This... this is where the actual work happens."

Gabe patted his leather satchel, "But not for much longer."

"Wait, what are we, you, going to do here?" asked Purity.

"Don't worry," replied Delphi. "It's like you said, it's Sunday. All the staff will be at home, no one will get hurt. We're going to burn this evil place to the ground."

"Simple as that?"

"Simple as that. You with us, Purity?"

Purity never had a particular affinity for animals and never had a pet - the regulations and background checks were prohibitive - but all she could think of right now was the constables torturing that dog in the back garden with unrestrained glee.

She nodded. "Wouldn't doing this at night be a better idea?".

Warren shook his head. "Statistically speaking, security is 25% higher overnight. Sunday morning is the quietest time, especially if we hit during the shift change."

He glanced at his watch, a retro silver Casio with red LED display. "Which we are."

"Anyway hun, who's going to pay us any notice?" said Samson heaving a placard high over her shoulder proclaiming TRANIMAL

RIGHTS!

"We're just more protesters on a day out."

They followed the exterior wall of the facility along the public footpath. Ahead was a fire door, to the casual observer, at least. Embedded in the brickwork was a small plain metal rectangle - a scanner of some kind.

"So how do we get in?"

Warren held his phone in both hands, thumbs flashing across the keyboard.

"There's this new thing out, you might have heard of it," he said, tapping the last button with a flourish. The door clicked and swung open a centimetre.

"It's called 'science.'"

Purity stuck two fingers up at him and followed the others through the door.

They found themselves in a long, straight corridor with worn vinyl flooring and low overhanging strip lights. Doors to offices and storerooms fed off the walkway and the air was heavy with fur and chemicals. High in the far corner was a camera covering the area, but they ignored it. Warren had already taken care of that.

Delphi put her finger to her lips and the team fell silent. Quietly, they tiptoed to the end of the corridor where it veered left. Delphi stopped, holding her hand up flat. She peered around the corner at another corridor, shorter this time, but with parked trolleys of medicines and medical apparatus. Beyond that lay an office door and the two large chrome doors. Above the gleaming metal doors, a plaque read:

ANIMAL ROOM

Putting her hand down, they moved forward again in silence. Cautiously glancing left and right, looking for signs of movement, anything out of place. As they drew level with the office door Delphi raised her hand again, waiting. Listening. After what seemed like an eternity, she dropped her hand and they continued until they reached the metal doors. She placed a hand on the horizontal bar and Gabriel did the same. Staring at each other, she silently counted down.

Three.
Two.
One.
They pushed together.

The doors swung open smoothly revealing a large square space. A dozen or so cells or cages lined the walls, some empty but most with dogs of different breeds and sizes. They were expecting a cacophony once they had reached the cells, but instead were met with an eerie silence. All the animals were clearly under some kind of sedation, but had pipes feeding into their mouths. As much as they might want to bark or cry, they couldn't. The creatures stared at the human intruders, silent but for the sound of laboured breathing.

"Dear God," whispered Purity.

Gabriel dropped his bag to the floor and unzipped it loudly. One by one he lifted out several small black and red devices wrapped in wires and laid them in a row at his feet.

"Wait," said Purity. "The animals! What about the animals?"

"Yeah it sucks," he answered. "But look at them, they're going nowhere. At least it'll be quick."

"You promised me no-one would get hurt!"

"No *people* would get hurt," he corrected. "Technically..."

"No! We're not murderers. Even of animals."

Gabriel ignored her and laid out the last devices. Warren lowering the explosive. "No, she's right."

"Okay, okay," said Delphi, taking control. "This is what we're doing. Warren, Purity... you take care of the animals. Do what you need to do but remember, we're against the clock here. Everyone else, as you were. Now go, go, go."

Samson, Gabriel and Delphi scooped up detonators and split up, planting the devices on load-bearing walls.

Warren rummaged through the backpack, pulling out a long pair of bolt cutters. He marched to the first cage and tightened the jaws around the padlock. With the lightest of pressure, it shattered instantly and clattered to the floor.

Good, he thought. This wasn't going to take long.

Silently he moved to the next cell, quickly working round the room.

Purity eased the cage open. Inside was a chocolate Labrador panting heavily. It struggled to stand, and Purity stroked his head.

"It's okay, it's okay," she whispered soothingly. She gripped the tube going into the animal's mouth and gave it a tug. It moved only slightly and the dog shook, emitting a faint whine.

"Oh God."

Warren was still busy working his way through the locks. There was no help to be had there.

Painfully aware that time was running out, Purity squeezed her eyes shut. "Sorry. I'm so sorry."

And pulled the tube as hard as she could.

The dog yelped, and the pipe popped out coated in bile and saliva, leaving the creature retching and coughing.

Warren shouted over. "You alright?"

She nodded, quietly stroking the animal behind the neck. "Good boy, good dog. You're okay." She wrapped an arm around the dog, hugging it hard and lifted her phone up panning around the sad creatures in the remaining cells. #MOREEQUALTHANOTHERS #ANIMALRIGHTS.

She returned the phone to her pocket and looked at Warren.

"Okay. Let's get this done."

Samson held the explosive against the support beam as Gabriel secured it with cable ties.

"Was thinking," he said. "There's this new Sushizza place, just opened off Soho. We should try it when this is over."

"Sushizza? What the hell is Sushizza?" asked Samson.

"I dunno. Maybe it's like sushi and pizza?"

Samson wrinkled her nose. "That sounds disgusting. We so definitely have to go there!"

Gabriel tightened the last tie and shouted to Delphi. "Clear!"

Delphi took the timing device from her breast pocket. It resembled a rotating dial with notches pushed down. Analogue, deliberately old-school… and impossible to hack remotely.

She set the timer to three minutes.

"Let's go."

They ran into the Animal Room just as Purity was easing the last dog out of its cage. It stood shakily on all fours and eyed the new humans with distrust.

"Come on. We are leaving!" shouted Delphi.

Samson and Delphi led the way, returning to the fire door where they had entered the building. Behind, Purity and Warren shooed the dogs, herding the crippled creatures like sheep towards the exit. The animals had now found their voices and were howling and yapping as they darted back and to between the steel trolleys, boxes of medicine and drugs falling to the floor.

"Purity," yelled Warren.

Samson crashed through the door with a bang, flooding the interior with sunlight and the hounds piled through to freedom.

"Purity!" said Warren again. Much louder this time.

Purity turned around, dogs running between her legs.

Warren was standing still, arms in the air. Behind him, a man, old with a bushy grey moustache stood pointing a taser at his back. On his pressed blue shirt, a badge showed a lightning flash through a stylised shield and a stencilled name MACKAY. A security guard.

"What do you think you're doing?" he shouted.

"Its... it's not what it looks like," stuttered Purity.

Only it was. It was exactly what it looked like, how could it be anything else?

"Both of you lie on the ground with your hands behind your head."

"That's not going to happen," said Delphi, suddenly at her side.

"There's five of us and one of you," said Samson towering over the group. "Let it go, honey."

"I already called backup, there's a team on the way."

"You didn't call anyone. You're as surprised as we are, I can see it in your eyes."

Mackay appraised the ragtag team. He had the experience, but they had youth and, looking at Samson, strength on their side. They were right about one thing at least - he was severely outnumbered.

"Why? Why would you do this?" he asked.

"What?" spat Purity. "You know what they do here, don't you? These sick tests on defenceless animals while you just take the money and turn a blind eye. Experiments on animals? You're the animals! You disgust me!"

The guard frowned. "I... don't know what you think happens here, but you're wrong."

"Wrong? How can I be wrong? We saw the dogs. We're stood in the middle of the proof... you experiment on animals!"

Mackay lowered his taser, flicking the safety back on. He squeezed his eyes shut and rubbed the bridge of his nose.

"This facility specialises in cancer research. They're working on a cure." He gestured to the trolleys parked against the wall. "Just look at the notes."

Purity grabbed a clipboard and licked through the first few pages. None of it made sense, of course - she was no doctor - but on every page the same word over and over. Cancer.

She waved the clipboard at him. "So, you're injecting the dogs with cancer just so you can find a cure! This changes nothing!"

The guard held his hands up, palms forward. He spoke slowly, earnestly, like a teacher with a student, or a doctor breaking bad news to a patient.

"They *already* had cancer. They came here to be saved."

Purity staggered back, stunned.

Came here to be saved.

Her heart pounding in her ears.

Saved.

Mackay's face dropped, and he crumpled to the floor, unconscious. Gabriel slid the cosh back up his sleeve.

"Sorry to break up this beautiful moment folks, but…" He tapped his wristwatch. "Gonna get real warm In about thirty seconds."

"What about him?" shouted Warren pointing to the body on the floor.

"The security guard?" sneered Gabe. "He knew what he was signing up for. Come on."

Gabriel rushed past Delphi through the open fire door.

Warren shook his head and grabbed the

guard under his arm.

Seeing what he was doing, Purity lifted his other arm and together they dragged him, his shoes squeaking on the shiny floor. Purity had no idea how long they had before things started exploding, but she knew it was soon. The door seemed so very far away, and he was so, so heavy.

"Come on, come on..." grunted Warren. Mackay's arm flopped out, catching Purity behind the knee. Her legs tangled and losing balance she fell to the floor with the guard.

Panicking, she scrambled to her knees. Warren pulled the body as hard as he could, but it was like wrestling with a bag of potatoes.

Time. There was no time.

They weren't going to...

In a blur, the security guard was lifted upwards and thrown over Samson's shoulder - her huge hands effortlessly lifting Purity like a rag doll and marching through the exit.

"No child left behind, honey."

In astonishment, Warren sprinted out as Delphi slammed the fire door closed behind them.

They staggered a few meters before the soft WHOOMP of an explosion was heard inside the building. Then another. And another, until a dozen small eruptions came together as one. Blackened windows blew out in every direction and viscous, thick smoke poured out. Along the roofline flames flickered high, taking hold and greedily devouring wood, plastic and insulation and an alarm bell rang out incessantly.

Away from the building, Samson laid the guard out on the pavement. She touched a finger to his neck, feeling for a pulse.

"He'll survive."

A column of billowing smog reached into the sky, the blaze intensifying and sirens could be heard a few streets away. People were emerging from homes and offices, cell phones in hand, filming the disaster. The guard still lay motionless but now he was not alone. Three escape dogs had already found him and were curling up on his body, licking his face. As Purity watched, others were joining them.

A lump formed in Purity's throat and she remembered the man's words. Words that would haunt her.

They already had cancer.
They came here to be saved.

Delphi fired up the double-decker bus and Sting suddenly blared from the speakers gibbering 'De Do Do Do De Da Da Da' - a song long banned for cultural appropriation and promotion of illiteracy. Inside, Gabe held the sliding doors open and Samson nimbly leapt into the vehicle.

"Quickly!" he yelled, "Before the police..."

He didn't finish the sentence, but he didn't need to. The constabulary were already here.

Two Kaesong Police Interceptors skidded into view at the end of the street, lights flashing, sirens wailing. Gabe slammed the bus doors shut as Delphi revved the engine hard. The tyres screamed and the bus bounced along the cobbles, veering away, Gabriel and Samson's faces pressed against the greasy back window.

"Run!" urged Warren.

Together they dashed to a break in the terraces and cut down a cement footpath between houses.

The sound of skidding tyres caught Purity's attention and she braved a quick look back over her shoulder. The Interceptor had stopped, mounted on the kerb and already a small, wiry constable was climbing out of the passenger seat, pointing at them.

It was Officer Lister.

Really? Thought Purity. *Are there no other police officers in this city?*

They ran down an alley behind two sets of terraces and emerged onto the square. In their hundreds, people of all colours, shapes and sizes carrying banners and placards were surging away from the Power Station, away from the noise and smoke. A panic of protestors.

Warren merged into the mass of people first, immediately swept away by the unrelenting tide of humanity. Purity put her head down and submitted herself to the pull and push of the horde, embracing the anonymity of the crowd

- allowing the flow of protesters to move her away from the scene of the crime. She looked back but saw no sign of the pursuing constable.

The movement of the crowd became slower, more erratic and Purity strained over shaved heads and bobble hats to see what the cause was. Ahead, a figure stood perfectly still like a rock in a stream, the masses struggling to move around her.

It was a girl in a coat.

A long white trench coat.

Purity went cold, recalling the suicide bomber in KostlyKoffee. What was more troubling, however, was she recognised this girl instantly: Warren had introduced her.

What was the name? Elle? Angel?

"It's...it's Ariel, isn't it?" she remembered.

The girl blinked in confusion, as if waking from a dream and surveyed the masses, wide eyed like a politician caught leaving a massage parlour. Purity studied the coat - although there were no obvious bumps or bulges, it's length was more than capable of concealing a bomb.

"Look," pleaded Purity, fighting to keep her voice level, "Look, you don't have to do this."

Alarmed, Ariel flung her trench coat wide open, holding her arms wide. Strapped to her torso was a series of tubes and wires; in her hand, a detonator. There was a scream from the crowd followed by others and the crowd pushed back, protestors scrambling over protesters to get away.

Purity and the bomber stood barely an arm's length apart in a loose clearing surrounded by frozen, terrified onlookers.

"Please Ariel, whatever you think this is fixing, I promise you, it isn't. These are just innocent men, women. There are children here."

Ariel hesitated, taking in the enormity of the situation. Haltingly, her arms lowered.

Purity held her hands out, palms forward. "It's okay, it's okay," she whispered. "Just put the detonator down and we can talk about it. This is not the way it has to go."

Ariel's breathing slowed and a single tear ran down her cheek, staining her lapel. Her watery blue eyes locked with Purity's and her expression melted. Shifting from hysteria to… what was that, exactly? Serenity?

Arial raised the detonator and spoke loud and clearly, "In the name of the Father!"

Purity screamed and hit the ground, crouching with her arms over her head. The suicide vest popped and hissed.

And popped.

And hissed some more.

Then fizzled out.

Tentatively, Purity lowered her arm from her face.

Arial was shaking the detonator, pushing the button over and over as a thin patch of fire crawled up her sleeve. She waved her arm in an attempt to extinguish it, but the flame caught her coat and ate straight through to her dress. Screaming, she tried batting the blaze with her bare hands but it was too late. The wild fire spread like wildfire - in seconds consuming her entire body. She thrashed around maniacally as a guttural, unearthly sound escaping from her, before collapsing in a blazing heap.

Purity wiped her eyes. She knew nothing of Arial other than she had suffered a senseless, pointless death. She had died for a belief, but it had changed nothing. Did she have parents? Loved ones?

This can't have been what she wanted, thought Purity. *Maybe she...*

The shokstik struck the base of her spine and she fell to the concrete, unconscious.

"Terrorists," spat Officer Lister, standing over her. "You're like buses. You wait for hours then three turn up at once."

BOOK 2
Hi-De-Hi

18. SUMMER HOLIDAY

"Squawk!" squawked the seagull.

Purity woke, blinking hard as her eyes struggled to focus on the angry grey and white bird only inches from her face. A large swathe of green moved past slowly and she was aware her whole body was swaying gently. The chilled salty air stung her face which, while uncomfortable, very quickly focused her.

She was in a cable car. A compact wrought iron cable car and judging by its design, built sometime in the fifties. It was basic and had no windows, simply consisting of two hard wooden seats facing each other and a hinged door. There was no lock of any kind on it. She sat up straight gripping the iron railings, smooth and bumpy from decades of overpainting and the car rocked with her movement, creaking and groaning wearily. The seagull squawked again and took to the skies.

Purity froze waiting for the cab to settle, suddenly feeling very exposed. The car returned to its previous rhythm and Purity peered cautiously over the side at the grassy hills below. It wasn't a long way down, considering, but it wasn't a drop you would walk away from. The car was suspended from a single, thick iron cable that stretched ahead and behind her as far as she could see, a view broken only by intermittent pylons carrying the weight. Another cable, only meters to her side carried cars back the way she had come. All the other cars she could see appeared to be empty. To her right, water stretched to the horizon - a sea of grey merging with a sky of grey, tiny boats bobbing in the distance.

The sea, she thought. *Is that the North Sea? English Channel?*

She patted her pocket, feeling for the familiar shape of her mobile phone but it was gone. Taken. Purity suddenly felt very naked and very lost.

The car rattled and shook as it traversed a pylon noisily, then settled again. A large, wide billboard was planted in the fields below, angled in such a way it's only purpose could be for the benefit of the cable car passengers. In a retro post-war design, it said:

TRUST YOUR DOCTOR - NOT THE INTERNET

The sign was sun-bleached, and weather beaten.

A knot, small and tight formed in her stomach with a sickening realisation.

"No," she gasped.

The next billboard featured a grotesque hook-nosed character dressed as a Victorian shopkeeper in a striped pinafore and flat, wide brimmed hat. The elements had not been kind to him though, his leering face warped and pock-marked by decades of sea-salt erosion. He held out a huge white gloved hand in the foreground revealing two sugar lumps in his palm. A speech balloon asked, "ONE LUMP OR TWO?" while the title warned:

JUST SAY NO! SUGAR - THE GATEWAY DRUG.

Beyond that, another billboard came into view, but Purity didn't need to read its contents - it was quite clear where the cable car was heading. Where *she* was heading.

The National Health Camps.

The government public information films had been in common circulation since Purity was five or six and were responsible for many children's nightmares ever since. Jumping out unexpectedly in advert breaks in kids shows, the weird, nightmarish character would dispense sage advice on topics such as safety and crime prevention with catchy slogans such as 'Immigrant or Innocent? We decide so you don't have to!' and 'Seen a tramp? Call the Health Camp!'

The National Health Service, twitching and groaning on its own form of life support for decades, finally shuffled off this mortal coil when the Purity Act became law. Years of bureaucracy and inefficiency had sucked all the life and influence from its body, leaving a hollow empty husk of an organisation existing from day to day on the power of goodwill alone.

The National Health Service, twitching and groaning on its own form of life support for decades, finally shuffled off this mortal coil when the Euvid-21 virus arrived on Britannica's shores. Years of bureaucracy and inefficiency had sucked all the life and influence from its body, leaving a hollow empty husk of an organisation existing from day to day on the power of goodwill alone. Under the Purity Act, the government seized buildings and land - anywhere large enough and remote enough to isolate the victims of the disease - converting the facilities to vast treatment centres. These new complexes brought fresh efficiencies and economies of scale. Waiting lists were halved and halved again. Whole tiers of middle management and administration were removed leaving the doctors and nurses to get on with their jobs.

But then there was the talk. Nothing ever written down, no pictures. Stories of these so called Health Camps far away, places where they sent the dying and the feeble, the lost and the broken. Rumour had it, once you were sent there you never came out.

On the billboard below, the ugly caricature wore a striped nightcap and billowing granny bloomers. He held the elastic out at the waist and was pointing a torch inside at the crotch. His wide eyes suggested some concern at what he was seeing.

THERE'S NO MEDICINE FOR REGRET - GET IT CHECKED.

The next board featured the same grotesque fellow wearing a black suit and bow tie and spiky, long haired wig. He cackled insanely at his own private joke and brandished a multicoloured feather duster that had seen better days.

LAUGHTER - THE BEST MEDICINE

Movement below caught her eye. Three or four figures in white overalls had erected ladders and scaffolding at one end of the board and were busy pushing wet brushes up and down a section of the poster in an effort to clean something. As she drew closer, the problem became apparent. Someone, it seemed, had added their own graffiti. A single decisive, sprayed stroke in red.

The letter 'S'

*S*LAUGHTER - THE BEST MEDICINE.

"Hey!" she shouted, waving over the side. "Hello!?"

The workers didn't look up.

That appeared to be the last of the billboards and the cable car shuddered as it crossed another pylon. Ahead a set of buildings of differing colours and sizes were laid out in a grid system, long low terraces intersecting with tall blocky warehouse sized structures. A single high wire fence bordered the complex and as she drew near, Purity could see barbed wire coiled along the top. A sudden wind whipped in, fierce and insistent, rocking the car fiercely. Purity swore and gripped the iron tightly.

The cable car crossed the perimeter and passed over rows and rows of terraced chalets with sloping roofs, their stucco walls painted in pastel pinks, greens and blues. The chalets thinned out around a tear shaped lake where giant plastic swans bobbed in the water, their passengers pedalling leisurely inside. Beyond the lake, paths led to a large angular glass roofed building decorated in faux Americana while outside on a thick striped pole, a huge red neon DINER sign revolved, blinking. As she passed over the roof of the diner, Purity peered through the glass roof to see people eating at dozens of tables or walking around a wide-open plan checkerboard floor. The car drew alongside a tall red brick chimney - easily the tallest structure here, towering over her, even from her lofty vantage point. Noxious, black smoke belched into the sky.

A cheery whistle caught her attention and below her a brightly coloured land train ferried people in white dressing gowns along wide sandy paths. Smaller featureless buildings were scattered together, meandering downhill to a sandy beach and a tired looking pier. Past that, and way, way out out to sea, wind turbines jutted out of the water in their hundreds.

Purity's stomach fluttered and she was conscious the cable car had begun its descent. The cable stretched down to a cluster of low concrete buildings on the outskirts, some distance to the rest of the facility. Outside the station, a small brass band in pyjamas and dressing gowns played 'Congratulations' enthusiastically. People gathered on the platform dressed in white. Where they nurses? Doctors?

The car hit the guide rails roughly and the car swung wildly for a moment before locking into its landing position. A large, burly man reached in pulling the handle and the flimsy metal door swung open with a pathetic groan. He held out his hand and Purity steadied herself on it as she climbed out of the iron cage.

Flanked by figures in white coats and surgical face masks, a woman in a lab coat stepped forward. She was in her late 50s, white hair pinned back harshly in a bun with spectacles balanced on her forehead.

"Good afternoon. Purity is it?" she asked jovially, shaking Purity's hand. "We're so glad you could join us. I hope you had a pleasant journey?"

Not waiting for a response, she put an arm around Purity and walked her to the foyer. "Good. Good. Well follow me, let's get you checked in and then you can make your way to your room."

"Room?" said Purity, confused.

"Of course, of course. What were you expecting? A cardboard box?" She giggled at her own joke, a shrill, unpleasant assault on the ears.

"No, no... the 'make my way' bit. I'm not a prisoner?"

"Oh my!" the nurse laughed. It was still no easier on the ears. "Prisoner? Prisoner?! This is a Health Camp my dear, not Strangeways!"

"Then why the fence?"

The nurse stared down her arrowed nose. "This is a very exclusive establishment, my dear. That's to keep people out!"

Purity followed her down a well-worn corridor smelling of wet paint, to a tall vertical touchscreen standing by a set of double doors labelled 'ARRIVALS'.

On the screen it said simply:

> WELCOME TO NATIONAL
> HEALTH CAMP 06 EAST
> WE HOPE YOU ENJOY YOU'RE STAY
> PLEASE PLACE YOUR PALM ON THE SCREEN.

A green silhouette of a hand pulsed gently below the text.

Purity hesitated for a moment, troubled by the misplaced apostrophe but it really didn't seem like the time or the place to mention it. She planted her hand gingerly on the image.

A single chime and the screen was replaced with:

> THANK YOU
> PURITY ST. GEORGE
>
> YOU'RE ROOM NAME IS
> RED 29

Purity's hand was suddenly uncomfortably warm and she withdrew it sharply. She turned it over, the cause of the discomfort glaringly apparent. In the centre of her palm, about a centimetre high were the digits 29 in red.

"What?"

"Oh that? That's nothing, dear," said the nurse. "Guests were always forgetting their rooms! This just makes it so much easier! It'll fade after a while. Don't worry about it!"

"Now you just need to go through 'orientation', then you can be on your way!"

"Orientation?"

"Just a short informal presentation for new guests. Show you what we have here, our facilities, services we have available to you. That sort of thing. Don't worry! It's just a bit of fun."

With a hiss, the doors opened revealing a hall with a low stage at the front. A dozen or so other people were stood around, some in groups or couples talking, most stood alone. Young, old, affluent, poor… there didn't seem to be any consistency in the audience.

New arrivals, Purity figured.

"P!" came a shout, and Warren's arms were suddenly around her.

"Warren!" she exclaimed. "They got you too!"

"I know, I know. It's crazy isn't it?"

"What about the others?"

"I don't know, as soon as she heard the sirens Delphi just floored it, fingers crossed they got away. Don't remember much after that."

He rubbed his shoulder. "Apart from the woman with the cattle prod!"

"Yeah, we've met before."

"Then, when I woke up I was in that stupid old chairlift." He raised his eyebrows. "That can't be safe."

"You get one of these?" he asked, holding up his hand showing a blue 13.

Purity nodded and showed him her stamp. "Lucky 13" she said.

The lights dimmed and brass band music burst into life. Purity recognised it instantly. The tune from the adverts, the public information films for the PHS. It was a classical piece by Edvard Grieg - 'In the Hall of the Mountain King'

The notes built and built, layer upon layer, rising in urgency as the lights became darker. Purity looked at Warren and he shrugged. Then, as the room was in almost total darkness the music peaked, there was a pyrotechnic flash and a plume of green smoke. And there at the centre of the stage stood the character from the billboards, the creature that had haunted the dreams of a generation - the crooked man with his crooked smile, arms outstretched in a theatrical welcome, brandishing a huge fake prop syringe.

It was a man in a costume, obviously, but he wore a long white doctors coat with a stethoscope around his neck and a comically large silver watch dangling from his breast pocket. His collar was turned up framing the massive animatronic puppet head, a good four or five times the size of a normal head. Dead eyes blinked from deep sockets above a bulbous nose and a manic grin stretched from pointed ear to pointed ear.

"Well hello, hello, hellooooo! Good afternoon ladies, gentlemen and everything in between! I realise it's been quite a while since last I graced your telly box, and the old memory ain't what it used to be... old timer's disease I reckon! Some of you may have fond memories of my antics but for the rest of you, allow me to introduce myself. I'm the master of mirthful medicine. The MD of madness, the physician of fun. Yes, it's me: The National Elf. At your service!"

Recorded applause filled the room as the audience watched, stunned.

"I'm so glad you could join us here today at this National Elf Camp." he proclaimed, accompanied by canned laughter.

"I'm sure you're all going to have a lovely time here, we have so much to see and do. We've got exercise classes, hydrotherapy, swimming pools. For the less energetic we have a delightful boating lake - I hope you can swim! - and entertainment centre!

"Now if you're ready, your carriage awaits to take you to your state of the art accommodation."

He spread his gloved fingers revealing a crudely painted number one in his palm. "And don't forget your room numbers!"

The Elf bent down on a knee and tipped an imaginary hat to the audience. "We hope you enjoy your stay. We want your time here to be memorable, enjoyable but above all... life changing!"

The house lights came up again and Grieg's classic instrumental faded in as background music. A door to the left of the stage opened and people hesitantly made their way out.

"What the hell was that?" whispered Warren.

Purity shook her head. "Never trust an elf," she said.

The Health Camp Land Train was parked outside. Three open sided carriages decorated with multicoloured flags and bunting waited, hitched up to an unconvincing blue steam train. Or at least a golf buggy heavily made up to look like one. Facing forward, at the head of the boiler smiled a model of the National Elf's face, a blue train driver's hat welded to his head at a jaunty angle.

"All aboard! All aboard!" shouted a recording of the Elf.

They sat side by side at the back of the last carriage on stiff blue rubber seats and waited as the train filled up.

"We could make a run for it" said Warren casually "Don't see much in the way of security."

"Make a run to where? We don't know where we are. No, let's just get a feel for the place first."

The engine tooted an over-enthusiastic toot and jerked forward sharply and an unconvincing chugging sound emitted from tiny speakers in each carriage.

'The Hall of the Mountain King' faded in again, a musical soundscape to their journey and the train left the cable car station and headed in towards the main complex. The music faded slightly and a pre-recorded narration by the Elf started to play.

"Now before we enter the main area, take a moment to look to your right at the azure blue of the North Sea. Natures finest defence, did us proud in both World Wars and now works hard protecting this Glorious Septic Isle from the European hordes."

North Sea? Thought Purity. *We're in Margate? Southend?*

The train clattered across a cattle grid and began a slow climb to the outermost buildings.

"And further out you can see the wind farm supplying natural renewable energy to this facility and our neighbouring counties. Passengers on our left can admire the miles and miles of rolling hillside which gives us that get-away-from-it-all feeling we strive so hard for. You could literally run for hours and never encounter another soul. Its true... people have tried! Hahahaha!"

The train passed through a freshly painted iron gate with bent hammered lettering arched overhead.

REPAIR. REJUVENATE. RECYCLE
PRIMUM NON NOCERE

"Primum non nocere!" The Elf repeated. "First do no harm! The Hippocratic Oath. These are the words all doctors are sworn to and have done for hundreds of years, and words we all aspire to at every Health Camp."

Purity couldn't help noticing the iron lettering NON was new.

"On your right is the original reception centre where all guests would have originally signed in while their luggage was taken to their rooms.

"And here you can see various treatment rooms. No matter what your ailment we have something for you. From a gentle massage to acupuncture... whatever that's all about! Who decided sticking needles in you could help? And just how did the first guy who did it discover it? It's not like you accidentally stab yourself with a hundred pins! Still, it's not for me, but it might just float your boat. Speaking of which..."

The buildings opened out and the train followed a wide path around a lake. The swan shaped boats Purity had seen earlier bobbed and wobbled, pedalled by occupants in white dressing gowns.

"Our boating lake, formed from a natural spring provides fresh, natural, mineralised water which offer all kinds of health benefits. Like these sauna and hydrotherapy rooms. Hydrotherapy.... Isn't that just a fancy word for water-boarding? Hahaha!"

Warren whispered to Purity. "This guy's a psycho."

Overhead the cable cars swung past serenely. The train reached the end of the lake and turned left onto an avenue of pastel blue chalets.

The train tooted eagerly and slowed to a halt.

"Well it's been short and sweet, like my good self, the National Elf. But I'm afraid it's time for some folks to leave us. This is the blue zone. So, if all of you with blue numbers would like to exit the vehicle you can make your way to your luxury chalets."

Warren stared at his palm. "Guess this is me."

Roughly half of the passengers climbed off, looking at the rooms with suspicion.

"Where shall we meet? The lake?" asked Purity.

Warren shook his head. "Too exposed. How about that diner?"

The blocky fifties style American Diner towered over the chalets, the red sign revolving with an electrical hum.

"Okay. I'll be as quick as I can."

The train tooted again and pulled away and Purity watched Warren shrink into the distance. She studied the remaining occupants of the carriages - there were only six other people left and she had already glimpsed red digits on some of their hands.

"Of course, it's not all hard work," continued the Elf. "After a day of gruelling exercise, sometimes all you want to do is sit in a dark room and be entertained. Here at Le Theatre Medicinal, we have nightly live shows and movies all designed to feed the mind and the soul. I recommend it. But then again, I would... I'm usually in it!"

The vehicle passed a number of windowless red brick buildings and the huge chimney belching black smoke into the clouds. Music played, but the Elf was conspicuous in his silence. After a few minutes the train slowed again, tooting loudly. Pink roofed chalets lined either side of the street.

"This is the red zone. That's zone red. Could all passengers allocated to red rooms leave the carriage now where their palatial apartments await."

Purity stepped onto the pavement. Four others had also got off and two passengers remained looking decidedly uncomfortable.

"And so I bid thee farewell as I take our last passengers on their final journey," intoned the Elf, with a veiled threat. "To their rooms, that is! Hahaha!"

The train tooted away, the music loop echoing eerily down the quiet street.

Hesitantly, the others had already made approaches to their rooms, but Purity stood in the middle of the street, fists clenched tight. She didn't need to be reminded what was printed on her skin.

From the outside, the chalets all looked identical. Horizontal whitewashed wooden slatted panels covered the front and pastel pink roofs repeated over and over. A single window with pink shuttered blind was positioned next to a single pink door. There was no keyhole on the door, but dead centre, underneath the room number was a small black palm reading panel.

Purity held her hand up and the door clicked open.

The chalet was larger than she was expecting, split over two floors. The ground level had a lounge and kitchenette separated by a breakfast bar with a retro chrome stool, upstairs was a single bedroom and a bathroom. The whole interior was decorated in a faux 1950s style and had a smell of peppermint that stuck in the back of the throat and stung the eyes.

In the corner of the room an old black and white television played a public information film on the benefits of the Health Service. Overlaying the image, a message read:

REJUVENATE THERAPY
SPA INDUCTION - 3PM

On the arm of the settee, a change of clothes was folded neatly. A red one-piece jumpsuit and a pair of cream slippers rested on top of a fluffy dressing gown.

She rolled her eyes. "Sod that."

And closed the front door and headed to

the diner.

19. TOM'S DINER

"Can I have one of those Strawberry lattes please?" The diner was a canteen built to feed hundreds at once, though currently held barely twenty or thirty souls. Faded white and red padded vinyl seats with laminate tables were laid in aisles on a black and white checkerboard floor. Running the length of the hall under a bank of tall windows, a row of old Morris Minors had been cut apart, roofs and engines removed, the bodies converted into private dining booths. Television screens hung from the ceiling silently playing news feeds and in the centre of the room, a chipped and flaking statue of Margaret Thatcher held down a billowing blue skirt as it blew upwards. A haunting rendition of Gracie Fields' 'We'll Meet Again' rearranged as Gregorian chant, drifted through the air.

Purity headed straight to the back of the diner, past a genuine, reconditioned Brexi-Cola refrigerator and sat on a tall stool by long counter next to a cylindrical straw dispenser.

"Strawberry what?" repeated the bartender.

"Latte. Strawberry latte," said Purity, pointing to an old man at the other end of the bar in a dressing gown nursing a creamy pink beverage from a tall glass. "Like that."

The bartender smirked, lifting a glass from a rack of drying cutlery. As he prepared the drink, she admired the wall art behind the bar - a graffiti painted map of the world with words scrawled artistically across the continents:

REPAIR. REJUVENATE. RECYCLE.

Purity's geography wasn't great but even she was pretty sure Britannica wasn't larger than Africa.

"There you go," said the barman, sliding the drink in front of her. She reached into her trousers for cash, suddenly realising her pockets were empty. But he had already gone.

Was everything free here?

She left the bar and sat down in an empty cubicle, the vinyl seating squeaking as she relaxed. On the table were red and yellow squeezy ketchup and mustard bottles and salt and pepper shakers styled as Winston Churchill and Enoch Powell. On the wall a bright pink neon sign flashed BRE-XXX-IT.

She took a sip of her drink, nearly spitting it straight back out again. That wasn't strawberry. Or latte.

What was that? She thought. *Beetroot?*

"Gross," she said under her breath.

A hand fell on her shoulder and a voice boomed in her ear, "Expresso?"

She turned to see man in a dressing gown, obviously the go-to fashion item around here. He was a big man, clean shaven with tightly cropped hair, pockmarked complexion and a faded scar running down his cheek. He had a generous smile and all his teeth.

"Tom?" she asked, as her brain played catch up. She stood up and flung her arms around him.

"Tom! You look..."

"I know, I know," he laughed.

"You look really well!"

And he did. Gone was the hairy, dishevelled shell of a man, buried under the weight of his own failure. His scruffy blankets replaced with clean white one-piece jumpsuit and a simple, silver locket hanging from his neck, this Tom was refreshed, renewed. Reborn almost.

He let go and brushed her down. "They certainly take care of you here. They've taken care of us. All of us. I feel better than I have done in years. They feed us, keep a roof over our heads. There's an exercise program and I can see you're already getting into the healthy eating!"

She wrinkled her nose and pushed the foul drink away. Tom put a big arm around her shoulder as they walked.

"They even train us with new skills."

He stopped in front of a dozen shaven headed men and women arranged in two rows. They also wore robes over white jumpsuits and sang the virtues of 'The White Cliffs of Dover' in perfect harmony.

"That's the in-house choir. Can you believe they could barely hit a note three weeks ago? I don't know why they don't advertise these places more."

Yes, why is that exactly? Purity thought.

They stood for moment listening to the mournful chorus when a movement caught her eye.

"Warren!" she shouted. One or two choristers frowned disapprovingly at her interruption but held their heads up further and sang louder still.

Warren saw her and made his way over. He wasn't hard to spot, neither of them was - they were the only people in the camp not dressed in white robes and slippers.

"What is this place?" asked Warren. "It's like World War 2 never ended in here."

They hugged and Purity introduced her to Tom. They nodded at each other awkwardly like complete strangers do.

Warren couldn't contain his disgust any longer. "Can you believe they've given me a job too?"

"A job?" asked Purity, bemused.

He pointed at the large panelled windows looking out over the manmade lake and the swan shaped boats bobbing lazily on the calm surface.

"Yeah, handing out tickets for bloody boat rides. I mean, me and boats? Really?

Above them, the screens showed fresh news footage. Prime Minister August was visiting the site of the Battersea terrorist incident, grinning like a Cheshire Cat on sugar, shaking hands with anything that had a pulse. In a stage managed and painful interview, he chatted with the security guard on patrol that night. Even with the sound turned down, his insincerity dripped from the screen.

Spotting something in the background, Warren said, "Would you look at the state of that?"

Behind August, a large character balloon rose into the sky filling the view behind the two men. The blimp, a bloated caricature of August in a lemon polka dot dress floated serenely in the sunlight.

Sniggers burst out in pockets around the room, the patients laughing and pointing at the news. August's attempt at uplifting positivity was working here at least.

Warren shifted his attention from the television to the patients in the diner. They were all relaxed, all happy.

"I don't get it," he said.

Purity cocked her head to the side, "Get what?"

"This place. If we're not going to be tortured or interrogated... why *are* we here?"

She looked at the painted map behind the bar and the words there.

REPAIR. REJUVENATE. RECYCLE.

For some reason, something about them troubled her.

"I have no idea."

20. DOCTOR, DOCTOR

Jasmine scented water trickled over machine polished marble stones, running through crafted troughs and gullies into a small lily pad shaped pond in the centre of the room. In each corner, tall reeds grew from simple vases, swaying gently from some artificial wind source. Pan pipes played a soothing melody over a backdrop of rain on glass.

Purity sat enveloped in a fat, heavily padded easy chair in front of a low coffee table. Another chair, more rigid, less comfy sat opposite.

It was safe to say, this was not what she had expected.

The door slid open silently and the doctor entered the room. He too was not what she was expecting. It was the elf, that damned elf again. He was dressed in corduroy pants and white shirt with a tweed jacket featuring leather elbow patches. His huge artificial chin sported a scrappy ginger beard and a single bulbous rolling eye was magnified even further by a saucer sized monocle. An ornate, hand carved smoking pipe protruded from his smile, puffs of steam pulsing mechanically.

"Well, hello, hello, hellooooo! It's me! The National Elf! At your service!"

He towered over her, grinning maniacally. "And who have we here today?"

Purity stared at him.

He leaned closer, his crooked nose huge in her face. This close, the decades old paint was visibly cracked and flaky as if he was suffering some bizarre and unpleasant skin condition.

"And who," he repeated slowly, "Have we here today?"

From deep inside the head, a tiny worn engine could be heard labouring away and sickly, oily clouds from his pipe gathered unpleasantly in Purity's face. She opened her mouth to speak but instead started coughing, the fumes irritating in her throat. Almost simultaneously the Elf started coughing. He staggered back wheezing, his big comedy gloves grasping at his throat. He shook his head left and right sharply and pushed up hard. The head detached with a hiss and he dropped it onto the coffee table. It landed nose first, depositing flakes of paint on the glass and leaving no doubt to the severity of the Elf's deteriorating skin condition.

Inside the suit was a man in his fifties with a bald head and ruddy cheeks, sweating profusely. Shocks of white hair sat over both ears like small creatures perching on the cliffside. He pulled the large gloves off and retrieved a handkerchief from his breast pocket.

"Terribly sorry about that, miss," he said, dabbing his forehead. "I know a lot of people aren't fans of the Elf, but they're keen we promote him wherever we can. A friendly face and all that! Just seems a bit…"

"Creepy?"

"I was going to say 'tacky' but, yes. I suppose it is a bit."

He rubbed the soggy hanky around the back of his neck.

"Gets warm in there, particularly in the summer."

He gripped the Elf head and stood it upright on the table facing him.

"He was one of the first things they did, you know, back when the government finally decided to rebuild the health service. Got a Soho agency in, you know the sort: a gang of hip and trendy, chai latte drinking beard strokers. Ran focus groups, workshops. Eventually decided we needed a mascot, a figurehead. A positive, get things done kind of guy, determined but with a sense of fun, personable but with mass market appeal. The National Elf."

He folded the handkerchief neatly and returned it to his pocket.

"Cost millions in the end."

Purity pictured the beds and equipment that could have been bought instead. "Money well spent" she said sarcastically,

The Doctor nodded, missing her point entirely. "He's not everyone's cup of tea, but I am rather fond of him."

He clapped his hands together brightly. "And here we are. Apologies, I didn't get a chance to introduce myself. I am Dr Roper and I am the Chief Medical Profiler at this camp. I know, it all sounds very grand! But all it means is I get to chat to every new arrival, find out what makes them tick. "

He opened the folder and glanced at the first page. "I mean, we know why you're here, but this should give us a better idea of how we can help you. So, according to your records you were arrested under the Terrorism Act of 1999 and brought to this facility for correction. Says here you were part of a plot to kill our Prime Minister."

"No, that's not…"

He held up his hand, a huge gloved paw.

"I get it: I'm not a terrorist, I only hang out with terrorists. I've heard it all before. Don't worry, I'm not here to judge you, I'm a doctor after all.

"Before we decide on your course of treatment we need to run a psychological profile, get a better idea of how you work, what makes you tick. Nothing too intrusive, just a series of soft questions. You simply give me a one or two-word answer. First thing that pops into your head."

"What's the point?"

"Works on a subconscious level. Your answers will fall into patterns from which we can discern the real you. It's all very clever stuff! For example, in one word how would your parents describe you?"

Purity shrugged. "Responsible?"

"Good. See, easy isn't it? Remember, there are no wrong answers here."

He scribbled the answer in the notepad. "Not all questions are personal, in fact some may seem very random, some may be familiar sayings. For instance: a dog is for Christmas, not..."

"For life. "

The doctor settled into his chair.

"Okay, you seem to have the hang of it. How would you describe yourself?"

"The oppressed."

He allowed himself a thin smile, they all thought they could beat the test.

"Life is full of?"

"Misery. "

"The worst form of violence?"

"Poverty"

"Who do you want to fix this?"

"The government."

"Want or needs?"

"Needs."

He turned the question sheet over, allowing the rustling to fill the dead air of the tiny room. He paused, drawing the moment out then changed tack.

"So Purity, how many times have you been arrested?"

"Two."

"And after this did the police think you had a) carried on, or b) stopped?"

"b) stopped."

"But you didn't stop, did you? Do you think you will?"

"I will be."

He flipped the page back and resumed from a different section.

"London Bridge is?"

"Burning down."

"The lunatics are running the?"

"Parliament."

Her defiance didn't bother him, he knew the test well. It was extremely reliable.

He continued. "We need the Police for?"

"Killing"

"Justice is for?"

"Everyone"

"Thoughts and dreams?"

"Inside"

"Work or?"

"Steal."
"People?"
"Power."
"1980?"
"Four."

The doctor searched through her earlier answers, circling a word in blue ink. He read it out.

"Power?"
"The people."

He nodded to himself, aware that he had reached a dead end. He held up his pen.

"The colour blue?"
"Murder."
"Midnight?"
"P.m."

Dr. Roper sat back in his chair and exhaled loudly. "Thank you, Purity. I think I've heard enough."

He placed the notepad on the desk between them, her answers scribbled on the page, circles and arrows connected them.

"You get what you need?" Purity asked.

He rubbed his temples. "Yes. Yes, I believe I did."

"So what's the verdict. Am I a terrorist?" she laughed.

Roper sat upright, his face stern. "You tell me."

He rotated the notepad 180 degrees until

it was facing her. Her answers, written in blue capitals stood out. Leaped out.

How would your parents describe you? **RESPONSIBLE** A dog is for Christmas, not?
FOR LIFE. How would you describe yourself? **THE OPPRESSED**. Life is full of? **MISERY**. The worst form of violence? **POVERTY** Who do you want to fix this? **THE GOVERNMENT**. Want or needs? **NEEDS.** how many times have you been arrested? **TWO**. And after this did the police think you had 1a) carried on, or b) stopped? **B) STOPPED**. Do you think you will? **I WILL BE**. London Bridge is? **BURNING DOWN**. The lunatics are running the? **PARLIAMENT**. We need the Police for? **KILLING** Justice is for? **EVERYONE** thoughts and dreams? **INSIDE** Work or? **STEAL**. People? **POWER**. 1980? **FOUR**. Power? **THE PEOPLE**. The colour blue? **MURDER**. Midnight? **P.M.**

She mouthed the highlighted words, *her answers*, aloud.

"Responsible for life, the oppressed, misery, poverty - the Government needs to be stopped. I will be burning down Parliament killing everyone inside. Steal power for the people. Murder PM."

"Murder the Prime Minister?" asked Roper. "Your answers, I didn't lead you. The test is the test."

Purity blinked at the paper.

What was that? How did he do that?

Roper closed the folder and stood up.

"Thank you for your time, Miss St. George. I hope you enjoy your stay."

He placed the Elf head upside down under his arm and dropped the gloves through the neck. "It really is rather lovely here when the sun's out."

He maneuvered his way to the door.

"Wait!" said Purity. "What happens now?"

"What happens now? Go out, catch some sunshine, try the boats. Do whatever you like!"

"I'm... I'm free to go?" she asked, confusion in her voice.

Roper frowned. "Of course you are, my dear. It's not a prison, you know!"

21. UNDER COVER OF THE NIGHT

"Not a prisoner, my ass," whispered Purity.

She grasped the door handle of her chalet and rattled it again. It was locked alright. Purity rested her forehead on the cool wood and sighed.

"So much for paradise."

When exhaustion came, it came fast and Purity lay down on her single bed closing her eyes. Just as she felt the arms of Morpheus around her, she was woken by a hum - an annoying mosquito buzz next to her ear. She sat up in bed, tilting her head to get a better fix on the sound. The bedside clock blinked 2:04am in a sickly green fluorescence - she had been asleep for nearly five hours.

It took a moment before she realised it wasn't a mosquito inside at all, but an electric motor outside. The golf buggies. Swinging her legs off the mattress, she peered through the blinds at the street outside. The road was quiet and lifeless. The chalets, like hers, in darkness observing the nightly curfew. Dim sodium street lamps bathed the view in an eerie washed out, amber twilight. The sound, louder now, was coming from further down the street and she strained at the window for a better view. A light source caught her attention.

Moving.

A buggy, turning from the main thoroughfare trundled between the chalets towards her. Purity squinted - it was hard to see the occupants past the glare of the headlights. As the vehicle drew level, Purity sank lower in the window. She didn't want to draw attention to herself.

Two figures sat at the front of the buggy. Like the staff she had seen on arrival, they were both dressed in white coats with surgical face masks and thick, black goggles. Behind them, raised like the Pope in the Popemobile, sat the National Elf - his huge head bobbing in rhythm with the car. He stared vacantly at the chalets, his eyes rolled back in their sockets and jaw hung slackly.

"Yeah, that's not creepy," Purity muttered to herself.

The buggy was towing a low, four wheeled flatbed trailer upon which a man was strapped. He wore a white jumpsuit, had a shaved head and was quite motionless. He was either asleep or dead.

"Not creepy. At all," she said.

The strange vehicle with its strange occupants and its strange cargo continued quietly to the end of the street and turned left away from the main complex and chalets. Purity knew what was down there.

The featureless building and the chimney.

22. GREEN DOOR

"What do you think?" asked Purity. Warren scratched his head through the thick curly hair.

"What do I think?" he smiled. "I think we're somewhere we shouldn't be."

She had told Warren all about the previous night's weird sighting and they now stood before a squat, featureless red-brick building just a few meters around the corner from the pink roofed chalets - the buggy had to have come down here. There were no fences or barriers, no guards or markings, just a simple brass engraved plaque.

STAFF ONLY

"Well, we do work here," he joked. "Kind of."

The only visible entrance on this side was a rusted iron-shuttered door, roughly the width and height of a double garage. To its right, a small rectangular panel was recessed into the wall.

"Biometrics. Again," sighed Warren.

Purity rested her hand on the panel. It buzzed, the border glowing red.

"Why can't these people just use locks like everyone else?" she asked. "Guess we'll just have to chop someone's hand off to open this."

Warren's face paled and Purity burst into laughter. "Really Warren? Really?"

She wiped a tear from her eye - the first tear of joy she'd had in a very long time. "Seriously though. Any way you can crack it?"

Warren pondered for a moment. Back in the outside world with all his tools and hardware available this wouldn't even have been a question. But in here?

"Might struggle to find the materials but we could make a fingerprint copy. It's easy enough, I've done it before. But…"

"But?"

"A standard fingerprint scanner uses about thirty data points. Whole hand scanner like this, about two hundred. And that's just an off-the-shelf scanner, this looks more… serious. Maybe a couple of thousand data points."

"It'd take months," he added, "And might not work anyway."

Purity bowed her head, her hands on her hips.

"Damn it. Could we cut the power?"

"Doubtful - they made a pretty big deal about their windfarm powering this place."

She shook her head. "Why would a hospital need military grade encryption?"

Wingnut stroked his chin and said, "They must take data protection really seriously."

Purity tipped her head to one side and stuck two fingers up at him.

"God Warren, you're such a bung."

23. JUMP

Like clockwork, it happened again the following night. Purity had tried to get some sleep, but it had come in fits and starts until eventually she just gave up entirely and pulled the armchair into the window. She slouched in the soft leather in darkness, her head propped against the headrest and watched the empty street outside.

At 2:02am she heard the familiar sound of the electric engine in the distance and she reached across, narrowing the blinds.

The scene unfolded the same as the previous night. A buggy driven at a leisurely pace, two identikit drivers and the sad, worn National Elf presiding over events from the back seat. Again, the trailer carried a man in a white jumpsuit except this time he looked... familiar.

"Tom?" she whispered.

Even from there she could see the scar across his cheek, but she zoomed in on the camera phone anyway.

It was Tom. Toothless Tom: ex-soldier, ex-vagabond and soon to be ex-Tom.

Purity shot to her feet and ran to the door.
"No. No, no, no."

She grabbed the door handle and shook it violently, as if it would somehow, miraculously be unlocked this night.

It wasn't.

She kicked the door and span around, facing the room. The car was just moving out of sight. She pulled the handle again but there was no give in it, it was clear that it was never going to budge.

Locked door - wood. Locked window - glass.

"Oh sod it," she said.

The retro stool crashed through the window in a bloom of broken glass. It tumbled down into the street and bounced onto the tarmac, warped and mangled, coming to rest in the middle of the road. A few chalet lights came on and nervous faces blinked through the windows.

So much for subtlety, she thought.

Purity elbowed the fragments of glass away from the edges of the frame and heaved herself through, emerging on the inclined roof. Her foot slipped on the slate tiles and she gasped, grabbing the drainpipe. It suddenly felt a lot higher than it looked from the ground. She straightened herself up and took a tentative step forward. Nothing slipped. Better.

Up ahead the buggy was reaching the end of the road.

Purity took another careful step, then another, well aware this was not the time for caution.

The car and its trailer turned the corner and she picked up the pace, settling into a rhythm of sorts. The plimsoll's rubber squeaked on the tiles as she made her way across the roofs. Joists and beams creaked beneath her, but thankfully held. Fortunately, since the chalets were built in rows, it was essentially one long roof - all she had to concentrate on was moving forward and staying alive.

Below, the trailer was moving around the corner, but from this vantage point she had a much better view. It was definitely Tom, alright. His body bouncing and rocking on the trailer. Asleep or.... No, he had to be asleep.

"Come on. Come..."

Her foot slipped out beneath her and Purity screamed. The pink tile under her foot dislodged and clattered down the roof, bouncing and spinning before vanishing over the side. Purity skidded to her knees clutching at the raised areas of tile. She slid for a moment before the rubber soles of her shoes stopped her.

The tile crashed onto the pavement and shattered, an explosion in the silence.

Over her shoulder she could see more windows lighting up.

Purity heaved herself up and scrambled forwards on her hands and knees. She reached the end of the row and peered over the side. Down below, the buggy was already driving through the wide entrance and the metal shutters were descending behind it with an understated clink. There was no way she could climb down, sprint across the yard and get through before they closed.

"Bollocks," whispered Purity.

Tom was inside. They had taken him.

To do what, God only knew.

The faceless building stretched out before her, the chimney ominously towering above, belching thick black smoke into the night. While it was true they had seen no other doors or windows at street level, up here told a different story. The roof of the facility was flat and dotted with raised glass skylights. Most were lit from within, some had steam escaping from them.

Purity was fixed with grim determination. If steam could get out, it was open and if it was open, she could get through it.

The complex comprised of low, single storey units; the last unit stopping only feet away from the pink chalets. Purity glanced over the edge. Although the facility roof was slightly lower than her and flat, they were separated by a narrow walkway maybe three feet wide. Not a huge distance to jump at ground level, but up here? The distance seemed like an eternity.

Maybe there was another way across. Maybe she could climb down and circle round, find a ladder...

The shuttered door clanged against the ground, closed.

No, she had to move.

Now.

Purity shuffled backwards on her hands and knees, retracing her steps. She wiped the soles of her shoes against the tiles checking their grip and raised herself into a sprinting position like a racer awaiting the starting pistol.

Here goes nothing, she thought to herself, heart pounding in her ears.

And ran.

In five short steps the chalets ended and she was in the air, arms flailing, the cold night air whipping her face. She hit the facility roof on both feet, trying to maintain her balance but fell, tumbling sideways. She bounced once, rolling across her shoulders and came to a rest facing back the way she had come.

It really wasn't that far, after all.

Purity lifted herself up, her arm and back throbbing - they were going to hurt in the morning, that was for sure. She limped across the bitumen roof, this surface providing a far better - and quieter - grip. She crouched, keeping her head low for fear of being seen as she approached the first skylight. It comprised of four identical hinged glass panels smeared with years of dirt and neglect. Two were open slightly and warm air escaped through the gap, carrying with it a scent of bleach and smoke. Light poured up through the glass, it's shifting and flickering suggesting movement below.

She looked down onto a narrow corridor with a worn green floor and chipped nicotine yellow tiles. One of the medical staff was wheeling an empty hospital stretcher back along the passageway away from the chimney, it's wheels squeaking rhythmically. Something about this man was different and Purity noticed that as well as the tinted goggles and surgical mask worn by others, he also sported thick black rubber gloves and rubber boots. He hummed a jaunty tune - off key - and it took Purity a moment to place it. *Sunday Night at the London Crematorium*.

He was clearly a fan of the tv show.

The man heaved forward, banging the trolley hard against a pair of double doors. He pushed the gurney through as they swung closed behind him.

Purity waited, straining to listen. The hum with squeak accompaniment receded followed by the bang-swish of more double doors, then silence. Delicately, she lifted the glass panel. Initially it resisted, before opened smoothly until the aperture was wide enough to climb through.

Purity moved her head through the gap, listening again. Silence.

Here goes nothing, she thought.

She swung her legs over the side and dropped through the opening.

Her feet hit the linoleum floor with a loud slap, echoing down the hallway and she froze in a crouch, holding her breath.

Still nothing.

Slowly she stood up, suddenly feeling very exposed.

At both ends of the corridor were sets of sturdy swing doors; solid constructions with square frosted glass windows. Following the direction of the hummer seemed unnecessarily risky so Purity quickly moved in the opposite direction.

The glass allowed no visibility to the rooms beyond, but she could tell there were no lights on, at least. Cautiously, she pushed the door open an inch. The smell of smoke was stronger here - this was much closer to the chimney. As she opened the door, the ceiling lights flickered on in staccato, bathing the room in a cool, harsh glow.

Three large rectangular, wheeled containers lay in a row along the wall. The first had a dozen or so blue jumpsuits scattered at the bottom. Purity noticed dark, wet marks on some.

Blood.

A sense of unease gnawed at her and she looked in the second container.

This too held jumpsuits, but red. Twenty or thirty of them. The stains showed as black on the fabric, but she knew exactly what it was.

Her unease had not only grown but had invited a friend.

The last container held white jumpsuits, like the one Tom and his homeless friends were wearing. The blood on these was sharp and vivid. There were considerably more suits here, ripped and torn, bloodied and soiled, piled high, spilling over the rim and littering the floor.

Unease and its friend had now moved in completely and were planning a family.

Purity lifted a torn pale sleeve, the fabric rough between her fingers.

Was one of these Tom's?

She threw the garment back onto the pile.

Was this what happened to patients here?

Behind the last container, a small bin contained keys, coins, scraps of paper - personal artefacts removed from pockets, presumably. Purity had no desire to rummage through other people's possessions, but a familiar silver shape caught her eye. She pulled it out, squeezing the power switch and the display faded to life.

It was a Korean AOJI 9 phone. Old and obsolete, but still a phone.

The battery showed 16% but the good

news ended there - there was no signal and no carrier.

She swiped the camera on and filmed a quick sweep of the room. It might not make calls, but it recorded just fine.

"Excellent," she whispered.

Scruffy tire marks scribbled on the floor ended at double doors, suggesting a lot of traffic through this area. The door handle was warm to the touch, warmer than the previous doors, and Purity pushed gently on it.

As before, the room lights flickered into life. This time however, Purity wished they hadn't.

Even without the lights, it was clear what this room was. Iron pipes and dials filled the wall, arranged around a circular hatch. A single round window on the hatch revealing flames flickering and dancing inside.

A furnace.

It was a furnace.

Purity wanted to look inside, but even from a few metres away the heat was considerable. From deep within the ancient machinery a rumble grew then faded, over and over. Laboured breathing, as if alive, punctuated by the hiss of escaping steam and the rattle of pipes. Tall free-standing shelves lined the opposite wall, tools, jars and boxes littered messily across them. Beyond the last shelf, upright wooden pallets formed a makeshift parking bay where three trolleys currently stood. Two of the trolleys were empty, the other however, carried a long, shiny zippered black sack monogrammed in simple text.

PROPERTY OF THE PHS

Even with the heavily censored and sanitised broadcasts of PBC One, Purity had seen enough police procedurals to know exactly what the sack was, and what was in it.

A body bag.

People vanishing in the night, piles of bloodied clothing, body bags. All the evidence was there - she didn't actually need to see what was inside the bag, did she?

Really?

"You've come too far to bottle it now," she murmured to herself.

With one hand, she recorded with the AOJI phone, her other palm probing the rough material and the soft, misshapen *something* inside.

Purity's fingers, shaking now, grasped the zipper. It slipped around in her sweaty fingers and she squeezed tighter. She closed her eyes and pulled gently. The canvas parted with a rasp and a foul stench assaulted Purity's nostrils. She gagged, covering her mouth, fighting back a rising tide of vomit keen to make an appearance. She turned her head away, breathing rapidly through gritted teeth, waiting for the nausea to subside. After a moment. the worst of the smell had passed and she pulled on the zipper again.

The bag opened easily, eager to reveal its secrets.

In the humid, flickering light, Purity could make out the shape of a body, the skin pale and waxy. It was a male, naked, mid-forties with a shaved head. He was gaunt, thin and very, very dead.

Purity's eyes widened, not at the corpse - that, in itself, was hardly a surprise - but at what had been done to it. Gaping black sockets stared at her where eyes once belonged and the mouth had been scrappily sewn shut, thick wiry thread twisting through the cracked lips like barbed wire. The skull was deformed and misshapen, crude stitching running around its circumference. Threads continued across the chest straight down the centre to the pelvis, the ribcage sagging to one side. Bones, broken and twisted, pushed grotesquely at the skin like some horrific tentpole.

It's not Tom, she thought.

A wave of relief swept over her, replaced almost instantly by guilt. It wasn't Tom, but this man was still the victim here. He was alive once, had hopes, dreams. And now... this.

"Oh my God," Whispered Purity. "What did they do to you?"

She zoomed in on her phone and gripped

the man's forearm, turning his hand over. The wrist was stiff and immobile but rotated enough to show his palm and the tiny digits tattooed there.

Grey 1142.

The homeless block.

Was this what they did here? Was this the point of this place? Herd up the weak, the broken, the dispossessed, lock them all up miles away from everyone and quietly... *remove* them from society?

Purity stroked the red digits on her palm. She was in no doubt that this fate wasn't just reserved for the inmates of grey block.

A sound caught her attention, not in the room but quiet. Distant.

Bang, swish. Bang swish.

The sound of double doors being hit by a trolley, getting louder.

The nurse was coming back.

"No, no, no."

Purity quickly scanned the room looking for options. The room was big and sparse and offered precious little in the way of hiding spaces. The only way out was the way she had come in.

Bang. Swish. Closer this time.

Nowhere to run. Nowhere to hide.

It was a dead end.

24. SOME LIKE IT HOT

The nurse entered the bin room humming the theme from Strictly Come Hanging. He really did like his tv shows.

He was still dressed in the stained white overcoat, facemask and black goggles but had removed the thick rubber gloves. Wearing them all the time got extremely sweaty and he only really needed them around the furnace. The gloves lay side by side in parallel on the middle of the trolley. A pin on his lapel read:

HI! I'M BOB.

He stopped mid chorus, noticing something on the tiled floor.

A tattered and bloodied jumpsuit from the whites' pile had fallen from the container and lay abandoned in his path. He kicked the

footbrake on the trolley and crouched down to pick it up, his breath loud through his nostrils. Was no one else in this place capable of tidying up after themselves?
Neatly folding the jumpsuit, he returned it to the container admiring the symmetry of the stack of clothes. There really was no need for mess.

Cleanliness was next to Godliness, after all.

The nurse flipped the brake off with the tip of his toe and pushed the trolley hard against the doors.

Bang. Swish. Straight into the furnace room. The doors gently swung closed behind him and he stopped. He let out a loud sigh through his nose and his whole body visibly relaxed. This had always been his favourite place.

The furnace room was quiet, secluded and private with an air of peaceful finality and he had always found it more spiritual than the actual church in the camp. Down here, he felt much closer to God. He picked up the heavy rubber gloves and wrestled them on, conscious of the added weight on his arms, and stepped towards the huge iron hatch of the furnace. The locking handle would be impossibly hot to touch, but barely registered through the gloves. He strained against the wheel. It resisted briefly before turning laboriously with a groan. One rotation. Two. Then a loud clang deep inside the mechanism. Hi! I'm Bob pulled hard and the hatch swung open, heat and light pouring into the chamber. The hairs on his arms stood up and he felt a thin sheen of sweat form on his forehead.

He stood before the opening and stared into the heart of the furnace, drawn like Icarus to the sun. The constantly shifting patterns of flame and fire was quite hypnotic, and the auto-tint goggles meant he could stare for as long as he wanted without fear of retinal damage. 2000 degrees fahrenheit held constantly 24 hours a day, 7 days a week. Hot enough to melt iron or rock.

Or bone.

He sighed. As soothing as this was, there was still work to do.

Humming the theme from *The Great Britannical Cake Off*, he wheeled the gurney down a short incline and steered it into the parking bay in a well-practised manoeuvre.

He moved to pick up the body bag and paused.

There were two body bags on the trolleys.

Irregular. Highly irregular.

This wasn't right. He was the only one on shift tonight and he knew he had only brought one body down for cremation. Had they changed shift patterns again without telling him? It wouldn't be the first time.

A clipboard hung on the wall and he lifted

the cover reading the inventory. The papers for 1142 were correct but there was nothing for the other bag. He shook his head. As much as he'd like to, he couldn't cremate a body without the right paperwork, he'd never hear the end of it, have to attend multiple training courses and undoubtedly end up demoted. Again. If there was one thing the PHS excelled at, it was paperwork.

He pulled his hand free of its glove - there was no way he'd be able to open a bag with that bulky thing on - and pulled the zipper.

The bag screamed and Purity burst from the canvas knocking him to the floor, her hands around his neck. She landed on top of him and dug her knees in hard around his waist, squeezing tighter.

The nurse grunted in shock - he was not used to the bodies fighting back. He grabbed her arms in a desperate attempt to pull them from his throat, but he still wore one glove and struggled to maintain a hold. He swung the heavy gloved hand hard against the side of her head and Purity was knocked sideways releasing her grip. She kicked the tangled bag from her feet and scrambled up, dizzy from the blow. She backed towards the coal chute and grabbed a shovel. With both hands she held it up and pointed it at the man.

"Get away from me! I won't tell you again!" she screamed.

She swung it left and right, warding him

off and he stepped back keeping out of reach.

"You're not doing that to me!" she shouted and lunged forward.

The nurse grabbed the shovel in his gloved hand and yanked it out of her grip, tossing it away. It clattered loudly against the granite floor.

Panicking, Purity grabbed the abandoned trolley, pushing as hard as she could. It rattled down the ramp towards the nurse bouncing and shaking on its squeaky rubber wheels. He leapt out of the way, spinning on one foot as it shot past him and he watched as the frame crashed into the shelves, careening on to its side noisily. The nurse turned back in time to see another trolley hurtle towards him. Purity was pushing it, running at him, grim determination on her face. The gurney struck his stomach hard and he groaned as he was thrown backwards, pinned against the rusted pipework.

Purity turned towards the door - if she could just make it past him to the corridor she would have a chance to get away.

Sensing her escape, the man threw out his hand and grabbed her collar. They swung around, knocking the trolley aside and fell against the furnace. Purity screamed as iron and rivets dug into her back, the metal red hot through her clothes. The man pushed down on her harder bearing all of his weight on her tiny frame, grunting as he dragged her sideways.

Towards the hatch.

The wide-open hatch.

Heat gushed from the opening, an intense, almost physical force. Purity turned her head away, the hairs on her neck prickling, as his huge, gloved hand covered half her face. She pawed at the glove desperately trying to move it, to stop it. Her hands slid off the slick rubber surface unable to find traction and she clawed at his neck and face frantically.

With a grunt he pushed again, forcing her head even closer to the opening. The heat of the furnace hit the back of her head like a sledgehammer and she screamed, the smell of singeing hair in her nostrils.

Terrified, Purity lashed out as hard as she could.

"I'll kill you! I'll kill you! Kill you!" she shrieked.

Her nails slashed his cheek and caught the strap of his goggles and facemask, snapping them instantly. The tinted eyewear sprang from his face as if on an elastic band, leaving him staring head on into the heart of the furnace. He screamed and covered his eyes, clawing at his burning face mask. Purity scrambled back trying to put as much distance between them as she could, but she needn't have bothered. Bob was crouched on his knees with his head down, rocking back and to. Shaking. Shivering. He made a low groan like an animal caught in a trap.

Purity caught her breath. "Don't say I didn't warn you, you..."

But she didn't finish the sentence because the nurse had dropped his bloody hand and now faced her. His eyes, once brown and fierce, were now pale and milky and saw nothing. He had gazed into the face of God and paid the price.

Even more shocking however, was what the mask once concealed. Like the cadaver awaiting it's fate, Hi! - I'm Bob's lips had been sewn up, tightly stitched, the skin growing around and over the threads.

Purity blinked in confusion.

"What did they do to you? I don't understand," she muttered.

Unable to see or talk, Bob simply groaned, a single tear rolling down his face.

"Oh God. I'm... I had no idea," Purity began, but the words eluded her.

Only minutes ago, she had mourned the death of a complete stranger, promising revenge. Was that what revenge looked like? What it felt like? Because if it was, she felt sick to the stomach.

Purity had said once she would never kill anyone. But in that moment, that situation, with his hands around her neck and a fireball behind her, she would not have hesitated.

And she knew it.

"I'm sorry," she said. She stood up and cautiously approached him. "Let me help you up."

She placed a hand on his shoulder and he flinched at her touch before straining to his feet. His head darted left and right as if scanning the room, but he could see nothing.

"Come on. We need to get you somewhere safe, somewhere you'll be found."

Purity walked him away from the heat of the furnace and back to the main doors.

"Look, I don't know what they did to you or why. But," And she already hated herself for having to ask the question. "I came here tonight looking for someone. They brought him in this evening."

She looked him in the eyes. He didn't look back.

"Do you know where he is?"

The man that had tried to cremate her alive was gone. All that remained was a hollow, broken husk of a creature. An echo of life.

Slowly, his shaking ebbed away but his head carried on nodding.

Yes.

25. SPACE ODDITY

Major Thomas Blodwyn Jones woke to the sounds of shouting.

"...ing do it!" screamed a woman's voice.

He opened his eyes, but the world refused to focus. A grey, muddy smudge of shapes and lights swam across his view, blurry, indistinct, like a politician's interview answer. He blinked, shapes shifting and lights pulsing, but nothing became any clearer. Then a voice nearby, male said, "Okay, he's coming around."

He became aware of a hiss - pressurised air, and the sounds of equipment... beeps and pings.

"Okay miss, just calm down," implored another man. "He's waking up now."

The warm, fuzzy bubble enveloping Tom dissipated and the room, and Tom's memory of events, suddenly became very clear. He was in a simple operating theatre. It was basic with limited functionality, but an operating theatre nonetheless. He lay on the table in a medical gown, pipes and needles running into his arm, wires attached to his head. A circular lighting array hung above him, the main lights focused on his torso. Over his shoulder he could see the anaesthetist adjusting the handle on a canister, carefully monitoring his heart and blood pressure.

He turned his head to see the Elf, that stupid bloody Elf, dressed in surgical greens, stethoscope, a big mirror fastened to his cap and face mask covering his mouth. He cowered in the corner of the room as a teenage girl held a scalpel to his neck.

"Expresso!" he croaked.

The teenage girl looked at him and smiled in relief.

"Tom! Tom! Are you okay?" Purity asked.

He nodded shakily. "What... What are you doing here?"

"Rescuing you!"

"Rescuing me? I don't understand."

Aware of others in the room, Tom lifted his head and saw the frail figure of Hi! I'm Bob cowering in the corner.

"Bob?" he whispered. "That you?"

Bob twitched in recognition of the voice and he angled his head in Tom's direction giving him full view of his raw, bloodied features, his blind eyes probing in the darkness.

Bob nodded silently.

"Bob... what happened to you?"

Bob tipped his head vaguely in Purity's direction.

"She... did that to you?" Tom dropped his head back on the bed and closed his eyes. "Oh Expresso, what have you done?"

Purity lowered the knife, confused.

"What have *I* done?!" she asked sternly. "Look at him... They sewed up his mouth! Why would anyone do that?!?"

The Elf surgeon shrugged. "The Health Service needs to protect its secrets."

Purity had seen enough. She tore the wires from Tom's skin. "We're getting out of here and you're not going to stop us!"

Tom raised his arm weakly, stopping her.

"No," he said.

"What?"

"I said no. I'm not going anywhere."

Purity blinked. It was safe to say this was not going as she had expected.

"Of course you are! Do you have any idea what they're going to do to you? Because I've seen exactly what they do. It's obscene!"

The Elf walked around the bed, standing next to Tom's head.

"Oh, my dear girl, you've got it wrong. So, so wrong."

When Tom spoke, it was calm. Level. "I volunteered for this."

Purity shook her head.

Volunteered?

"I tried to tell you," spat a condescending voice from inside the Elf.

Tom raised his hand and squeezed the silver locket around his neck. Inscribed on the locket were the initials A.J.

"Alice Jackson," he murmured.

"Who?"

He prised the locket open with his thumbnail. Inside was a faded photo of a young blonde girl playing in a field. She smiled to the camera with a smile that could light up the world.

"Alice is twelve," he said. "Lives in Northumberland up near the Caledonia demilitarised zone. Her father died in the Meat Riots and now her mother has to hold down four part-time jobs just to feed her and keep a roof over their heads. Six months ago, Alice was diagnosed with a particularly aggressive cancer... they showed me the pictures, she has tumours everywhere. Kidney, liver, bowels, stomach. There's no repairing them. But they could *replace* them. With the right donor."

Tom closed his eyes. "Been a long time since I've had a purpose. Do you know how many years I've spent sleeping in doorways, begging for scraps? Stepped over, ignored, invisible to the world. People don't even see me anymore."

He shook his head. "I stopped living a long time ago. Spent a long time just existing... least this way I can make a difference."

Purity clenched her fists. She could feel herself getting angrier with him.

"Out there, I got no purpose," he said. "In here, I can make a difference. Used to save lives all the time in the army, this way I get to save one more. We all have something to contribute."

"You are going to die!" she yelled.

Tom squeezed the locket tighter. "Yeah, but this little girl is going to live."

Purity paced around the table, shaking her head. "No. Just no."

She grabbed a handful of tubes feeding into his arm and screamed at the anaesthetist. "Get this crap out of his arms."

The anaesthetist looked panicked. "Madam, if I..."

"NOW!"

Tom protested. "But I don't..."

Purity held up her hand, cutting him off. "You want to make a difference? You want to save lives? Then you're coming with us."

She put her arms under him, forcing him to sit up.

"But Alice..." he groaned.

Purity clasped her hand around his. "We get out of here," she said, "We'll save a hundred

Alices. A thousand. We'll find a way, I promise."

A sudden movement behind her caught her attention, but it was too late. The Elf slammed an emergency button on the wall with a balled fist and from deep within the complex a siren droned into life. The lights turned red casting the occupants of the room in an eerie glow.

Wide eyed, Purity shouted, "Run!"

26. RADIO GAGA

Warren leaned back in his ergonomically friendly chair and yawned. The television was muted, but lit the room in a cold, eerie glow. It was tuned to the PBC World Service and showed President Crass signing a legal document at his desk in the White House surrounded by officials and aides. Across the bottom of the screen scrolled the words:

CRASS SIGNS SURPRISING TRADE
DEAL WITH BRITANNICA.

Warren was sat at the kitchen table with the retro radio squarely in front of him. It hissed quietly. He had already spent the best part of an hour scanning the airwaves for a signal, a message... anything, but it was looking less and less likely this was going to work. He had no idea, no way of knowing if Delphi or the rest of the team were still active - they may have been caught in the bus at Battersea for all he knew - but he wouldn't give up. If the team were still functioning, he knew they would be looking for them both. And if they had figured out where they were being held, if they planned a rescue, they would send a signal.

That's a lot of 'ifs', he thought.

On the screen, Prime Minister August stood on the steps of 10 Downing Street waving a piece of paper and grinning like a lunatic.

Warren massaged the knots in his stiff neck and spun the dial back a quarter. No point watching the whole wavelength; if the signal he was looking for was going to be anywhere it would be around the top end. Slowly he rotated the wheel clockwise again, the old plastic bar inching up the scale. Static played out through the rattling speaker broken only by the occasional ghostly whistle or whine.

1516khz
Hisses and whispers, harsh clicking. An irritating buzz.

1517khz
A wall of white noise phasing rhythmically.
Was this really going to work?

1518khz
The noise receded, another sound revealed beneath fighting for attention. Structured. Me-

lodic.
Was that music?

1519khz
Definitely music. A rapid, upbeat jaunty piano piece.
Was that circus music?
It sounded old, maybe a music hall number or something like that.

1520khz.
The static dropped away completely, the music much clearer now.

It seemed familiar, a tv theme, some ancient gameshow from before he was born. He knew Purity would have identified it immediately, she had certainly made him watch enough classic shows. From what he could remember it was a fiendishly difficult competition with degree level questions coupled with a game of skill requiring superhuman levels of hand-eye coordination, the prizes the stuff of legend. Nothing at all like the simple shows today.
What was it called?
He remembered it featured some sort of cartoon farm animal.
Lamb's Tail? Goat's Leg? Sheep's Ear?
Abruptly the radio fell silent and the room was bathed in a maroon glow from the tv. The grinning PM had been replaced by a single red screen with a message in blocky white text.

PHS ALERT.
STAY IN YOUR ROOMS.

In the distance, Warren heard the wail of sirens echoing across the rooftops.

"Oh P... What have you done now?"

27. BODY TALK

"Come on!" yelled Purity.

She walked more than ran, but even supported by Purity, Tom could barely manage more than a shuffle. The sterile corridors were bathed in a pulsing red light, the shadows black and inky. The alarm, particularly shrill in the confined space dug into their ears like needles.

"Take me back!" shouted Tom.

She ignored him. It was for his own good, he'd understand one day.

After they had left the operating theatre, Purity had decided against returning the way she had come, instead heading away from the incinerator. Hopefully there would be a more obvious exit point this way, there would be no climbing up through a skylight with this patient in tow. They reached a junction, another faceless corridor stretching left to right before them. She heard a bang to the right and saw figures moving urgently behind glass. Many figures.

Security.

"Just let me go," Tom whimpered.

She turned left and they limped to a larger metal door. This was unlike all the others she had seen, polished and shiny like a mirror with a long single bar acting as both lock and handle.

She gripped it, surprised how cold it was to the touch, and lifted. It moved easily, the mechanism ratcheting quietly inside, and the door swung open on smooth, silent hinges.

A wave of cold air hit them immediately and bluey white strip lights flickered overhead.

"Just get in!" she scolded.

They stepped over the threshold and she looked back, pulling the door behind her. Down the corridor more figures were moving, there was some shouting.

The metal door shut with a clang and she pushed the locking handle down completely.

The room was spacious with a high ceiling, much more a warehouse in fact, with grey corrugated walls and bare metal racks. And it was cold. Very cold. Banks of air conditioning units hung from the ceiling pumping out a freezing breeze. The insulation keeping the room cool also dampened the noise outside; it was much quieter here. The only exits appeared to be the way they had entered and a full width shuttered garage door at the far end, large enough to accommodate two or three haulage trucks. The warehouse was scattered with a dozen identical containers. They were polished steel, about the length of a family car with no apparent locks or handles and a simple cluster of instrumentation on the end panels that blinked and flashed. Thick electrical wires ran from unit to unit, tangled and snaked across the shiny floor ending at a small portable console.

"What's with all the freezers?" asked Purity, her breath hanging in the air like a speech balloon.

"Who cares," groaned Tom.

She ran her hand along the smooth, chilled metal. "Don't you think it's... well, weird?"

"Whole place is weird. Thought you'd already figured that out."

He walked away, throwing his hands in the air. "You seem to have everything else figured out."

"Not everything," she said to herself.

The console consisted of a monitor and basic control panel on a tall, narrow wheeled trolley. Twelve boxes filled the screen, each showing the internal temperature and battery life of their respective containers. Each vessel was currently set between 4.5 and 4.9 degrees centigrade. On the control panel were a handful of buttons set around a central rotating handle.

It had three positions.

CLOSED/LOCKED UNLOCKED OPEN

She twisted the handle clockwise, all the way to the far end. Dull thumps emitted from across the warehouse as each unit unlocked. Then in unison, they all opened gently, hissing on pneumatic hinges.

Instinctively, Purity raised her phone and peered into the nearest container with some trepidation, a ghostly chilled vapour rising from within. Inside, stacked in neat rows, were small cylindrical metal canisters with clear lids. The glass was frosted with a thin layer of condensation and Purity wiped it off. Inside, sat in a shallow puddle of blood was something red and shiny, veined and wet.

Were they livers? Kidneys? Biology was never her strong point.

Clipped to the interior of the lid was a printed laminated sheet and she eased it loose.

Toms voice echoed down the length of the warehouse, "You should have just left me behind. What are you even doing this, anyway? Trying to prove something? Trying to make a name for yourself?"

Purity ignored him, scanning the sheet. It was a list, a manifest.

UNIT   BLOOD TYPE   EXPIRY   DESTINATION

LIVER	TYPE	C	23 AUG	NY, USA
KIDNEY		TYPE O	24 AUG	CA, USA
KIDNEY		TYPE O	24 AUG	IL, USA
LIVER	TYPE	AB	22 AUG	AZ, USA

It continued down the page and onto the other side. There must have been 150 items on the list and that was just this single freezer.

"No," she whispered.

The next container held shallow flat metal boxes with glass lids, again stacked neatly. She didn't need to look closely to see what they were storing. She yanked the manifest down sharply.

UNIT	BLOOD TYPE	EXPIRY	DESTINATION
CORNEA	TYPE A	25 AUG	CA, USA
CORNEA	TYPE C	25 AUG	CA, USA
CORNEA	TYPE O	24 AUG	CA, USA
CORNEA	TYPE C	25 AUG	NY, USA

"This can't be right."

The eyes staring back at her unblinking. Accusing.

"Tom! You need to see this!" she shouted, holding up the laminate. Tom ignored her and was instead focused on a plastic drum, or rather the shiny contents of the drum.

"I don't need to see nothing!" he barked. "I didn't ask to come here, you brought me. I was finally going to make a difference, save that poor little girl."

She ran to the next freezer and the next, barely glancing inside, snatching the manifests down one by one without stopping.

"Shut up!" she yelled, inches from his face. "Just shut up and listen!"

"Heart. Lungs. Intestines." She peeled the documents off one by one, tossing them at him as she read. "Pancreas. Intestines. Tendons. Veins. Veins?! How is that even possible? Dermal layer tissue. Skin! It's everything! They take everything!"

"They're saving lives."

"They're harvesting organs! It's an organ farm on an industrial scale!"

"And my organs would have saved that girl in Northumberland."

"No," she said quietly, the fight suddenly gone out of her. "No, they wouldn't."

Tom didn't reply. He was holding a handful of silver chains, long, polished with round pebble-like lockets at the end.

All identical.

He turned one over, the metal cool in his hand. On the back of the locket was a simple engraved message.

LOVE A.J

Most lockets were closed, but some were already wide open displaying their contents - a photo, grainy and weathered with age - a black and white portrait of a pretty blonde girl, aged maybe ten or eleven. She wore a striped summer dress and appeared to be stood in a flowery meadow, the sun backlit through her hair.

A low groan escaped his lips.

He didn't need to open any more to know the lockets were *all* exactly the same.

"They're not going to Northumberland," Purity whispered, "Any of them. I don't think they ever were."

None of the manifests listed destinations *anywhere* in Britannica, but they *were* all going to the same place.

Americana.

Tom's grip relaxed. The chains unwound from his fingers and fell back into the drum, re-joining the hundreds of others. He stuttered, "For the first time in my life, I thought... I thought I was making a difference."

Purity put her hand on his shoulder and he brushed it away, "They just played me. Played us. They played all of us."

Tom's body shook and she realised he was sobbing. Touching his shoulder again, he relented, so she wrapped her arms around him and hugged, his huge frame shaking in silence.

"Shhhhh, it's okay. You're okay," she said quietly.

With a bang, the huge shuttered door at the end of the warehouse ratcheted up and a slow hand clap echoed through the hall, the sound so out of place it took Purity a moment to understand what she was hearing.

"Well, well, well… isn't this cosy," sneered the Elf.

28. SHOOT IT UP

The National Elf stood hands on hips, framed in the warehouse doorway backlit by silver moonlight, behind him the grassy hills rolled down towards the pier and beyond that the wind farm out to sea. He was flanked by four security guards, two on either side, all kneeling prone and pointing tasers directly at Purity and Tom.

"I hope you're both happy with yourselves, you've led us a right old merry chase!" cackled the Elf.

"Fuck you." said Purity.

"Now now, there's no need for profanity!"

"We know what you're doing here. We've discovered your dirty little secret."

The Elf held his hands up in surrender.

"You kids, you think the Health Service is a mess now... you have no idea the state it used to be in. You think when Aneurin Bevan came up with the idea he'd ever imagine it being run into the ground by immigrants and scroungers? If people can't look after themselves why should *we* have to?

His voice dropped, adopting a conspiratorial tone. "To be fair, it's still better than the American offering, which is why our lovely PM managed to secure such a good trade deal."

"What does Americana need with all this?" said Purity.

"Everyone wondered how we managed to get such a good trade agreement with The Colonies, but the Americans… they *do* love a transplant! So much easier than trying to fix the problem or change their lifestyle. A perpetual supply of organs in return for tariff free trade. Their Government gets rich on medical aid and CrassCare while our Government gets a free no-strings trade agreement with the second biggest economy in the world, removes immigrants, undesirables *and* reduces the need for more housing."

The Elf clapped. "It's actually genius if you think about it."

"You'll never get away with this." said Purity.

"Get away with it? Have you seen the news? Crass signed the agreement today. It's already a success."

"When the people find out…"

"Aaah yes, about that."

The Elf outstretched his arm dramatically, as if offering Purity the first dance.

"Your phone, please," he purred.

"What? What are you talking about? I don't have a phone."

The Elf tilted his head, saying nothing.

"No really, they took them off us before we arrived."

The Elf wiggled his fingers, shrugging. He stared at her with a big wonky eye.

"Look, I haven't got…"

"Shoot the tramp," the Elf sighed.

The lead guard pulled her trigger and the dart shot out trailing a glittering microscopic filament behind. The barbed needle struck Tom in the chest pumping electricity into his body in rapid controlled bursts. He grunted through gritted teeth and fell on his back twitching spasmodically, accompanied by the sound of the electric TACK-TACK-TACK.

"No!" cried Purity.

Thrashing wildly, Tom barely suppressed a pained groan.

TACK-TACK-TACK.

"Stop! You're killing him!" yelled Purity.

TACK-TACK-TACK.

"STOP!!!" she screamed and threw the smartphone at the Elf as Tom's body shook and writhed, fitting uncontrollably.

"Hey!" shouted a voice outside. "I believe the lady asked you to stop!"

The Elf turned slowly, his giant head creaking on well-worn hinges towards the source of the noise.

On the flat roof of the outbuildings silhouetted by the full moon, stood Warren. His arm, held steady by his other hand, was raised and pointed a bulky pistol directly at the people below.

"The terrorist," spat the Elf. He raised a gloved hand and the guard disconnected her taser. Tom lay still and Purity ran to him.

"He alright, P?" yelled Warren.

She lifted his head, wiping the sweat from his forehead. His breathing was rapid, but he was still conscious.

"Yes. I… I think so!" she shouted.

"Sorry I'm late, wasn't expecting it all to kick off so soon!"

He surveyed the chaos before him. "Was this part of the plan?"

Purity yelled back. "Not quite!"

The Elf tapped his foot comically. "Far be it from me to break up this heartwarming reunion, but what exactly do you think is going to happen now?"

Warren steadied himself. "I'll tell you what's going to happen now, my pointy eared friend. You are going to let us all go, or I am going to shoot you."

The Elf squinted, lenses in the animatronic eyes whirring and whining as he magnified his view of Warren. Or rather what Warren was carrying.

"Shoot me?" chuckled the Elf. "Forgive me, but... is that a *flare* gun?"

Warren frowned, he hadn't counted on the mask having a zoom lens.

"Might be," he said. Being in charge of the boating lake had one advantage, at least.

"You intend to shoot me with a flare gun. That's your plan?"

Warren shrugged. "I dunno, that old costume of yours looks pretty flammable. Figure it'll go up like the 29th of March."

The Elf paced the length of the courtyard, the bells on his curly shoes jingle jangling with each step. "You've never worked for the PHS have you? Everything the hospital uses has to pass over two hundred safety checks... and I do mean everything. Beds. Machinery. Pencils. Hell, if a paperclip has to meet regulations, I'm damn sure this suit will. We both know it'll be fire retardant."

Warren pondered for a moment. "I'm sure it was... when it was made. Just how old is that suit anyway? I remember seeing the Elf adverts when I was a kid and that was at least 10 years ago. Are you really confident it won't go up in a ball of flames?"

The Elf stopped pacing and stroked his sharp chin.

"Hmmmmm… You know what? Yes, I am!"

He puffed his chest up and stretched out his arms. "Fire away!"

Warren faltered. This was not how it was supposed to go. "Wh… What?"

The Elf raised his head and shouted, "You said it yourself - you're not killers. Let's see, shall we?"

Warren had indeed said as much many times, he wasn't expecting to have to put it to the test tonight though. The gun, now heavy in his sweaty grasp shook nervously and he tightened his finger against the trigger.

Concerned, Purity shouted, "Warren!?"

The Elf spread his arms even wider, nodding faster, the mechanical grin stretching from ear to ear. Warren squinted down the barrel, his chest squarely in his sights. There was little chance of missing at this range and he was fairly sure that suit wouldn't put up much resistance. Burned alive in a creepy Halloween costume. As ways to go, it was pretty grim. But the National Elf was right about one thing - he wasn't a killer. He had never killed before and he sure as hell wasn't going to start now.

"Damn it," he said.

And fired the gun straight up into the sky.

With a pop, the small fireball hissed and

sputtered up into the clouds, flickering and flashing in hues of salmon and coral. Higher and higher it rose, a trail of pink, puffy smoke in its wake. The flare hung in the clouds, momentarily the brightest star in the sky before beginning its descent. Energy spent, it arced gracefully along the coastline and broke up into sparkling fragments.

The Elf turned to the young man on the roof, "You missed."

Warren smiled - that cocky, stupid know-it-all smile that Purity loved.

"Did I?"

29. THE UNFORGET-TABLE FIRE

Out to sea, bright flashes of orange and silver appeared on the water. First one or two, then a dozen. Then the sound finally reached the shore. The sound of an explosion. Multiple explosions, all wrapped together and served with a flaming side order of chaos. One by one the wind turbines erupted in balls of fire, bent scorched blades spinning off into the waves.

"WHAT!!" cried the Elf, the mask offering a poor approximation of shock.

Another explosion went off, closer this time, near the fence. Close enough to feel the heat.

"We're under attack!!" the Elf shrieked.

"Sound the alarm! Sound the alarm!"

The lights in the camp flickered briefly, then as one, faded. The campsite was plunged into darkness, lit only by the moon.

"P!" yelled Warren, "The phone!"

The smartphone lay on the tarmac, jagged cracks spidering out from the bottom corner, just feet from the bewildered Elf. Purity sprinted across the yard towards it, but the Elf had seen her. The phone was closer to him and he closed the gap in a few steps. He lifted his comical pantomime boot above the phone, poised to crush it under his heel and wagged a finger at Purity.

"I don't think so!" he said slyly and stamped as hard as he could.

As his boot dropped he was struck by a figure. Tom ploughed into him in a violent rugby tackle, his huge body knocking the Elf sideways onto the lawn.

"Bastard!" he screamed as they both fell to the ground in a tangle of limbs, Tom punching he bulky suit frantically. The guards spun around aiming their tasers at the struggling pair, but it was hard to separate them in the failing light.

Purity snatched the phone up and pushed the power switch. The screen flared into life and she saw immediately it had a signal. One bar.

Tom brought his knee up, kicking the Elf hard in the groin. Even under that excess padding he was sure that would have hurt.

"You tricked me!" he punched, "You tricked us all!"

A guard fired, the electrified needle hitting the grass uselessly and Tom heard the familiar TACK-TACK-TACK of the weapon.

He clambered to his feet, dragging the Elf with him - he wasn't putting up much of a fight, and seeing their chance, the guards fired again. Tom span, hauling the Elf around in a smooth motion. The projectiles hit the padded costume dead centre instantly pumping 1200 volts down the glittering wires. Tom let go and the Elf screamed, jerking and shuddering in a flurry of sparks. TACK-TACK-TACK. The mechanical jaw chattered insanely and the eyes blinked and rolled in smoking sockets, the electrical systems flooded with energy.

"Come on!" yelled Warren.

Together, they ran from the courtyard across the neatly manicured lawns down towards the lake. Behind them an eerie metallic oscillating screech came from the Elf, echoing into the night sky but they didn't look back. The explosions seemed to have stopped and fires had broken out across the facility, ashen smoke filling the air. There didn't seem to be much property damage, Purity noted, the bulk of destruction limited to wide gaping holes in the peripheral fences. Purity stabbed at the AOJI.

"A phone?" asked Warren, incredulous. "Where did you? Never mind. What's on it?"

She smiled grimly. "Proof."

An orange fireball bloomed behind them and cinders blew through the air.

The phones battery was on 3% now and she quickly opened the VIDEOS folder, tapping on each thumbnail as they ran, finally hitting the UPLOAD TO FEED icon.

A popup window overlaid the display.

USERNAME:
PASSWORD:

For a second, Purity was confused. She couldn't remember the last time she'd had to physically type a username or password, she was so used to logging in with voice, face or fingerprints. In fact, she wasn't even sure she actually remembered them. She slowed to a walk, typing was hard enough on a screen that small.

USERNAME: PURITY29

That was easy enough, but the password? It was set up so long ago. She typed.

PASSWORD: PASSWORD

Rejected.
She tried again.

PASSWORD: QWERTY

Rejected.
The battery icon dropped to 2%.

"Oh come on," she said, exasperated. She was trying to think where she was the first time she had used the feed for herself. Her dad had bought the phone for her, a scuffed second hand AOJI from a charity shop. She remembered sitting at the kitchen table together as he set it up, one of his old cartoons playing on the video recorder.

"Oh Daddy," she smiled and typed a single word.

PASSWORD: DANGERMOLE

The speaker played a micro symphony and the screen was replaced with a progress bar.

PLEASE WAIT - PREPARING FILES 1%

She was so used to instant transfer of files on her own phone. How could anyone still use these old 5G models?

They reached the lake where plastic swan boats, melted and charred, floated on their sides in disarray. There were patients here, some running and shouting, others merely shambling along the verges and pathways, dazed and confused. Guards ran amongst them swinging shoksticks, desperately trying to regain control but clearly outnumbered.

A lone figure caught Tom's eye.

"Bob?"

Hi, I'm Bob stood motionless, a statue amid the chaos. His gown was torn and dirty, eyes wide with fear. He was clearly in shock.

"Bob? It's me," said Tom.

"We need to leave!" hissed Warren.

"I'm not going without Tom," explained Purity.

"No. You go."

"What?"

"Look around you, look at them.," he said. "They don't know what to do, they don't know what's going on.

"You can come with us!"

Tom wrapped a huge arm around Bob. "The camps... they were right about one thing. Out there, I'm no-one. Here, I can make a difference, a big difference. These are my people. They need someone to lead them. I turned my back on them once, it won't happen again."

He was right, of course, and Purity knew it. After spending so much of his life adrift he had finally found purpose, direction. A reason to live.

"We'll stay then!"

"We'll what?" said Warren.

Tom shook his head. "Go girl. You'll not change the world from here. Get out there... shake some shit up. Always said you were destined for great things, Expresso. Don't you go making a liar of me."

She hesitated, but seeing his sincerity, flung her arms around him and hugged tightly. She began to talk but he merely hushed her and winked. He hauled Bob up straight and they limped away into the smoke together, his voice booming into the night. "Same time tomorrow, Expresso. Two sweeteners."

30. NIGHT BOAT TO CAIRO

The pier was sectioned off with lengths of yellow tape bearing the repeated words HAZARDOUS AREA KEEP OUT. It was threatening but offered little defence. They pushed through the ribbons and stepped onto the slippery decking, the cool, salty sea breeze hitting them face on, now they had left the protection of the land. The wooden flooring sloped up towards a large square building with steps leading to an entrance framed between ornately carved columns. Gaudy, handmade letters ran along the front of the structure, some at odd angles, others barely hanging on.

MORGANS PIER

The doors, like the windows had clearly

been boarded up for decades so they made their way around the side of the building. There, a narrow walkway meandered past empty, decrepit huts that once sold hot dogs and postcards, sticks of rock and kiss-me-quick hats to eager, gullible customers. They climbed over faded boards promising better times and the abandoned cafés BURGER QUEENZ and GRUBWAY until they emerged on the main pier walkway. The pier ran some 300 feet bordered with rusted iron railings and dotted with small huts and benches along the length. Majestic Victorian street lamps stood in darkness, strings of dirty, discoloured flags dangling between them, flapping in the wind. The end of the pier had fallen victim to fire decades ago and had long since fallen into the sea.

PLEASE WAIT - PREPARING FILES 62%

They treaded carefully on the rotting beams, slowly making their way along the pier. From here they could see people on the beach. Patients had escaped the confines of the facility and were dispersing across the sand and fields. She felt a pang of sadness and wondered if Tom was in there somewhere.

"Where are we going?" whispered Purity.

The wooden beams creaked and sagged beneath their feet and they exchanged a worried glance.

"Trust me."

The wood snapped like a gunshot and Warren's foot disappeared into the gaping hole. Purity grabbed him and held on as they watched the timber pieces fall away into the crashing sea below. Purity studied the pier ahead. It was just a craggy and broken mass of splintered wood. There was nowhere to go. In the moonlight, she could just pick out the remains of the windfarm, the towers clawing free of the water like witches' fingers. Fires ran unchecked and thick black plumes of smoke poured off them, enveloping the pier in a choking, blinding fog. Flickering embers danced through the sky like amber snow.

PLEASE WAIT - PREPARING FILES 78%

Purity peered over the side into the sea. "So, what do we..."

"Well, well, well," cried a voice.

It was strained, metallic, but there was no mistaking who it belonged to.

The Elf stood halfway along the pier, wobbly and unsure. His jaw hung off completely, connected loosely by sparking wires and an eyeball hung down the cheek, blinking constantly. His face and side were black and charred, and thin plumes of smoke drifted off his body - a grotesque parody of a parody. He limped forward, every step a struggle.

"It's only... me!" he rasped, "The National...

Elf."

He raised a taser and pointed it shakily at them.

"At.... your... service.... You should have... killed me... when you had... the chance."

Warren stared at the gun.

He had already had the same thought.

"You're wasting your time. Look around you." Purity held her phone up, screen facing him. Her thumb over the SEND button.

PLEASE WAIT - PREPARING FILES 99%

"Look! You're too late! This is *all* going to the feed. Its over. It's all over."

On the AOJI, the screen blinked out.

The battery was dead.

If only the Elf could smile. "It is for you, " he rasped. "*And* I'll get the satisfaction of killing you both."

The Elf raised the gun pointing it squarely at Purity's chest and the dirty clouds of smoke billowed and churned around the pair, suddenly moving with unexpected urgency. The Elf peered above them at the sight.

What was this?

The smoke rolled and pulsed with unnatural symmetry and two faint glowing lights formed in the smog, spectral eyes getting larger and brighter. If the Elf's face was capable of emoting confusion, it would have. With an almighty blare of a horn, a tall bow cut through the oily mist and a ship's hull emerged, spotlights bathing the pier in a fierce white light.

The Elf threw his good arm in front of his good eye, but it was good for nothing. The light, magnified and amplified by the mask's visual receptors instantly blinded him and he staggered backwards with a cry, his clunky boots slipping on the wet surface. His heel struck the weakened planks and he dropped with a crack.

For a second he stood with a foot in the floor, an unlikely Rumpelstiltskin.

"What!?" he shouted. "Wha...!"

Then the wood shattered and he plunged into the icy waves screaming.

The ship, an ex-Greenpeace trawler, drew alongside the Victorian structure blaring it's horn again. Painted on the bow was its name.

BULLY'S SPECIAL PRIZE

The trawler bobbed gently in the shallows and Warren saw familiar figures lined on the deck waving.

Delphi. Samson. Gabriel.

Warren hugged Purity and threw his head back, punching the sky.

"And that's a bullseye!"

BOOK 3
Fawlty Towers

31. WE BUILT THIS CITY

"Beautiful, isn't it?" said Delphi.

The observation deck of Monolith One was arguably the project's crowning achievement. In a rare concession to aesthetics, the top three floors had been opened out into a glass roofed ornamental garden taking up the entire roof space. Instead of another 300 habitation units, trees and ponds with unconvincing animatronic ducks were dotted around the shallow grassy hills alongside picnic benches and tables. Large statues were dotted around the gardens, hand sculpted effigies of the nation's legends watching out over the capital. The sun was sinking over Hyde Park, an angry red eye casting a crimson glow with long umber shadows across the city. The wailing of evening prayer echoed up through the manmade canyons.

"You still set on bringing this all down?" asked Purity.

"That's the plan," nodded Delphi. "These are symbols and symbols hold power. Every religion has known that - that's why so many churches, cathedrals, mosques are such massive statements. These? These are this government's statement to the people and as long as these stand, the government will be seen to be right."

Purity raised her eyebrows. "Peace through war?"

Delphi shook her head. "Order through chaos."

Purity sighed. "When's the big day?"

"Purity Day."

Purity couldn't conceal her surprise. "That's in three days!"

"Hey, while you've been chilling in a holiday camp some of us have been very, very busy."

"Some holiday," Purity said to herself.

The modified fishing trawler had slipped away under the cover of smoke and darkness, leaving the burning Health Camp, sailing south on the North Sea. After the initial jubilation of the rescue passed, Purity had found herself uncharacteristically solemn. She spent much of the journey alone, hypnotised by the patterns in the surf and white noise of the sea, simply trying to wrap her head around everything she had just been through, everything she had seen. The lies and deceptions, the factory farming of humanity for profit. That bloody Elf.

And Ted... she hoped Ted had made it okay.

BULLY'S SPECIAL PRIZE made its way down the east coast in radio silence, skirting Coast Guard and French scallop gunship patrols, past Felixstowe and Clacton-on-Sea before taking a hard starboard towards the Thames Estuary. A kilometre out from the 19th Century gun tower of Grain Tower Battery, they killed the lights and veered into the River Medway navigating by moonlight. The vessel skirted a number of bluffs, emerging at a secluded rundown private jetty surrounded by heavily wooded farmland. A narrow dirt track wound up the hill to a nearby farmhouse where the double-decker bus waited under a camouflaged tarpaulin.

"Since when did we own a ship, anyway?" Purity asked.

"We know a few... like minded individuals," said Delphi. "Wealthy. Help us out now and again."

"Friends in high places."

How do you square that circle, Delphi? she thought. *Fighting for the redistribution of wealth from a millionaire's boat.*

"We just need to transfer the explosives to the base of Monolith Two," Delphi explained.

"The tower's uninhabited, it's essentially a controlled demolition."

Purity didn't reply but stared at the last vestiges of sun disappearing over the horizon, the clouds shifting from bright hues of purple to grey.

Delphi asked softly, "Cold feet?"

"I don't know, it all seems a bit… much. Just thinking about something my dad said once - you don't need to change the world, you just need to change one mind."

"That sounds very profound. What does it mean?"

Purity shrugged. "I'm still processing it, to be honest."

"We're supposed to be celebrating!" shouted Gabriel raising his can in a toast.

"Fantabulous, darling!" cried Samson, throwing her silk scarf over her shoulder and knocking the fizzy beverage back.

"C'mon kids. You forgotten how to party?!" shouted Delphi throwing a can across the table. Warren flinched but Purity caught it instinctively, the metal cool in her palm. She turned it over, studying the distinctive red design. Blocky, militaristic copy read NIKOLA KOLA while a pouting, cartoon-breasted female wearing a crimson bikini and matching furry cap said via a speech balloon, 'Take the COLD WAR to your taste buds!'

Gabriel had contacts in Little Poland who had contacts in Belarus and Latvia. Drug running in Eastern Europe was managed heavily by the big cartels, but sugar... that was relatively new. Certainly new enough for regular, small coordinated groups to smuggle crates of banned drinks across the Soviet border and onto light aircraft. The risks, as always, were huge but the profits unimaginable.

Sugar it seemed, was big business in Britannica.

"Expresso, two sweeteners, she muttered to herself.

Delphi frowned, "Sorry?"

"I was just thinking about Tom," said purity, handing back the can.

"Oh, the homeless guy," said Delphi, a little too dismissively. She corrected herself quickly. "He sounded very brave."

"He was. And we left him behind."

"Look, we couldn't hang around. We always knew blowing up the windfarm was going to attract the coast guard's attention."

"So, you left them to die."

"We don't know that. they might..."

"Like you always do. Like you left us, like you left that security guard to die in the explosion."

Gabriel butted in. "You still moping about that? He was just doing his job, he wasn't there to make friends."

Purity felt a flush of anger. "You were going. To let him. Die."

"We're terrorists, darlin'," he shrugged. "Clues in the name."

Terrorist? Is that what she was now? She turned her back on Gabriel, he was too much like hard work.

"Just remind me, Delphi. Why didn't Ariel come with us in the bus that day?"

"Ariel?" Delphi frowned, unfazed. "She was supposed to, she wasn't picking up when I called and missed the rendezvous. So, we left without her."

"Did Warren tell you we saw her at the demonstration?"

"You saw...? What was she doing there?"

"Trying to blow herself up."

Purity's eyes narrowed. "We blow up an animal experiment lab, the crowd panics. The crowd is funnelled into the square. Where Ariel is waiting with a bomb. You'll forgive me if I don't see that as a coincidence."

"No, no, no. That's not our style."

"Why? Because we're not killers? I'm hearing the words, Delphi, but your actions? Well, they're saying something completely different."

"Ariel was always the most... religious amongst us. And she was certainly frustrated at the speed of change. Or lack of it. Maybe she joined another cell?"

An image of Ariel, frightened, panicked, consumed by fire sprung into Purity's mind and she quickly shook it away. That was not something she wanted to think about. "Joined another cell? Have you any idea how ridiculous that sounds?"

"What can I say? She obviously chose to do it, it was her decision. We never really know what other people are thinking, do we?"

No. No we don't, thought Purity.

Lights, red and blue, caught her eye and she squinted down at the ring road circling the towers. From this height, vehicles looked like ants, but this was something more dangerous than insects.

Far more dangerous.

Warren's phone buzzed, not his usual ringtone but an unexpected synthesized melody, a theme tune from an old tv show that was impossible to ignore. Almost instantly, the other phones joined in doing the same. He grabbed it from the bench and turned it over. The screen was blue, flashing a single word.

THE BILL

Purity stepped away from the glass and shouted back.

"We've got company!"

32. DANGER ZONE

"Turn those bloody lights off!" yelled Officer Lister into the vehicle's walkie talkie.

The three Sangwon troop transporters were six-wheeled, unmarked and black, escorted by a police motorcade of bikes and cars. The blues and reds quickly blinked out and the escorts fell back, the trucks surging into the car park of Monolith One. With a screech of rubber, the lumbering wagons pulled to a stop in a line outside, their rear doors facing the main entrance.

"All teams prep for evac."

Roni left the engine idling and climbed down the ladder past the huge front tyres while Ronald jumped out of the passenger seat, throwing a hard metal case onto the tarmac. By the time Roni had circled around the bonnet, Ronald had already opened the case and was tightening a bulky glove by the wrist.

Roni swiped at a map on her tablet. "Can't run forever," she murmured under her breath, watching two blinking lights at this location. She spoke calmly into her headset.

"Reliable intel informs us the perpetrators are all currently in Tower One."

And the intel was, in fact, extremely reliable. The numbering branded on Warren and Purity's palms carried a very distinct, mildly radioactive signature - they were never going to escape.

Team Rod will be performing a floor by floor sweep starting at floor 13 - the first pod level. Team Jane will also perform a floor by floor sweep starting on floor 302 - the top of the building. Team Freddy will sweep the mall, service and maintenance levels. All teams will continue until the perpetrators are found, or more intel becomes available."

Ronald held his arm out and opened his gloved hand flat, a whirring noise suddenly firing up from inside the aluminium case. He raised his hand slightly and a drone, four blades, squat and flat, shot up out of the box into the sky. Roni watched it rise parallel with the tower, orange and white lights blinking as she felt the first spots of rain on her face.

"All teams be aware, once we're inside, we will be locking the building down. No one is going in or coming out. This is an extraction, but if that option is unavailable, lethal force has been authorised."

She paused, partly to let the message sink in, partly for dramatic effect. "And remember, we do not have the time or the luxury to evacuate the tower… so please *do* try to avoid killing civilians," she added. "The paperwork is a nightmare."

She faced the wagons.

"Team Rod, go."

On the first truck, the rear door descended and six soldiers ran down the ramp. They all wore black - gloves, uniform, boots and helmets. They all carried assault rifles.

"Team Jane, go. Team Freddy, go."

The other trucks followed suit and eighteen highly trained and heavily armed soldiers ran towards the glass entrance of Monolith One.

Roni withdrew her pistol from her holster, feeling the carefully balanced weight in her hand, and smiled.

It was a long time since she had used a proper gun.

33. SELF CONTROL

In the foyer, the soldiers split off into their respective groups - three teams of six soldiers each. Team Rod, having only to start on floor thirteen, made straight for the emergency stairwell while Team Jane, starting on the roof, waited for the service elevator. Team Freddy spread out in couples, approaching the shops in a crouched walk, rifles out, pushed hard into their shoulders. The mall, usually bustling this time of the evening fell silent as shoppers slowly noticed the armed women and men amongst them.

Roni raised her hand to her ear, looking back at the entrance they had just walked through. "Lock her down."

A single clang echoed through the foundations and thick metal shutters started rolling down over the entrances and windows.

A young woman with a pram suddenly realised what was happening and started walking faster towards the exit. Seeing her, an elderly couple did the same.

"Everyone," shouted Lister in her best official voice, "Please stay where you are!"

Shadows stretched as the copper sunlight was slowly squeezed out and more people were now jogging, some sprinting to the doors.

"This area is a live crime scene! Anybody attempting to leave will be arrested and..."

But she was being ignored. Nearly everyone was running and shouting, panic rippling through the crowd in an almost tangible wave. The woman with the pram was nearly at the door yelling something unintelligible.

"Stop!" shouted Lister, levelling her weapon at her back. The shutters had descended to waist height and the woman tipped the pram on its back wheels to squeeze it under.

"Stop! Armed police!"

She pushed the pram through and was hunched down when the bullets hit her spine and heart. Roni fired twice in an even controlled burst, squeezing the trigger gently, keeping the gun steady. The young mother hit the ground, her neck twisting at a horrible angle. Free of her grasp, the old pram wheeled to a stop outside the building. The iron shutter hit the ground loudly, settling in her expanding pool of blood, the fluid black in the clinical hue of the LED strips that now lit the interior.

The crowd stared in shock. Guns were not something that happened in Britannica, that was a Colonies thing. Whispering spread through the foyer as people lifted their phones filming.

"Oh my God!"

"That baby? What about the baby?"

"She killed her. She just killed her!"

A man, bald, muscular with a green Union flag tattoo on his temple marched towards Lister, phone in front of him recording.

"Murderer!" he screamed, "This woman is a murderer! She just shot an innocent girl in the back!"

He was a big man and Lister stepped back with not a little concern. The people gathered around her angrily shouting and pointing their phones in her face.

"Killer!"

"Government scum!"

Roni swiftly pointed her gun up and fired twice and the mob receded, cowering.

Union tattoo grunted, "Big woman with a gun, aren't you?"

She looked him up and down. "Big man without a gun. You lose."

Lister straightened up, regaining her composure and cleared her throat. "As I was saying. We have reason to believe Christian Extremists are being harboured in this building, and as such this area is now a live crime scene. Anybody, and I do mean anybody, attempting to leave will be arrested and charged with the offence of harbouring terrorists. Under article 57.2 of the Prevention of Terrorism Act, all phones, wearables and recording devices will be collected and destroyed."

His comments were answered with annoyed grumbles.

"If you have any complaints, feel free to write a strongly worded email for your local MP to ignore."

Lister studied them: docile, compliant. It never took much for human nature to reveal its true cowardly self, she thought. But even now some were still filming on their phones, a small act of defiance or just an automatic, ingrained reaction she didn't know. Or care to be honest.

She snatched a phone from a teenager's ear and threw it to the floor, her boot smashing it into glass and plastic splinters. The boy opened his mouth to speak, but Lister put up a hand. "Now if you don't mind, I'd like everyone to lie face down on the ground and shut the fuck up."

34. LOVE IN AN ELEVATOR

"Soldiers," said Warren peering at the grainy image on his phone's display, "a dozen, maybe twenty."

He had connected to the tower's CCTV camera array and was swiping frantically between views. With the council spending as little as possible on what they regarded as non-essentials, the resolution was blocky and updated slowly. While the picture wasn't the best quality, the story it told was still very clear.

Foyer cameras showed civilians lying on the ground, their hands behind their heads while soldiers weaved between them kicking in shop doors. Warren swiped up selecting a different bank of cameras. He selected ELEVATORS and a grid of live thumbnails of lift interiors filled the screen. Most showed empty elevators, two or three carried bored civilians, but one was full.

Of soldiers.

"Service elevator," said Delphi. "Can you tell where it's headed?"

Warren tapped the thumbnail, filling the screen. Data across the bottom of the screen showed an array of technical data: speed, weight, altitude. And there in the corner, the selected floor.

FL 303

"They're coming here."

"I don't get it, how do they know we're here? How do they know we're on this floor?"

"They can't, it's just procedure. One team at the bottom, one at the top. It's a pincer movement to squeeze us out."

"How long before the lift reaches us?"

Warren did his best thinking out loud. "Six metres a second, 300 floors... erm, I dunno. Two, two and a half minutes tops."

"Can you stop it?"

"No," he said waving the device in the air, "This app just scrapes data. Can't write back without a direct connection. But..."

He jogged to the service elevator doors. The display above read 104 and was climbing. The CALL button pulsed gently and he ran his fingernails along the edges of the brass panel. He called over his shoulder, "Hey Gabe, you got a screwdriver?"

Gabriel reached into his back pocket and retrieved a flick knife.

"This do?"

"Why does that not surprise me?" replied Warren, taking the weapon and easing the blade into the groove of the panel. He balled his fist and brought it down sharply against the handle. The cover offered no resistance and pinged off revealing a mass of coloured wires and circuit boards. He reached in blindly feeling around.

"What? You just going to plug your phone in or something?"

He smiled, holding up a micro connector.

"That's exactly what I'm going to do, "he grinned.

They gathered around him and he kneeled, plugging the wire into his phone.

"It's no different to what the service monkeys do," he shrugged. He opened a black command window and a list of controls scrolled past. Recognising one, he typed it on the command line, appending figures and symbols in brackets.

Delphi spread her arms, "Okay, don't crowd him. Let the expert work his magic."

Then quieter to Warren, "You do know what you're doing, right?"

He made a non-committal whine.

The elevator read 211, still climbing and Warren ran the command. Instantly, the numbers leapt up in a blur.

223.
234.
246.

Too fast. The lift had speeded up.

Warren whined again. Not so much non-committal, more abject panic.

He typed the line again, changing a one to a zero and hit ENTER.

271.
282.
294.
293.
294.
293.

"It's stopped!" he shouted. By the way the display was flicking between digits, Warren assumed it was stuck between floors but still, that was only eight floors away, far too close for comfort. From there they could just as easily get out and walk. He switched between apps and called up the video feed from the elevator car. Soldiers on either side of the car were prising the doors open slowly, a slice of the 294th floor visible through the gap.

"Aw give me a break," Warren muttered.

He pinched the screen into a split display and opened the command prompt again, typing a string of codes and characters beneath the monochrome video. The soldiers had pulled the doors three quarters open and were lifting a man up to the open space.

"I don't think so," said Warren and hit ENTER.

Nothing happened.

"Huh?"

He punched the button again. Nothing.

The soldier's arm and head were through the gap but his backpack was caught against the top of the door.

Warren squinted at the command line he had just written, mouthing the characters silently. It didn't make sense.

The soldier pulled the quick release buckle and his backpack fell into the elevator, caught by a colleague.

"Oh," said Warren with dawning realisation, "Typo, you great bungle."

Both the soldier's arms were now though the opening and he squeezed his torso through the tight space.

Warren swapped two numbers around and pushed ENTER again.

The elevator shuddered and the soldiers started yelling, urgently grabbing their team member in the doorway, hands clutching around his legs, feet and belt.

Warren paled. In his eagerness to stop them he hadn't considered anything like this, he had only wanted to stop them, not kill them. The soldier was going to be decapitated.

The car dropped.

"No!" screamed Warren, closing his eyes.

The service elevator descended at speed away from the penthouse gardens, destination ground floor. Nervously, Warren raised an eyelid and looked at his phone. All six soldiers sat on the floor of the car in shock. All heads intact. With a wave of relief, Warren unplugged his phone and tore the connecting cable free of the console in a bloom of white and blue sparks. He turned to his friends and bowed.

"And that's magic!" he said.

"Warren?" said Purity, nodding at the display over the elevator door. "It's slowing down."

They watched as the numbers slowed to a crawl then stopped on 202.

"They're regained control," barked Delphi. "Stop them!"

Warren held up the frayed connecting cable, "That... might be difficult."

202.
208.
220.
232.

"They're coming back," said Samson.

244.
256.
268.

"And fast," added Gabriel. "Run!"

35. TURN TO STONE

Sergeant Pat 'Phoenix' Ortega and Private Nora 'Batty' Bateman emerged from the elevator, their Sepo assault rifles sweeping the area in abrupt arcs. Three steps out they crouched on the synthi-grass and two more soldiers flanked their sides, guns raised.

The sun, a narrow scar on the horizon, was clinging on to the day and the park was tinted in muted pinks and purples, deep dark puddles of shade pooling in recesses and alcoves. Uplighters in the pavements had already come on but their size and scattering did little to boost visibility, leaving the trees and statues in eerie silhouette against the night sky. Other than tic tac of rain against the ceiling glass, the park was silent.

Phoenix tapped the visor on her helmet

cycling through the display options. LO-LIGHT, INFRARED, ZOOM, settling on HEATMAP. Immediately the grass around her lit up, orange and yellow blurry footprints trampled messily around the elevator then dispersed along paths in two distinct groups. She raised a gloved hand, three arrow-straight, upright fingers raised together. She gestured left-left in a swift, fluid wrist movement and Batty led the soldiers beside her away silently along the virtual trail, scanning the park. She stood and moved forward, following the second set of footprints.

Ahead of them was the bandstand. Shimmering footsteps led towards it then split, as if two people had run around it in opposite directions. She brought her gun up and took the left route, Batty taking the other.

A quick glance into the bandstand revealed it was empty, if indeed it had ever been used, and they continued on around it. On the far side the footprints re-joined and continued down a grassy hill where they reached a duck pond.

And stopped.

Cold water would have masked the heat trail, they could have gone in any direction from here. A sudden movement in the water caught her eye and she levelled the rifle at it, finger braced against the trigger.

The plastic duck stared at her along the gun barrel with dead eyes.

"You saw them," she whispered, "which way did they go?"

But the moulded beak stayed tightly shut. The duck wasn't giving up its secrets today.

Phoenix aimed at its head. "Bang," she said, lowering the weapon.

The visor should still be able to pick up whole body heat signatures, they would be much harder to mask unless someone was entirely submerged in cold water, that is. She fired off two rounds into the pond and waited for blood or a body to surface.

Nothing.

But two statues were within sprinting distance of the pond - Manning & Dawson. They would certainly be dense enough to block body heat.

Behind Les Dawson, Samson, Gabriel and Purity huddled together pressed tightly against the plinth. From this angle they could see the figures of Warren and Delphi crouched behind another statue.

And the soldiers cautiously approaching.

Kneeling behind the base of Kenny Everett, Delphi and Warren could see the soldiers reflected in the glass of the dome. They had watched in silence as the strike team had left the elevator and split up. Warren tugged at Delphi's sleeve and nodded at the reflection. Three soldiers were heading their way, armed. Warren was suddenly very aware of his own mortality and groaned.

Delphi put her finger to her lips. Shush. Don't worry.

They had been in tighter spots before.

Probably.

Batty Bateman raised a clenched fist and the soldiers stopped. She was sure she had heard something. She tapped the multi-control on her visor and selected AUDIO-BOOST. She slowed her own breathing as she tilted her head, enhanced sound feeding into her earpiece in a steady hiss. The background patter of rain wasn't helping, but behind that white noise was something more rhythmic. More consistent.

Breathing.

Batty adopted a combat stance, levelling her weapon at the statue. The team spread wide and did the same.

Phoenix stood at the base of the Bernard Manning. It was humbling to be in the presence of one of the giants of entertainment, even if it was only a statue. She could only imagine what it was like to be alive at the time of the greats.

Her earpiece squawked, "Target acquired."

She turned, facing the other team. Tapping ZOOM, she could see outline of the hunched pair behind the statue of Everett.

"Target sighted. Target sighted." she reported, "Two individuals. Unarmed."

Phoenix adopted a combat stance and peered into the telescopic sight. "Taking them out."

"No!" cried Purity, running out from behind the statue waving her arms. "Stop!"

All three soldiers aimed at the sudden intruder, Purity squarely in their sights. Facial recognition software in their visors confirmed her identity immediately.

"Belay that," said Phoenix, "We have the package."

Purity put her hands behind her head and kneeled down.

"Don't shoot them. Please. You've got what you came for, take me," she pleaded. "Just let them go."

Through the earpiece, Bateman asked, "What about the others, Sarge?"

Phoenix lowered her rifle and spoke calmly into the mic, "As you were."

"No!" screamed Purity. "You don't need to..."

A noise, unusual, out of place, creaked above them. Phoenix looked up to see Manning wobbling precariously, the bronze mass suddenly unsteady on its feet. With a herculean cry, Samson braced against the statues thigh and pushed the effigy beyond its tipping point. It toppled over the edge of the base, shadows growing longer as the grinning comedian plummeted onto the soldiers. Batty heard the screams and ran towards the fallen structure, her comrades sprinting beside her.

"They're going," Warren whispered with relief, "the soldiers are going."

Getting no reply, he looked back, "Delphi?"

But he was alone in his hiding place.

Delphi had gone.

While Phoenix had almost managed to jump clear of the falling star, her companions had not been so lucky. The sergeant's leg was crushed from the knee down under Bernard's weighty shoulder and was bleeding out onto the manicured lawn. Of the remaining two soldiers, one had vanished underneath completely and the other's boots stuck out beneath the iron belly.

Gabriel kneeled down, relieving Sgt Ortega of her weapons. He took the rifle, her pistol and a few grenades.

"You won't... get... away..."

"Don't waste your breath, darling," he interrupted, "we already did."

Samson helped Purity up.

"Oh my God. They're... You just..."

Sparks flew from Manning's jacket as bullets ricocheted away. Glass shattered from deflected ammunition and icy rain poured in through the cracks of the exterior windows.

"Get down!" barked Gabriel, ducking under the statue's arm. He jumped up and squeezed off a round at the oncoming soldiers. The soldiers dived to the ground and returned fire in short bursts.

"Delphi?"

Staying close to the statue, Warren peered across the park. Where was she? Stray bullets winged past and he covered his head with a yelp.

Delphi stood in the service elevator squeezed tightly against the side wall, hammering the lift controls with a fist. She looked up and for a moment, the longest possible moment, and their eyes locked. He tried to read her expression, a combination of fear, anger, determination and ... was that sorrow?

"What are you doing?" he mouthed.

Delphi looked at the floor then returned his gaze, an empty, hollow smile on her lips.

As the elevator doors closed, she mouthed the words, "I'm sorry."

And that was the last time he saw her alive.

Samson squeezed off two shots with the Hyoksin .45 pistol and the last soldier fell to the ground. Gabriel moved in swiftly liberating them of their weapons.

"What are you doing?!" shouted Purity.

"I don't think they'll be needing them, darling."

He held out a pistol, grip first, to Purity.

"I've never fired a gun in my life," she said, "I'm not bloody starting now!"

They met Warren near the bandstand. He was alone and looked shocked.

"Where's Delphi?" asked Purity

Warren hung his head, still unsure of what just happened. "She's gone."

"Gone? What do you mean, gone?"

"Took off. Ran," he stuttered. "When the shooting started she jumped in the lift. She's gone."

Samson shot Gabriel a concerned look. "She wouldn't leave us," she said, but the truth of the matter was, she had. Gabriel knew the soldier's radio silence wouldn't go unnoticed for long. And when it was, they would send more. Much more.

"Come on, we need to be somewhere else."

Even before they had reached the elevators they could see there was a problem. Every floor display was rapidly ticking down, all lifts were descending.

"What are they doing with the lifts?" said Purity.

As each car reached the 36th floor, the numeric display blinked out.

In the foyer, Lister frowned at the bank of elevators. One by one each lift arrived at the 36th floor and the lights flickered out.

"What have they done to the lifts?" she muttered to herself.

The lifts were dead.

36. SECRET SMILE

"I understand, my child," said Archbishop Runcible. He stood alone in the drawing room of 10 Downing Street in darkness lit only by the stale sodium street lights outside. He leaned against the oak desk and spoke gently into his mobile phone in a hushed tone.

"And the Lord came down to see the city and the tower, which the children of men were building. And the Lord said, Behold, the people is one, and now nothing will be restrained from them which they have imagined to do. Come, let us go down, and there confound them."

He listened patiently to the voice on the other end, nodding slowly.

"You do what you need to do, child. You

are in my prayers."

Runcible finished the call. "In the name of the Father."

"Bad news?" asked Hattie.

Hattie Simms perched by the door, backlit by the bright hallway. He had no idea how long she had been there or how much she had heard. Not that it mattered - there was no going back now. As she watched he leisurely, deliberately closed his gold-plated smartphone and returned it to the silk drawstring pouch on his cassock.

"No, no, no," he said softly. "Not at all. Just one of the flock seeking advice."

He turned to the window and the view of the Monoliths on the horizon.

"It's all sorted now," he said. "All sorted."

37. LIVING ON THE CEILING

"This will take hours!" panted Warren. The stairwell, a square spiral, ran parallel to the elevators as part of the central column of the building and was surprisingly clean and well lit. People generally kept to the lower floors for social - and anti-social - activities and it was more effort than it was worth for the average scrote to come all the way up here for a bit of graffiti.

"You got a better suggestion, I'm all ears, sunshine!" shouted Gabriel, breathily.

They bounded down the steps two at a time, a light touch on the brushed metal handrail to maintain balance. Passing the exit to level 284, Warren realised that even at this speed - without slowing down - it would still take over an hour to reach ground level.

"This is... ridiculous" he gasped, stopping to catch his breath, calves burning.

"No stopping!" shouted Gabriel. "We ain't got time for..."

Noises echoed up through the stairwell. Footsteps. Shouting.

Samson leaned over the railing.

Twenty, maybe thirty floors below were the recognisable shapes of helmeted, black clad figures carrying guns.

"We need a plan B," she said.

Gabriel kicked the door to floor 284 open and it clanged loudly in the confined space.

"Plan B?" Warren blinked, "What... wait... there was a plan A?"

They emerged from the stairwell onto one of the many, many dormitory levels. As with every other floor, a single wide corridor ran around the perimeter of the building with residential pods repeating endlessly in the walls. They all followed the same pattern, layout and design and Purity had an uneasy feeling of Deja vu. Rumour had it an elderly woman had left her pod one night to visit the bathroom and wandered the floors in confusion for three days trying to find her way back. She was eventually found collapsed dead from exhaustion outside an identical pod a hundred floors away.

So the rumour went.

The pod doors were stacked in columns,

one above, one below, repeated down the length of the corridor on both sides. The floor appeared deserted but about half of the lights on the pod doors were red; people were inside.

By the stairwell doors, a rectangular red box was affixed to the wall next to a bucket of sand and an extinguisher.

IN THE EVENT OF FIRE

Gabriel thrust his elbow through the glass front, shattering it, and tore the tool free from inside.

He nodded at the pods shouting, "You need to clear the floor, get everyone out."

"*We* need to? Why?" asked Purity. "What are you going to do?"

He held the fire-axe up and smiled. It had a long, rubber handle and ended in a fierce razor-sharp blade.

"Plan B."

Gabriel turned back down the corridor and pushed open the public toilet door.

Purity was incredulous. "Where's he going?"

Warren shrugged and headed towards the pods, "Hey, when you gotta go, you gotta go!"

Gabriel ran into the restroom past the gender-neutral stalls, ignoring the graffiti and used sweet wrappers, and stopped at the row of ceramic wash basins. He went to turn the taps on only to discover they had no handles - the water was activated by the movement of a hand in the sink. He waved his hand under the first tap and water dribbled out feebly. He moved the length of the bathroom, waving his hand beneath all five taps, but the first cut out a long way before he had reached the last.

He let out a groan. A tap is a tap. Why did people feel the need to overcomplicate things? One by one, the water clicked off and he watched the water drain away with a soggy gurgle.

"Okay," he said, lifting the axe high. "Plan C."

He swung the axe down hard, severing the first tap from the basin completely. A fierce jet of water erupted from the jagged hole, hitting the ceiling and raining down onto the floor tiles. He swung again and again, bent chrome and ceramic chips flying through the air, until all basins were spraying freely. Gabriel stood back, his feet splashing in a shallow pool of water that was rapidly getting deeper.

"You need to leave!" said Purity.

A pale, skinny man dressed only in underpants stared back from inside his pod, blinking.

"Get lost, I'm not going anywhere!" he said, his accent broad and scouse. He pulled the door handle to close it and Purity forced it open.

"You don't understand, it's not safe. You have to!" she pleaded.

"We were told to stay in our pods, do you not listen?" the man said, as if reasoning with a toddler. "There's terrorists in the building! They could be anywhere!"

Samson reached over Purity's shoulder, her Hyoksin .45 pistol pointing into the pod. She smiled that beautiful smile. "They're closer than you think, honey," she purred. "Now do one."

Gabriel ran back into the corridor. Of the occupied pods on this floor, only three were open and civilians stood around looking confused.

"People come on!" he despaired. "We don't have time for this!"

He pointed at an elderly lady with white hair tied in a ponytail, a crocheted woollen shawl in floral oranges and greens wrapped tightly around her shoulders. A vintage hearing device ran from her ear to a small electronic box hanging around her neck.

She eyed him suspiciously and he lowered his voice, keeping the tone light and informal. "I'm sorry, Miss...?" The question trailed off and she felt obliged to answer.

"Slocombe," she replied nervously. "Mrs Maud Slocombe."

"Thank you, Maud," he said, pulling the pistol from his belt. "This might be a bit loud for you."

He unplugged her hearing aid and pointed his gun at the ceiling, firing three shots off.

"Can I have everyone's attention?" he yelled.

"I want everybody out of their pods now. This is not a negotiation. This is not a drill!"

"They may have told you there are some bad people in this building. Well I'm here to tell you they were right."

The people looked on, confusion turning into something much, much worse.

"Now I don't know how well you know your neighbours on this floor, but assuming you do, right now I'm looking at your friend, the lovely Mrs Slocombe."

He raised his voice, fully aware Mrs Slocombe wasn't hearing anything. "Everybody. You have ten seconds to leave your pods. Or I paint the walls with Mrs Slocombe's brains."

Maud nodded and smiled.

"No!" shouted the half-naked scouser and he leapt at Gabriel.

A hand, huge and strong clamped around his arm, stopping him immediately. Samson shook her head at him.

"Time starts now!" Gabriel shouted.

Tiny green lights blinked out and doors creaked open the hiss of compressed air. With surprising speed, the pods emptied and their occupants gathered in the hallway, panicked and scared.

Gabriel hugged Mrs Slocombe, plugging her hearing aid back in. "You remind me of my Grandmother, she was tough," he said, kissing the back of her hand, "And exceedingly beautiful."

He addressed the panicked occupants.

"There *are* some very bad people in this building. But it's not us. Now leave, get off this floor as quick as you can."

He lowered his voice.

"The bad people are coming."

Gabriel paced along the length of pods finally settling on a unit facing the stairwell doors.

Pod 99.

He heaved it open shouting, "Sam, get me some extinguishers!"

"There's a fire?" asked Purity, confused.

Samson pulled a red canister from the wall and smiled, "Not yet, honey."

Grunting, Gabriel manoeuvred an extinguisher into the pod, laying it flat on the padded bed. Samson appeared carrying three more; two under one arm and a third over her shoulder.

"This enough?"

He nodded and she tossed them in as if they were toys. They clanged noisily against one another, coming to rest in a scrappy heap.

Purity was even more confused. "What are you doing?"

Sam didn't answer; she had seen this before.

Gabriel quickly released the safety pins from all four canisters, breaking the anti-tamper seal. He held the axe upside down and smashed the head hard against the handle. Carbon dioxide hissed free of the damaged mechanism and he swiftly moved onto the next. Within seconds all four extinguishers were leaking pale clouds of gas into the dark cubicle. He twisted onto his side, finding the control panel inside the pod. There, underneath the lighting and media controls was what he was looking for - a single mechanical lever.

PANIC LOCK

He yanked on the handle and jumped out, the door slamming shut behind him. A pneumatic whine echoed from deep inside the wall and the exterior lights blinked out, just the faintest hiss escaping the module.

Gabriel threw the axe to Samson who caught it with ease. She slid her manicured nails into a vent on a wall panel and tore it free exposing dozens of coloured wires and cables.

"Everyone back!" she yelled, lifting the tool high in the air.

She swung it down, the blade severing a thick electrical cable. It exploded in a shower of silver sparks and fell into the pool of water twitching and writhing spastically like a wounded animal.

The overhead lights flickered momentarily then went out.

As a group they retreated down the corridor, away from the water and the stairwell doors.

With the curve of the corridor providing a degree of protection they crouched behind some open pod doors and waited for the soldiers to emerge.

They didn't have to wait long.

38. WAR

Sergeant Benitez 'Beni' Hill kicked the door open wide, emerging from the brightly lit stairwell into the gloomy corridor and noticed the wet floor immediately.

She held her fist up.

Stop.

But it was too late. Private Mark 'Curly' Watts had already advanced on their position, foot landing firmly in the shallow pool. He opened his mouth in a silent scream, his weapon falling from his shaking hands. His arms and legs convulsed wildly as he performed a macabre jitterbug until finally his legs gave out and he fell face down in the puddle, motionless.

In a thoroughly inappropriate thought, Beni realised she was going to be late for salsa class tonight.

She tapped her visor, switching to infrared. The area around the door was flooded and on the far wall she saw a loose mass of wires, a particularly thick one feeding into the black water. Beyond that, at the far end of the corridor figures moved and shuffled behind some open pod doors.

"I *can* see you, you know," she shouted.

Beni wasn't expecting a response and didn't get one.

She kneeled and pulled a tablet device from a sleeve pocket, the rest of the squad standing with rifles poised, aiming into the darkness.

"I see what you did," she said loudly, looking at the wet power cable. "It's not exactly subtle."

She tapped the glass and retrieved the building schematic, quickly scrolling up the screen to floor 284 then swiping left to reveal a new set of controls.

| LIGHTING | SECURITY | AIR-CON |
| POWER | COMMS |

She tapped POWER and hovered over the new set of commands.

"You really think a little trick like that was going to stop us? You'll have to try better than that!" she shouted.

She tapped OFF, cutting the power to the entire floor.

Including Pod 99.

With no electricity supply, the panic lock

disengaged. Unable to contain the mammoth pressure inside the pod, the iron door exploded free of its hinges in a jet of carbon dioxide and shot across the corridor, spinning uncontrollably. It flew over Benitez' helmet and ploughed into the standing soldiers behind her like a bowling ball striking pins. Unlike a bowling ball striking pins however, the soldiers exploded in a grisly pink mist as the iron hatch continued its trajectory through the wall behind them, punching a hole into the outside world and tumbling silently down to the streets below.

Sergeant Benitez struggled upright, her uniform coated in a fine red spray. She held up her gloved hands, smeared in maroon droplets.

This was her team.

She was wearing the remains of her team.

The wind howled through the gaping maw, rain lashing against exposed concrete and steel as the City slept impassively, unaware of the terrible tragedy that was unfolding high above it. Lights, blinking orange and white caught her eye and she realised the drone was watching her through the hole, hovering rock steady in the rain.

Numb, Beni simply shook her head.

Turning away, she wiped blood and water from her visor and stepped into the corridor. Ordinarily she would wait for backup, adopt a stealth approach but she had just lost her team.

Her entire team. In one go. The time for caution, for verbal warnings, for capture... well, that was long gone.

She braced her assault rifle against her shoulder and fired.

Warren's shoulder exploded in a shower of meat and gore and he span to the ground screaming. Gabriel and Samson drew their pistols returning fire but the soldier's assault rifle did not let up. Long continuous bursts lighting up the corridor with impact sparks and ricochets. They ducked behind the protection of the pod doors waiting for a break in the gunfire.

Purity knelt by Warren and grabbed a flannel from the open pod. It wasn't very large but it would have to do. She bundled it into a ball and applied pressure to the oozing wound, absorbing the blood. Within seconds it was sodden and black.

Samson glanced at the wound, "That's right, do it again. Apply more pressure." She fired off three more shots blindly and ducked for cover.

"Here, take this," she said. She pulled her scarf off and handed it to Purity. "Wrap it under his arm and tie it behind the shoulder."

Warren groaned in pain as the scarf tightened around the damage, nerve ends screaming in protest. More gunfire battered their defences and Samson noticed Gabriel breathing heavily.

"You hurt?" she asked, concerned.

Just above his belt, a wet patch of red spread from Gabriel's right side. He tugged his jacket down concealing the wound.

"It's nothing," he said, firing off three rounds into the darkness.

The automatic rifle fire slowed, then ceased, the ear-splitting explosions replaced by an irritating whirr. The drone flew in, hovering amongst them at waist height. It span 360 degrees, scanning their faces in an instant then rotated onto an exit path.

"Not this time," muttered Gabriel and he grabbed the drone by the propeller. The blade cut into his hand and stopped. Gabriel turned the drone, pushing his face close to the camera.

"I assume there's someone down there watching this," he said. "If you are, then I've got a message."

He snapped the ailerons and flaps on the vehicles arms, sharp pieces of moulded plastic dropping to the floor.

"You treat your people like cattle, an annoyance. You are not better than us. We are all born equal. It just seems some are more equal than others. "

He unclipped something from his belt and hooked it onto the landing struts.

"You hit us. We hit you back twice as hard. You hurt us, we make you suffer. You kill one of us, we kill ten of you. You blow us up? Well..."

Gabriel tilted the drone away from his

body, its tiny motors straining against his grip, and let go. It drifted back down the corridor listing slightly from the weight of its fresh cargo.

Sergeant Benitez lifted the Hyoksin .45 from her holster as the drone approached and frowned. There was something unusual about it. Was it the way it struggled to maintain its height? Maybe the odd angle it was flying at? Or was it the round metal object hanging underneath it?

Round metal object?

Beni's eyes widened as she realised she wasn't going to make that salsa class, after all.

And the grenade exploded.

39. END OF THE ROAD

The blast killed the last member of Team Jane instantly, destroying half a dozen pods on either side and tearing the ceiling apart like paper. The floor collapsed in a landslide of rubble and tiles, a neat round hole revealing the corridor below.

Gabriel clutched his side and nodded at Warren.

"Pick him up," he grimaced. "We can use the southern stairwell."

Careful to avoid his shoulder, Samson wrapped a giant arm around Warren and lifted him to his feet. He was pale and shaking, but conscious.

"Now don't you go bleeding on my new dress honey. This is Versace."

Warren's face strained, forcing the thinnest of smiles.

"Today really... sucks," he groaned.

Purity took his weight on his other side. "You're okay. You'll be okay," she whispered. "We're getting out of here."

They shuffled deeper into the corridor in silence, the cacophony of gunfire and demolition now replaced by rain on glass and coarse breathing.

"We need to find Delphi," said Gabriel

"No, we need to get out of here," spat Purity. "We can deal with that traitorous cow after."

"You don't know..." he replied.

"She ran out on us. Again, I might add. But I guess you're used to that."

"I..." Gabriel began, then fell, one leg giving out, the other knee taking the force of the landing. He sat on the floor barley upright, his leg sprawled out behind him uselessly.

"Oh God, Gabe," whispered Samson.

His jacket had fallen open to reveal the extent of his wound. The wet shirt had very little white remaining, the bullet hole in the fabric now torn wide to reveal a deep, scabrous puncture in his side. Pooled in blackened blood, the veiny smooth surfaces of internal organs were clearly visible. With grim determination he placed his hand on the rupture, pushing hard.

At the far end of the corridor, doors clattered open and the exit to the southern stairwell filled with figures. It wasn't the civilians, they had long fled.

Team Freddy had arrived.

"Oh hell," said Purity.

"Go," strained Gabriel.

Samson looked at the troops advancing and opened her mouth to speak.

We won't leave you behind, she was going to say. The old platitude. But it would have been a lie. Their eyes met in a silent exchange - they both knew how bad he was and how this was going to end. She pulled the spare pistol from her bra strap and placed it in his hand, wrapping his fingers around the handle gently and holding his hand tight.

She didn't let go.

"What are you doing?" said Purity. "We can't leave him!"

Samson didn't answer but simply shook her head, blinking back a tear.

"We never did... try that... Sushizza restaurant... did we?" he whispered.

She smiled, but it never reached her eyes. "Honey, I don't even know what Sushizza is."

Gabriel fished around in his jacket pocket and lifted out two small white cubes. He had been saving these for a special occasion and now, well this seemed as good a time as any.

"I was... wrong about you... kiddo," he stammered to Purity. "Turns out... blowing up... shit... ain't always the answer."

He coughed a wet, bloody rasp. "Figure if...

anyone can fix this... mess. S'gonna be... you."

He held the cubes up admiring the craftsmanship then popped the squares of granulated sugar in his mouth, savouring the feeling of the blocks disintegrating on his tongue. The pure, undiluted sweet stuff absorbed into his system rapidly and he felt the effects of the drug almost instantly. A profound calmness fell over him and his pain eased. As his eyes dilated the world snapped into sharp focus, an intense clarity. He bent his working knee and rested both outstretched arms on it, two pistols pointing at the figures in the distance.

He turned to Purity, coughing, a thin line of blood running down his chin. "Now I figure it's... your turn... to run out... on... me."

And he opened fire.

40. A QUESTION OF TIME

Samson dropped through the grenade hole, landing in the tiled corridor of the 283rd floor. Warren was already braced against Purity and she promptly scooped him up and threw him over her shoulder. They stared up at the hole in the ceiling, the sound of gunshots and explosions in the corridor echoing above.

Purity glanced at Samson. Did she and Gabriel have a 'thing' going on? She had no idea, but it did make her realise that although she didn't know them, not really, any one of them would lay down their lives to save another.

What would it take, she wondered, *for you to sacrifice your life to save someone you barely knew?*

Abruptly the shooting above stopped and wordlessly, they turned and started walking.

There was nothing to say, nothing anyone could say. The south stairwell would be too risky, but the north stairwell would be accessible from this floor - and from there, the long walk down. They descended the stairs as fast as they could, which was to say *not fast at all*. Warren grunted at each step but kept his pain and discomfort to himself, it was the least he could do.

Purity pulled her phone out while they walked - the case was cracked but it was still functioning. The phone lines were down, but it still showed a weak data connection. She unlocked the phone and started typing with her thumb. Before Warren or Samson could even open their mouths, she spoke, her voice calm and steady. Unwavering.

"That bitch is going to give us some answers," she said, and pressed SEND.

Nearly 250 floors below them, Delphi's phone pinged.

41. MESSAGES

PURITY: delphi

PURITY: you there
PURITY: hello

DELPHI: I'm sorry, Purity
PURITY: sorry? what do you mean
PURITY: where are you. where did you go
PURITY: gabriels dead

DELPHI: I'm… sorry. He was a good man
PURITY: a good man? a good man?!? is that all you have to say
DELPHI: I had high hopes for you, Purity. I really did. I really thought you were the one
PURITY: the one
DELPHI: The one to turn this fight around. I've

been doing this for so long and the victories are few and far between, but you...

PURITY: This isn't what we signed up for. Any of us

DELPHI: The world's broken, just no-one can see it. Or rather, those that can see it are happy to keep it that way, maintain the status quo. Keep the masses subdued on a diet of reality TV, celebrity gossip and cheap gameshows. Keep the *feed* fed so nobody even thinks to look up and question what they've sleepwalked into.

DELPHI: People, governments, entire nations only change when the old system, the system that they're used to breaks down. And breaks down completely. Disastrously. Then, and only then does real change happen.

DELPHI: I have a confession to make, Purity. Would you take it?

PURITY: i'm not a catholic

DELPHI: LOL. Do you want to know the irony? I don't even believe in God, I'm just following a script

PURITY: then why are you doing this

DELPHI: You can't just unite a nation against their government overnight, It's like herding cats. And everyone wants their say, wants their opinion heard. It's soooooooooo slow.

DELPHI: So we created this extremist threat, these Christian terrorists. Created a common enemy to rally against the government, bring it

to task, hold it up for scrutiny.
PURITY: you keep saying *we*. who's *we*? who are you working for
DELPHI: Ah ah ahhh. You don't get all the answers
PURITY: sorry i thought you were confessing
DELPHI: Quite, but that's not it. My confession is a little more pressing, I'm afraid.
DELPHI: You remember I told you we were going to burn down Monolith Two, expose the government for cutting corners and putting lives at risk? Publicly shame the Prime Minister into closing the housing program down?
PURITY: yes

DELPHI: That was never the plan.

DELPHI: You really thought waving a few placards and banners outside number 10 would change anything? I mean, I knew you were naive but... really? Look outside, people protest every day. And when protesting is so commonplace it ceases to mean anything. It's the new norm. And as such, is completely ignored.
DELPHI: No... and this is my confession, or the first part at least:

DELPHI: We were going to bring all three towers down at once

PURITY: and the people inside?
DELPHI: That would have just have been unfortunate, for them I mean. Omelettes and eggs and

everything. On the plus side, it'd be the biggest peacetime atrocity in recorded history. No way the government would survive that. No way at all. Such a monumental tragedy caused directly by their policies would have forced them out.
DELPHI: Like I said, real change only comes when the old system breaks down on a grand scale.
DELPHI: And this was the grandest scale of all.
PURITY: you're insane. you're actually insane

DELPHI: But when those soldiers arrived, all I could see was the plan slipping away. We hadn't even distributed the explosives between the towers yet.
PURITY: what are you saying

DELPHI: I loaded them all into the lifts
DELPHI: The bombs are here. They're all still here.
PURITY: where
DELPHI: With me. In the car park.

PURITY: WHAT

DELPHI: I'm sorry, Purity. I really am.
PURITY: delphi wait

DELPHI: In the name of the father

42. TWO MINUTE WARNING

The floor lurched suddenly to one side. Purity and Samson both grabbed the handrail steadying themselves as a thin layer of dust drifted down on them like snow.

"What just happened?" asked Samson.

In response, a thundering roar crashed through the stairwell from far below, resonating through the very fabric of the building. Exterior windows shattered and the ground lurched again with an ear splitting groan and dropped sharply. The entire floor fell a metre then stopped with a bang, tiles and insulation showering from the ceiling in a thick cloud of dust. The handrail sheared away from the wall in chunks of plaster and all three were thrown to the floor violently.

Warren screamed as his shoulder erupted

in searing pain as clumps of debris pummelled him.

The wall split with an ear shattering crack, water and steam spraying out with a hiss.

Purity lifted her head, blinking dust from her eyes. Warren and Sam were sprawled on the floor but conscious. Wind howled through the aluminium frames where glass once sat and cold raindrops swirled and danced in the currents. Aside from a long crack which zig-zagged along the steps and up the interior wall, the stairwell seemed intact, though somehow… off. The barrage receded into a distant rumble, the sound of some ancient wounded beast dying in its cave.

Purity stood up amongst the debris of plaster and glass, sensing the problem immediately. She looked at the city skyline outside - it was only out by a few degrees but the floor she was standing on most definitely was no longer horizontal.

"You okay? Everyone okay?" She grasped Warren's good hand and helped him to his feet. He was wide eyed, confused.

"Was that? Did she?" stuttered Warren.

Samson stood up, brushing dust from her dress. "Crazy bitch went and did it."

The floor shifted slightly again but the rumble slowed, breaking into a staccato creak like an old wooden ship or squeaky door, multiplied infinitely.

Purity nodded, acutely aware that they

were still over 200 stories above the ground. "We need to move."

They took the stairs as fast as they could manage, Samson almost carrying Warren. Each new sound, each random unexpected bang or crash caused them to flinch. Was it the building settling or a precursor for something much worse? Every few floors, ragged cracks and crevices had appeared, snaking up walls and down steps. Some light fittings still flickered providing a degree of illumination but most were either dead or spitting sparks.

They had almost reached the 259th floor when Purity held up her hand.

The repetitive creak below slowed, gaining volume on each beat. Slower. Slower. Stopped.

Then two huge thuds, an impact, something big against something bigger sent a shock through the structure. The stairwell trembled momentarily then settled.

"Listen." said Purity.

A hiss, distant at first, grew louder. Louder and deeper.

"What is that?" asked Warren.

Samson gripped the handrail and peeked over the side.

The stairwell spiralled downwards, lit only by broken lamps and moonlight. At the limits of her sight she saw movement - something grey and undefined growing in size. Pulsing. Shifting.

She squinted hard trying to make sense of it before realising exactly what she was looking at.

"Get to the door!" she panicked. "We need to get off the stairs! Now!"

The air was suddenly warmer with a distinct diesel smell, ashes and cinders drifting upwards. She scrambled down the remaining steps and hit the fire doors shoulder first. They smacked open and Purity and Warren limped through as a dust cloud, thick and heavy, flooded the stairwell. In an instant visibility was reduced to zero, just an intense, rushing, churning wall of grey. Warren fell, choking as angry plumes of pale fog poured through the entrance and consumed him.

Putting all her weight behind the door, Samson heaved against the force of the deadly mass, straining hard. The door inched closed, but slowly. Purity braced her back against the door, digging her heels in, tensing. The gap narrowed, the torrent reducing. One more step, two more steps and it clanged shut.

Exhausted, they collapsed with their backs to the door as the mist dispersed. Propped up on his good elbow, Warren gave a feeble thumbs up.

"Dust cloud," panted Samson. "That's not good."

Purity said nothing; she knew Samson would elaborate in her own time.

"Major structural failure, I'd guess... Somewhere near the base of the tower. I don't get it, we had the explosives stored on the 36th floor. They were safe there, it wasn't structurally important. The whole stash could have gone off and the worst that could happen would be a big hole on the outer wall. No, Delphi must have moved the explosives."

Purity recalled Delphi's final message, "She did."

"She did?"

Samson pictured the schematics of the Monolith. "She would have had to load the explosives into elevators. Would fill four, maybe five if she took them all.

"She said she was in the car park." explained Purity. "In the... basement."

Purity couldn't help but notice Samson go pale. "What?" she asked.

Samson buried her head in her hands and for a minute didn't say anything. When she opened her mouth, she spoke slowly. Really slowly. There was no room for confusion.

"The Monolith is constructed around a single central column, yes? It supports the entire building. The elevators all run up and down this central column."

She paused, letting that sink in.

"Now imagine the elevators - full of explosives - are all at the base of this column. All together on one side, in fact. They explode..."

She opened her fingers, spreading them wide in slow motion. "And the Monolith will just..."

Purity's mouth opened wide, the penny had dropped.

"Fall over," she finished.

43. HUMAN RACING

They staggered along the corridor of floor 259. Open pods lined the walls - if anyone was living on this floor, they were long gone. The floor was littered with possessions; shoes and magazines, coats and toothbrushes, and they stepped through them carefully.

Sound was more subdued on the habitation floors making the creaks and bangs distant and somehow less threatening. A coarse, unnerving scrape clattered somewhere beneath them, the vibrations running through their feet and they froze waiting for it to pass.

So not that much less threatening.

The north stairwell was now unpassable, so they made their around the perimeter of the building back to the south stairwell. Worrying about the presence of soldiers no longer felt like a priority.

Halfway around the building Purity paused at a tall gallery window. Or what was left of it. About a third of the panes had smashed, but this side of the building seemed to avoid the brunt of the weather and only a light breeze whistled through the gaps. A broad trail of smoke and dust bled into the sky, so opaque it seemed solid, glowing embers diving and gliding around it like fireflies. The slight incline blocked Purity from seeing what was happening at the foot of the tower but over by the Thames the frantic red and blues of emergency response vehicles lit up Blackfriars and Waterloo Bridges. Help was on its way, for what it was worth. The tower was so tall they could never get practical help up here, and assuming the south stairwell was clear all the way down - which was a huge assumption, Purity knew - it would still take longer than she liked.

A lot longer.

From this vantage point Monolith Two was visible through the smoke, squatting silhouetted in darkness. It was empty, or mostly empty with only a handful of floors lit - as the grand opening was still days away it only had a few security and maintenance staff working inside.

Then she saw it, they all did.

The long tubular iron and glass corridor, suspended between the Monoliths. Uniting them. Connecting them.

Of course, she thought. *Why didn't we think of that earlier?*

The skybridge.

"Is it safe?" asked Warren, eyeing the structure suspiciously.

A deep thump reverberated through the building followed by a series of sharp twangs and the three gripped each other tightly.

"I think that's kind of relative, right now," replied Sam.

The bridge rocked gently, buffeted by gusts. Some glass panels were smashed and It didn't look quite as straight as they remembered it. Each Monolith had two skybridges, one on the 75th and the other on the 225th floor. Essentially, the bridge was a separate construction - not actually part of either tower - the design allowing it to slide in and out as the buildings swayed during high winds. Constructed in aluminium and glass, the bridges were built to facilitate travel between the Monoliths and in the event of a suitable emergency, escape to the other tower.

There could be no denying this was a suitable emergency.

Purity pointed excitedly, "Look!"

There was movement on the skybridge. Figures hobbled and ran, some in clusters but most alone. Purity counted maybe twenty people making their way across to the safety of the other Monolith.

"They're escaping," she said, her heart filling with unexpected hope.

The skybridge wasn't far below them. Not far at all compared to the long walk to the ground.

Feeling like she had just turned over a 'Get out of jail free' card, Purity said, "Come on, it's only a few floors! We can do this! We're getting out of here!"

But they couldn't, and they weren't.

Not all of them, at least.

44. GET THE BALANCE RIGHT

The ground fell away without warning. There were no subtle series of noises, ticks or clicks. No build up. Nothing. One minute they were discussing their escape, the next floating in mid-air as the entire building dropped three floors. They hit the polystyrene ceiling panels, shattering them into chunks of microscopic white balls then fell back to the floor, landing hard. The remaining glass panes exploded in lethal shards.

Warren's arm pushed into his bandaged shoulder, a gout of fresh blood squirting free. Samson tried to stand, her foot sliding in the crimson puddle and she crashed to the floor alongside him. Purity grabbed a pod door and hauled herself up, arms and legs shaking.

Except it wasn't her that was shaking, it

was the tower.

The structure vibrated, shrieking as if in some kind of death throe.

Which in truth, it was.

Snap! Dust and debris fell from cracks above the ceiling. The tremors increased in force, getting louder and louder and the tower shook. It was all Purity could do to cling on and close her eyes.

Crackle! Electrical wires strained and snapped, sparks spraying chaotically. Warren and Samson held on to each other braced against the wall, heads down.

Pop! Pipes pushed through the floor, vomiting water and sewage.

The tremors grew and grew. Louder and louder. Faster and faster still. Peaked.

Then abruptly stopped.

Purity held her eyes squeezed tight, waiting.

It was suddenly eerily quiet, the only sounds her breathing and the wind whistling through the wreckage of the window frame.

Cautiously, she opened her eyes.

Purity squinted through the remains of the window. Miraculously, *literally* miraculously, the skybridge was still there, intact. And she could see people moving along it. She watched this incredible piece of engineering and thought about all the things Delphi had said about how the government had cut corners on the Monoliths. The fireproofing and cladding had held; the building had not caught fire. Everything she had said no longer ringed true.

Samson was shakily lifting Warren to his feet and they looked around, shocked and confused expressions on their dust-streaked faces.

Purity wobbled towards them, arms wide, and hugged them in silence. They stood for a while supporting each other, literally and metaphorically. Warren's blood soaking into Purity's sleeve, Samson's muscular arm around her; this wasn't a hug of victory or conquest, but survival.

Maybe they were going to be alright, after all.

"P?" Warren's voice was strained, quiet, his face expressionless. "The horizon."

With a frown she shifted her gaze away from the bridge and looked out beyond Monolith Two at the lights of London scattered far and wide like stars reflected in the sea.

At first, she didn't get it. The horizon? What about it? It looked no different than it ever looked.

But then... but then... she saw it.

Almost imperceptibly, the horizon moved.

Down.

Only a fraction, but down nonetheless.

"Oh no," she whispered.

The horizon moved again.

Up. She felt it this time, they all did. Their stomachs flipping, their inner ears telling them all was not right with the world.

The tower was rocking.

And not in a good way.

The floor tilted and Monolith Two loomed outside the window. The skybridge twisted and contorted, straining to maintain the connection between the two huge masses with a metallic screech of iron against iron.

Inside the bridge, people screamed and yelled, running for the exit. Windows shattered outwards as metal beams bent and shook under unimaginable stresses.

Monolith One swung wider, the angle increasing each arc.

Purity grabbed a pod door and they hung on in a chain as debris and belongings slide past their feet.

The skybridge jammed and buckled as metal struts reached breaking point, its entire length shuddering violently. People inside fell to their knees screaming, holding on to anything solid.

The Monolith rocked again, lurching towards the second tower and the bridge gave a final chilling shriek. It sheared in two, both halves folding and bending into each other before finally snapping completely - the hollow tube of glass and aluminium no match for 300 stories of iron and concrete. The bridge bent impossibly in on itself still clinging on to both buildings then Monolith One swayed backwards again.

The gap was now too far, the damage too extreme and Purity watched in horror as the wreckage of the skybridge and its occupants tumbled to the streets below, their screams receding earthwards.

Freed from the constraints of the connecting structure, Monolith One rocked back even further this time, holding its position for what seemed like an eternity.

Unconsciously they knew this was the last swing. They were not running down a few flights of stairs to the safety of a bridge; they were not taking an emergency elevator; a fleet of helicopters were not appearing outside the windows to tow them to freedom.

The tower was going down.

Never give up, DangerMole. Fight to your very last breath.

In that moment, that long, drawn out moment, she remembered something. Something Warren had said to her on her first night in the tower, oh so long ago.

Rednecks.

"The pods!" yelled Purity. "Get in the pods!"

She clambered in, dragging Warren with her. Unquestioning, Samson squeezed her body in alongside them - this was not the time for conversation.

Purity reached for the handle and the tower tipped forward, falling into its final, destructive arc. The pod handle swung away out of her grasp and she yelped. The building leaned forward, picking up speed and Purity scrambled for the handle but it was too far. Through the gap, Monolith Two loomed large.

Way too large.

She wasn't going to close it in...

A muscular arm shot past her. Samson grabbed the door and heaved it shut.

45. FALL AT YOUR FEET

"Get in the truck!" screamed Lister.

She was already installed in the driver's seat of the Sangwon troop carrier, hammering the START button with a sweaty palm. The passenger side gull-wing door was raised and Ronald sprinted across the courtyard of Monolith One peeling off his drone gloves as he ran. Hot fragments of cement bounced off the tarmac around him and he lowered his head as if approaching a helicopter. Lister revved the engine as her partner reached the vehicle, grabbing the ladder. "Cutting it a bit fine, aren't..."

The cabin rocked and Ronald Stott vanished in a bloody blur. The door had smashed down on him, crushed under the weight of a plummeting statue. The grinning bronze visage of Tommy Cooper stared at Lister, its spiky hair and fez streaked with blood, ash and scratches. Stott was gone.

Just like that.

Officer Lister slammed the gear stick into 'drive' and floored the accelerator. The Sangwon roared, tyres screeching, pushing her back into her seat. She heaved the steering wheel, swinging the vehicle between flaming rubble and smoking holes in the tarmac, past bulky burning tangles of steel and wire, bodies hanging like grotesque Christmas tree decorations.

Wind and diesel fumes blew through the blood-spattered doorway and Lister noticed a hand still gripped to the rung.

Just the hand.

It was annoying about Ronald, Lister had liked him, or at least liked his silence. Now it was goodnight from him and she would be assigned another partner. She prayed it wouldn't be a talker this time.

A hard rain of scorching debris battered the cabin roof and bounced off the strengthened windscreen leaving long sooty trails. Lister grimaced at the noise of the impacts but was unconcerned - if the North Koreans were good at one thing, it was building military vehicles. The wipers came on automatically, smearing bands of ash across the windscreen and she peered through a narrow gap in the dirt, watching the road ahead.

Her full attention however, was on the wing mirror of the truck.

Behind her, Monolith One fell in slow motion. The foot of the tower burst outwards from the foyer in an eruption of concrete, girders and thick voluminous smoke. With the sudden absence of support, the first half a dozen floors fell away in an avalanche of cinder block and stone exposing the tower's service and maintenance levels. The gas hub breached as the electrical generators surged and a huge explosion ripped through the tower base. An angry jet of flame erupted upwards, consuming Skybridge Two. Already clinging on at an alarming angle and jammed between both towers, it was engulfed. Superheated aluminium beams melted and fused with glass and bodies before limply vanishing into the dense fog.

Roni cleared the worst of the ground damage and accelerated onto the dual carriageway heading for the Thames. Fire appliances and ambulances shot past her going the way other way - *towards* the disaster - but she felt no guilt. She'd done her bit.

Admittedly she had failed, but she had done her bit nonetheless.

Sufficiently far from the danger zone, she eased off the accelerator and swung the Sangwon around, coming to a halt straddling both lanes. She reached across the exposed passenger side and popped open the glovebox revealing a packet of crisps. Roni pulled them open and settled back in her seat watching the disaster.

As the Monolith tipped, the balance of weight shifted. The front of the building - never designed to support the floors above it - collapsed instantly, imploding in colossal blooms of dust. In seconds the lower hundred floors were laid bare, rooms and hallways open to the City, pods pouring into the streets below. In the corridors, people clung on for their lives to no avail - their bodies crushed and spat out mercilessly.

Lister wrinkled her nose in disgust - the crisps were horrible.

She read the front of the foil packet. Purple and orange aliens danced amongst cartoon planets. MUNCHOSODIUM GLUTO-MATES. GENERIC FLAVOUR.

Bloody vegan-activist nonsense.

Still, she picked out a couple of crisps and bit into them carefully.

She *was* hungry, after all.

With all support gone, the tower tilted faster. The glass-covered penthouse gardens of Monolith One struck the second monolith on the 242nd floor, disintegrating in a flurry of artificial flora. Trees, plants and wooden benches fell from the sky amongst bronze effigies of comedy legends. George Formby toppled over the side of the building, his banjo spinning out into space while a surprised looking Ted Rogers clutching a dustbin plummeted to the ground in a halo of glass and dust.

Monolith One scraped heavily down the face of its neighbour, the rooftop floors peeling away one by one as if made of paper. A vertical chasm scarred its wake as the toppling structure gouged deeper and deeper into the opposite face, dozens of floors at a time. Smaller blasts erupted from the building punctuating the fall as fuel and power lines were hacked apart in abandon. In Monolith Two, newly built pods and dwellings were messily struck from existence - the tower ploughing through the face of the building by the biggest eraser in history.

But then the falling giant began to slow, finally acknowledging the gargantuan resistance pushing back against it. The hulking mass shook and strained, a last-ditch attempt to emerge victorious in the battle of the towers, before juddering to a halt embedded in the other building.

Smoke poured from the base, shrouding the buildings. The top hundred floors of Monolith One had gone, their only memory now a spiky mess of tangled pipes and cement, and the tower now leaned steeply against Monolith Two like a drunken friend.

Lister scooped a handful of crisps into her mouth and chewed thoughtfully.

"Well, that's something you don't see every day."

46. POLICY OF TRUTH

The battered pod door opened slightly with a creak, then jammed. Three hard kicks sounded from inside and it squealed free on damaged hinges, gravity opening it to its full extent. Purity emerged first, peering over the side of the pod. The floor stretched away at an alarming angle - at least 30 degrees off the horizontal - down towards a yawning maw of bent and broken iron, and a startling view of the ground over a hundred floors below. Microscopic lights flashed on Lilliputian emergency vehicles and people swarmed around them like ants. Only a few steps uphill, the opposite end of the corridor had sheared off completely and opened out on to what was now a new roof and a glorious view of the night sky.

Miraculously, the pod had held - they all

had, for the most part. While the structure around them cracked and crumbled, the individual habitation units were largely fine - their simple, sturdy construction working in their favour.

They peeled themselves apart as much as they could in the confined space. The pods were never designed to house three people at once but ironically that may have helped them - the closeness of their bodies distributing and absorbing the impacts. Samson sat up rubbing her neck and shoulders. They were sore and a long bruise ran down the back of her arm. "I can't believe that worked."

Purity nodded, recalling Warren's words.

"I figured if Indiana Jones could survive a nuclear explosion in a fridge," she said, "we'd have a chance."

Warren winced, "You *do* know that's just an old movie, right? A work of fiction?"

Purity ignored the jibe but could see his visible discomfort. "You okay, Warren?"

Warren was pale, much paler than before and very pasty. He panted as he talked. "Feel like... I've been run over... by a bus."

He cradled his bloodied arm uselessly in his lap. "I don't think... I'll play the piano... again."

He was in a bad way, but they didn't have time to worry about that. Now was the time for decisive action, they could wallow in self-pity later.

Purity's entire body ached, every joint, every muscle.

But they were alive.

Purity stood on the roof of Monolith One - or what was left of it. Twisted girders and rods poked from the rubble and a mountain of concrete and plaster was piled up against the second tower. Silvery white pods stuck out of the debris like loose teeth and Purity couldn't help but notice they were all intact.

God bless those rednecks, she thought.

The superstructure of the tower was more apparent from here, the collapsed floors scruffily encircling the smoking central column, a pillar of white fumes rising from it into the night and drifting out over Regent's Park towards Watford.

Although their tower leaned at an angle, the roof was relatively flat joining Monolith Two in a rough mound of scree and glass. The pile sloped off on one side revealing a dark cave-like entrance punched into the other building.

Purity allowed herself a guarded glimmer of hope and looked out across the City.

Her legs wobbled - it was a long way down. The cold wind buffeted her face, whipping her hair up. After the insanity and destruction, it was perversely peaceful. It was so quiet up here, even the sirens of the emergency vehicles were barely noticeable. The vertigo subsided and she took in the view - an almost unbroken 360 degree view of the City.

From Big Gwen to the Tower of London, St Pauline's Cathedral to Queen's Cross, London glowed. Under a blanket of stars, streetlights sparkled with an almost magical effervescence. Majestic. Grand. A fairy-tale city of endless dreams and hopes. A city where anyone could be anything. Where a pauper could become a princess, or a princess could become a prince. A city with endless possibilities. A city that could change the world. Once upon a time, this capital of the entire British Empire had ruled over a quarter of the planet. The city had changed the world before and could do so again.

Purity's breath caught in her throat. She felt privileged to be stood there, literally on top of the world. Privileged, grateful, energised.

Alive.

The wind abated and she became aware of a sound. Faint, weak but not through distance.

"You hear that?" she asked, eyes scanning the rooftop.

Whatever it was, it was nearby.

Samson stepped over broken slabs and sharp metal, unconcerned by the altitude.

"It's coming from over here!" she shouted. She reached the core and looked over the side.

Vertigo was definitely not something she suffered from.

A dense column of smoke blew past her and she strained to filter out the other sounds. There it was. Tapping. Rhythmic. Three fast and three slow.

"It's close," Samson yelled. "Think it's the floor beneath us!"

She moved parallel to the wall through a mess of smashed concrete and steel, touching metal surfaces, feeling for vibrations. The sounds were louder now.

"Hello?" she shouted.

The tapping stopped for a moment before resuming at a frantic speed. Amongst the clanging, the sound of voices.

"Here!" Samson shouted. "There are people here!"

Purity kneeled and they both grabbed rubble, tossing it aside. The shouting grew louder. Very quickly, they cleared a hole allowing them to see the floor below. A large flat metal panel masked the gap, but through the narrow space a dozen dust covered faces stared back.

"Hello?" said one, cautiously.

Samson smiled back at them. "Step away from the opening. I'm going to widen it."

She braced her back against the core wall and planted both feet on the iron panel. With a grunt she tensed, her whole body pushing against the obstruction. The wall behind her cracked and splintered and the sheet creaked backwards.

Purity reached out her hand and a man, old, pale with an elaborate moustache caked in dust emerged. He held on to her as he shakily climbed out.

"Th... thank you," he stuttered.

Behind him, more survivors followed - elderly men and women in pyjamas and dressing gowns. Samson joined Purity and helped them up until they were free. All in all, there were nine of them.

"Is that everyone?" asked Purity.

"Yes... yes, I believe so," said the first survivor. "Thank you, again."

Samson was helping a lady sit down on a block of concrete when the pensioner asked, "How is that nice young gentleman?"

"I'm sorry?" replied Samson.

"You know... that nice man who helped me from my pod, I don't see him anywhere."

Recognition was slow coming, but Samson realised that under the streaks of grey dust was a grey bob and shabby shawl. It was Mrs Slocombe. Separated from her neighbours, she had found friends closer to her own tender age.

"Gabriel," said Samson. "He...he..." But she couldn't finish the sentence, her throat tightened, breath short.

"He went on ahead," finished Purity. "To clear the way for us."

Mrs Slocombe smiled. "Oh, he's such a good boy, I knew the minute I saw him. Got that sparkle in his eye just like my late Jack. You make a lovely couple."

"We're not... we weren't..." Samson turned, blinking tears away. This wasn't the time or the place. No, the mourning would come later.

"I just wanted to thank him." said the old lady.

The ragtag group of pensioners gathered around them trying to shake their hands.

"Yes, thank you."

"Thank you."

"I really must..."

Purity held her hands up, "Look, we'll have plenty of time for this afterwards. Right now, we really need to concentrate on getting down from here."

The pensioners nodded eagerly.

Samson was still composing herself, so Purity turned her attention to Monolith Two.

The pile of scree bled down to a hole in the buildings face - a large man-made cavern allowing entrance to the interior. It was close and they should be able to pick a path through the rooftop detritus, the biggest concern being how close the path strayed to the edge.

Purity sighed. One step forward, two steps back.

"Sam. You ready?"

But Samson still had her back to everyone - she was picking at the cracked core wall that she had pushed into earlier. She tugged at the material, rotting chunks disintegrating in her fingers.

"These walls," she said. "They're all rotten."

Purity pulled a piece off with ease. It made no sense. This was the central core - the lynchpin of the entire structure - yet it was dry and brittle.

She pulled another. And another.

"The bastards," she muttered. "The miserable, money-grabbing bastards."

Anger ignited inside her.

"Everyone was so concerned about fire safety they spent all their money fireproofing the exterior. The countries eyes were on the cladding and materials. No one thought to question *where* they were making savings."

She shook the fragment and it turned to powder in her hand. "So they cut costs in the places people would never see - cheap materials buried deep in the heart of the building. The central core, the foundations."

The powder blew away in a spiral, caught in the crosswinds. Purity watched it snake around Monolith Two past the cave mouth, when a realisation hit her.

A stark, terrifying realisation.

"The Monoliths," she whispered. "They're all the same. Same builders. Same plans. Same materials."

She turned to Samson.
"They're not safe. Any of them."

47. A VIEW TO A KILL

Samson led the group. She picked her way carefully through the debris field with Warren unceremoniously strewn over her shoulder, while the others followed in single file. Purity stayed at the back keeping the team together, ensuring no stragglers were left behind.

The pensioners, they had learned, had mostly lived on the west side of the building about half way down and had already gone to bed before the carnage began. When the tower fell, the top levels and the east side took the brunt of the impact, the pods from the west face becoming buried deeper inside the structure as the collapse slowed.

They were less than ten metres away from the 'cave mouth' when a tremor struck. Compared to everything they had been through that night it was negligible, barely a rumble, but a note of concern rippled through the group. Nobody wanted the sleeping giant to wake up this close to freedom.

Samson picked up the pace. To their left, a mountain of rock and scree towered ominously, to their right a sheer drop of a hundred floors and a howling wind. The new building configuration channelled and accelerated the air flow and the wind canyoned up, catapulting loose jetsam into the sky. With every step, rocky fragments and gravel shifted and slid underfoot, the threat of an avalanche now very real.

The other side was literally a stone's throw away but the path around the hill had narrowed even further - it was little more than a ledge. Samson signalled for the group to hang back.

"Path's a bit tight here," she shouted, "going to have to move one at a time!"

About half way along the ledge, distant thunder rolled from the belly of the tower.

Samson froze, waiting for the echo to die away.

"We've stopped! Why have we stopped?" panicked Warren.

"I'm thinking," she said.

The other side was so close, she could jump it if she wasn't carrying another person.

"Well can't you walk and think at the same time? I thought women were supposed to be good at multitasking."

"Gender stereotyping now? I could always throw you over the side, you know."

Somewhere deep inside the building another rumble echoed. The loose ground shifted again and Samson staggered, swinging Warren out over the void. He screamed. The path disintegrated beneath her feet, plasterboard and panels breaking apart and spiralling away in the wind. She dropped to her knees desperately trying to maintain balance and grabbed hold of the floor beneath her. More stone and gravel fell revealing gaping holes either side of the path and streetlights below.

As quickly as it started, the tremor subsided.

"Okay! Okay! I get it!" shrieked Warren, "I'm sorry!"

The path - or what was left of it - was a metal beam, part of the superstructure of the building, a red, rusting, iron girder about half a metre wide. It was solid, inasmuch as it did not rock or shake, but the views either side of it were not for the faint hearted.

"Oh my God... oh my God... oh my..." chanted Warren.

Samson raised herself back to standing, carefully maintaining her balance, "Close your eyes, honey. You're not dying here tonight."

She took a deep breath and marched briskly. Four steps and they were on the other side.

On the far side of the chasm there was a small outbreak of polite applause. Purity cheered.

Samson stepped through the crack into Monolith Two, ducking to avoid the low overhang. She found herself, unsurprisingly, in an identical corridor to that of Monolith One with vacant pods filling the walls. It smelled of smoke and wet paint. To her immediate left, the hall was blocked with a barricade of building material and rubble, but directly in front of her was a bank of elevators. Warren winced as she slid him off her shoulder and sat him down under the elevator controls. Blood covered her arm and neck, soaked into the silk of the Versace dress.

She fixed him a steely glare. "You're getting the dry-cleaning bill for this."

She punched the DOWN button and was pleasantly surprised to see it light up.

Samson shouted to the group, "Okay, it's safe! Now one at a time, come over!"

One by one, the pensioners made their way across. There was no fuss, no complaints, no drama. Having lived through the Meat Riots and the Gender War, they had seen it all before. The oldest members of the group were toddlers during World War Two and had lived through the Blitz, scavenging the bombed-out streets and sleeping in the Underground. They just put their heads down and got on with it.

Purity looked on in admiration - they quite simply didn't make them like that anymore.

Very quickly, seven of the group made it across the gap. Purity guided them on while Samson poised on the far end taking their hands as the drew near. On the eighth, however, the tremors returned. Number eight, a Harold Cartwright had traversed the length of the beam when the tower shook. Properly this time.

Scree poured from the mountain inches behind him and he toppled forward. As if predicting it, Samson's giant hand wrapped around his flailing arm, holding his entire weight. Her other arm held onto the metalwork of tower two. She threw him backwards through the jagged entrance where he rolled to a stop amongst the other survivors.

The tremors continued. A torrent of wreckage bounced off the girder and the beam suddenly slid and dipped under the punishment.

This was not good.

More rubbish, and the beam dipped again.

No, this was very not good.

Framed in the entrance, Samson bent down and gripped the end of the girder with both hands, steadying it. Her feet slid in the wreckage then found purchase, rock cutting into her flesh. Dust and gravel rained on her as she pulled, letting out an animal moan. The bar shifted, sliding towards her. Through gritted teeth she grunted and manoeuvred the end of the beam, sweat running down her face and arms. The girder moved slowly and came to rest on a concrete block.

She braced herself in the entrance with her back against the wall, one arm holding the beam secure.

"I take it all back, Sam. You're one hell of a woman."

"Woman?" panted Samson. "I identify as a badass motherfucker, honey."

Purity studied the girder. It had taken quite a battering, and while it still appeared secure where she stood, the other end told a whole different story. No longer fixed in place, the tip of the girder now half-rested on a cracked stone crossbeam with only Samson's grip keeping the bar horizontal.

The muscles in Samson's scratched and bloody arms tensed and flexed.

"Whenever you're ready!" she yelled through gritted teeth.

"It seems to be our turn," said Mrs Slocombe.

But Purity was no longer looking at the bar, it was the cavernous drop beneath it that had her full attention. From the ground, the Monoliths were so glamorous, exciting - who wouldn't want to live in the clouds with spectacular views over the City. But right here, right now, the reality of balancing on a thin strip of tin over a collapsing rubbish tip with no safety net was biting hard.

"You alright, dear?" asked the old lady.

"I... I can't do it," stuttered Purity.

Yet everyone else just had. No arguments, no hesitation, they had just stepped up and did what needed to be done. Do, don't do... the difference between life and death.

Maud saw how sickly Purity looked.

"Come now, dear. You got us this far, would be a shame to give up now when we're so close, wouldn't it?"

She took Purity's hand between her frail fingers and looked her in the eye.

"I believe in you. We all do. We wouldn't have got this far without you, that's for sure. You saved our lives. You know that, yes?"

The pensioner squeezed tightly.

"While there's a breath inside us, we never give up, yes?"

Never give up, DangerMole. Fight to your very last breath.

Her father's words, a million miles from home.

Purity nodded.

"Not if it's something worth fighting for," she whispered.

A piercing clap, sharp like thunder whiplashed overhead and they all looked up. A crack, long and winding appeared on Monolith Two. Starting at the 'cave mouth', it snaked up and around the building in a loose crescent leaving a deep, dark gash.

And there was something else, almost imperceptible to start with but from her vantage point it was Purity who saw it first.

The face of the tower was sliding down.

"Sam!" shouted Warren, wide eyed.

Samson felt the weight of the building shift on her shoulders and she pivoted her free arm up, palm flat against the beam above her. She pushed as hard as she could, muscles bulging through torn silk, but she could still feel movement, painfully aware of the weight of the building bearing down on her. Quickly she released the girder and raised both arms over her head, straining. Snorting fast through her nose she adjusted her stance, bending her head down and bracing her shoulders fully against the crossbar above. She locked her powerful legs straight and looked back outside. Without her holding it in place, the girder was starting to tip sideward. With a cry she thrust her right arm out and grabbed the very end with her fingertips. It was just in reach.

On the far side of the chasm, Purity and Mrs Slocombe watched in horror.

"In your... own... time!" grunted Samson with undisguised sarcasm.

Purity couldn't take her eyes off the Monolith. The exterior wall was visibly moving now, windows and cladding shifting and sliding with only one person stopping it all coming down.

Sam was literally holding the building up.

"Purity... St... George," spat Samson, "Don't... make me... come and get you!"

The rusted girder was stable, but not for long.

Purity grabbed the pensioner's arm and ran. In reality it was more a brisk walk, Mrs Slocombe was 94 after all. They kept their gaze fixed dead ahead at Samson and the gap in the wall. One step at a time. One step.

Samson groaned, a low guttural rasp. Feral. Veins bulged aggressively on her triceps and biceps, purple flowers blooming under her skin. The ground under her feet cracked and shattered. Her breathing was fast now - she was hyperventilating. The rasp became a feral scream.

Purity and Maud crossed the threshold, setting foot on Monolith Two and Sam finally let go with her right hand. The girder slipped away, toppling end over end into the void chased by clouds of metal shrapnel and stone. Sam repositioned the hand over her shoulder.

Purity ran to her.

"Get... back," hissed Samson. "Not... safe."

"Sam, let us help you!" Purity yelled.

The Monolith creaked louder still, cracks spidering away from Sam across the ceiling. Across her shoulders, the beam splintered and shredded, cracking like gunshots under the intense pressure.

"We're not leaving without you!" shrieked Purity, her hands out pleading. "Please!"

Samson grimaced, brickwork digging into her skin. Her breathing became faster and she shook her head in tiny movements.

"Knew this... was a one... woman... show," she gasped. "Turns out... the woman... is you."

Purity blinked back tears.

"Just promise... you'll do... one thing... for me."

"Of course. Anything."

Sam sighed and her face, her arms, her whole body seemed to relax. She turned to Purity and smiled that perfect smile and for that moment, that long, drawn out millisecond of a moment that lasted forever, all the blood, bruises, dirt ceased to exist. Sam was beautiful.

She winked at Purity.

"Be fantabulous."

The roof fell instantly and Sam dropped, engulfed under a hundred floors of bricks and mortar. A deadly cloud of stones and dust rolled inwards and Purity felt a hand on her arm.

Mr Humphries pulled her backwards into the elevator as Warren punched the CLOSE button. The occupants covered their eyes and faces as the smoke entered but the doors were already shutting and the lift started to move.

48. IT'S OVER

They descended in silence, too shocked to talk. The elevator swayed, juddering occasionally, rocking the survivors in synchronised unison, their arms tight around each other. Samson was the first person Warren had talked to when he joined the extremists, she had shown him round and looked after him. He had no idea why she had chosen to join and he had never asked her. In all the time he had known her he wasn't sure they had ever had a deep conversation about anything. It felt like that should trouble him, but he knew that was how she liked to keep things - all surface. Thoughts were for thinking, not sharing, she had once said. An imposing, beautiful, genuine human being. More than the muscle, she was the heart of the team.

And now she was gone.

Out of the corner of his eye, he watched Purity. She was streaked in dust and blood and stared at the wall, expressionless, vacant, unblinking.

Broken.

And very, very unfantabulous.

The digital display above the doors was cracked so they had no idea which floor they were on or how long it was going to take, just a collective belief that it was heading in the right direction and was going to make it. Warren stared straight ahead at a small sign above the buttons.

IN THE EVENT OF FIRE OR EMERGENCY
PLEASE USE THE STAIRS

He'd had quite enough of stairs for one night. Given the severe impact Monolith Two had taken, Warren was surprised the elevators were working at all, but any concerns about safety he kept to himself. He wasn't one to look a gift elevator in the mouth and any good luck they were owed was long overdue. They felt their weight shift and the car shuddered to a grinding, bouncing halt. With a PING, the doors slid open onto the eerily quiet, deserted darkness of the foyer.

It followed the same layout as the other tower, but where shops should be were just rows of empty business units, ladders and scaffolding, dimly lit by maintenance lighting. As swiftly as they could, they exited the elevator and hobbled across the courtyard - none of them had any desire to spend any more time inside these monstrosities. Their scuffed steps echoed in the unfinished space as they walked past palettes of artificial bushes and shrubs, boxes of signage and park benches still wrapped in polythene, and out towards the main entrance.

Warren barged through the doors straight into a district of hell.

Sirens and screams hit them first, punctuated by the low burst of explosions. Acrid smoke stung the eyes and scratched at their throats.

Huge chunks of masonry, indeed whole sections of building were strewn in heaps of bricks and metal, tangled iron struts pointing to the heavens. A black Sangwon truck lay on its side, flames licking up the skewed and twisted trailer, tyres dripping off in shreds of melted rubber. Cars and vans, scattered across the road like discarded children's toys, burned and smouldered. Every so often a fuel tank ruptured and smaller blasts rang out.

Silvery white pods stuck out of the rubble, bent and crushed from the fall. Not as indestructible as they had thought, after all. In the firelight, lumpy black goo oozed from some of them and Warren quickly averted his eyes.

He did not want to think about that.

A sound from above him made Warren

look up. Monolith One leaned heavily against the corner of the tower they had just escaped, its oppressive weight almost tangible. The fallen tower creaked and groaned, cement and glass still flaking off in deadly clumps.

Amongst the devastation were fridges and ovens - the only things that could survive such a drop and there in a clearing, an ivory bathtub sat on four short legs looking brand new. Warren stepped over a dusty and torn teddy bear.

The personal effects weren't the worst thing though.

The worst was the bodies.

Half buried in the rubble, hanging out of windows, impaled on wreckage, the story was the same. Corpses, bloodied, charred and blackened littered the street. Twisted and contorted in a myriad of grotesque and impossible shapes, the bodies presented a morbid panorama.

Ambulances and fire engines idled further back, lights strobing relentlessly. A makeshift barrier had been set up holding back crowds of citizens and reporters, their phones held high recording the moment.

Pumping water directly from the Thames, teams of shouting firepersons futilely aimed hoses at the lower floors. Darting in and out of the bodies, medical staff in hi-vis jackets knelt by victims checking for pulses and heartbeats.

They hadn't found any yet.

"Medic!" cried Warren. "Hello? We've got

people here!"

No one looked up - he was just another noise in a tsunami of noise. He took a deep breath and shouted louder, "Hey! We've got survivors here!"

At the word 'survivors' people stopped what they were doing and looked their way. Disbelief gave way to surprise. Surprise gave way to elation. From behind the barriers, cameras flashed and reporters spoke excitedly into microphones.

Warren stayed back as emergency responders and field doctors swarmed around the bemused pensioners. These old people had lost their homes and their possessions, but looking at them now, proud, resilient, he knew they would be okay. More than okay in fact. Survivors of this disaster would undoubtedly get a huge pay-out - either as compensation or hush money, or both. He sank back into the shadows, away from the excitement. He desperately needed medical treatment, he knew that, but official channels most definitely couldn't be trusted - he was a fugitive. No, there were contacts Delphi had used before, he was sure he could find them again.

"P, we need to..."

But Purity was already walking away - a lone figure shambling through the chaos, silhouetted by fire. He limped after her, stepping over disembodied limbs and potholes, drawing alongside a mound of contorted iron and glass. It was long and deformed with the lopsided cabin of a Sangwon troop carrier slicing through its middle. Inside the structure he saw bodies, trapped and broken, and Warren suddenly realised he was looking at the remains of the Skybridge.

"P!" he shouted, "P! Come on!"

She stopped walking but didn't turn.

"What for?" she asked, weakly.

"We need to get away. Regroup."

Purity span sharply, facing him, her face full of anger.

"Regroup? There is no group!" she screamed. "They're all dead!"

Warren shrank under the outburst, but as quickly as the anger flared, it was gone. In its place - nothing. Just a hollow, empty, nothingness.

Purity's voice lowered, "I can't do this anymore."

"Do what?"

"This!" she spat, gesturing at the devastation around them. Mutilated bodies fused into the glass stared at them from inside the remains of the Skybridge - an obscene, silent audience. Purity's arms dropped to her side, the fight well and truly gone.

"It's me. It's all on me," she said quietly.

"What do you mean?"

"They were after me since the beginning.

If I'd just handed myself in right at the start none of this would ever have happened. These people would still be alive. All of them. Sam would be alive. Gabriel. Delphi. Ted."

Voice cracking, she added, "Dad."

Purity wiped her eyes with the back of her cuff and squinted at the stars.

"If I'd just gone with them when they had come to my house, everyone would still be alive. It's on me. Everything."

Suddenly, urgently she rummaged through her pockets.

"Dad was right. He was right all along."

Her fingers found the small, cold slab and wrapped around it. "If I hadn't been so reliant on *this*," she said, brandishing the old Korean AOJI phone like a deadly weapon. "None of this would ever have happened. So much effort building followers, chasing votes, chasing likes. And for what? What was the point?"

She threw the phone at him in disgust. He flinched as it bounced off his chest and onto the ground, a deep crack curved across its face.

"I can't do this anymore. I'm done," she said.

She turned her back to him and walked away.

"What? Where are you going?" Warren pleaded. "Purity! Where are you going?"

She didn't slow or stop but spoke quietly, her voice somehow carrying over the noise of the fires and sirens.

"Home, Warren. I'm going home."

49. OUR HOUSE

The windows of 52 Festive Road were boarded up with large rectangular plywood panels. Yellow tape crisscrossed the door and continued around the perimeter of the front garden draped through bushes and tied to fence posts. Small black text on the tape repeated:

SCHEDULED FOR DEMOLITION - KEEP OUT - DANGER OF DEATH

Every house on the street had the same treatment - boarded up and taped off, empty and in darkness. The government had finally pushed ahead forcing a compulsory purchase on them all to pave the way for Monolith Four, though after the events of that evening a fourth tower was now looking increasingly questionable.

Purity looked over the rooftop of her

home. Monolith One had slipped lower still against its partner while the half-built Monolith Three looked on, an embarrassed bystander. Higher up, small fires dotted the windows of both buildings like flaming numbers on the most disastrous lottery ticket ever.

Except there would be no winners tonight.

The garden gate opened gently, squeaking on rusty hinges. It was a simple, familiar sound. Comforting. The tired old gnome still guarded the front door with its pants around its ankles and a cheeky wink that didn't seem quite so funny anymore. The paint, flaked and cracked, had faded over the years and the once ruddy complexion was now a sickly, bleached yellow.

Gnomer Simpson, her father called it. It was only years later she discovered the name was a joke based on some old banned political cartoon. She twisted the ornament clockwise on its base. It turned with a rusty squeak then came free. Underneath, in a small waterproof plastic compartment, the spare house key still waited.

She slid the key in and unlocked the door - the council hadn't changed the locks, at least. It opened with some resistance and Purity stepped over a mound of unopened mail piled on the mat. The hallway, cloaked in shadow, was cold with a musty smell. Her fingers instinctively found the light switch and flicked it on lighting the narrow corridor in a harsh glare - her mother always did like a bright room, still, it was surprising that the electricity was still connected. She kicked a few envelopes on the floor - brightly coloured paper and cards promising GREAT CASH PRIZES and FREE INSURANCE.

At the end of the hallway, light spilled into the kitchen entrance and Purity saw her cup of tea was still on the worktop where she had left it a lifetime ago. Even from the front door there was no mistaking Howard Jones' unshakable smile and the almost luminous caption:

THINGS CAN ONLY GET BETTER.

Sorry Howard, she thought. *They really, really can't.*

Purity hovered on the threshold of the lounge. The last time she had seen her mother, she was in the armchair watching the television. The chair now, of course, was empty. Though a small part of her was hoping her mother was still sat there watching game shows, in truth she wasn't expecting it. The government had taken her, though taken her where?

Purity sank into the threadbare armchair, smelling her mother's perfume on the fabric straight away. The packet of SoyWeed crisps lay on the arm, unfinished. Purity turned her nose up at the Korean snack; as far as she was concerned they could stay unfinished. She reached a hand down the side of the padded seat and retrieved the remote control. She pointed it at the tv and turned it on.

The room was bathed in a cool, clinical glow and Purity was greeted with an aerial shot of the leaning Monolith, thick clouds billowing into the sky. The word LIVE pulsed slowly in the corner of the screen.

"...as a precaution, residents are currently being evacuated from the surrounding areas, but this is still expected to take a few hours before..."

No. She had already seen more than enough on this subject tonight. She hit the channel selector.

A ground view this time. Handheld camera. Very shaky. Medics and police scrambling over upturned cars.

She pressed the next channel. A cluster of hoses ineffectually spraying the lower half a dozen windows.

The next. Crowds of people behind police barriers, phones high, recording the event.

And the next. A closeup of a child's doll in the rubble, one eye fixed open staring blankly into the camera.

Every channel. Not just the news channels. It was live streaming on every channel.

Purity couldn't watch anymore. Her head ached - everything ached, in fact. Submitting to fatigue, she rested her head on the soft back of the chair and closed her stinging eyes letting the audio of the broadcasts wash over her.

"...at 11:37 last night when a huge explosion ripped through the lower floors of Monolith One..."

Her hand still on the controller, she moved the channel on.

Click. "...of the Monolith, which can only throw doubt on the government's flagship plan to build more of these so-called mass affordable housing projects. The grand opening of Monolith Two is now expected to be postponed until..."

Click. "...wondering just how safe the other towers actually are..."

Click. "...given that a single tower at full capacity can house 50,000 occupants, we can only speculate as to how many poor souls were at home in Monolith One tonight..."

Click. "...believed to be a terrorist bombing designed to spread fear and..."

Click. "...Christian Extremists have not yet claimed full responsibility..."

Click. "...Mayor of London has yet to comment but..."

Click. "...acting on information received, Police have arrested a woman in connection with tonight's bombing."

Purity's eyes snapped open and she sat bolt upright blinking at the images on the screen. An insincerely fake newsreader with fake boobs and fake lips read fake news from the auto prompt, the words BREAKING NEWS filling the backdrop behind her.

How could they have arrested a woman already? Had Delphi survived somehow?

"It is believed she is a ringleader with very close connections to senior members of the so-called Christian Extremist Group. Though they have yet to give her name, Police have released this image."

A photograph filled the screen, and Purity's blood ran cold.

"The woman is believed to be married, in her late forties and was said to be living very near the Monolith project with easy access to all three towers. She is currently being held for questioning at New England Yard under the Prevention of Terrorism Act, though a source on the inside tells us this is little more than a formality and they are working hard to fast track her onto this Sunday's public executions. Anyone with information on this or any other terrorist activity should call 999 or visit their nearest police station at their earliest convenience. And now, the weather."

Purity touched the screen with the tips of her fingers.

The photo was of her mother.

50. TELEPHONE LINE

"Thank you for calling 999 emergency," said the voice.

"Yes... I'm...my name is..." stammered Purity, rushing to get her words out.

"Which service do you require?"

It was just a recording, Purity realised - an automated call system. The voice was genderless, sounding at once like a deep voiced female and a high voiced male depending on the caller's mental expectations.

Purity sat at the bottom of the stairs with the telephone receiver pressed to her ear. It was a deliberately retro old pea green trimphone with a ring her dad always said sounded like Roger Whittaker on speed. In the living room, she could still see her the picture of her mother on the tv. The news caption read TERROR MILF?

"For police assistance press 1. For fire press 2. For medical assistance press 3. For all other emergencies press 4."

Purity pushed the 1 button on the telephone, feeling the cheap plastic mechanism bend under her finger.

"Thank you for choosing Police. If you would like to report a violent crime press 1. For financial crime press 2. Psychological press 3. Spiritual press 4. Civil press 5. For all other crimes press 6."

Purity punched 6.

"You chose 'Other'. If your crime is a based around religion press 1. For gender crimes press 2. For race press 3. For disability press 4. For sexual orientation press 5. For all other crimes press 6."

Purity's finger hovered over the keypad. Was it a religious crime or was it something else?

It was being reported as an act of extremism, so she hit 1.

"Thank you for choosing 'Religious Crime'. If your crime is terror related, press 1. If it is..."

She stabbed 1 on the phone.

"Thank you for choosing 'Terror'. Your emergency is very important to us. You are currently 384th in the queue."

Classical music abruptly cut in, tinny and distorted.

"Three hundred and what?" Purity shouted.

The music cut out harshly.

"You are currently 384th in the queue. To maintain your place in the queue, press 1. To leave press 2 or hang up."

She stared at the phone in her hand as if it was something strange and alien. She punched 1 and the music carried on.

384th in the queue. Was this how all emergencies were dealt with? Was she just supposed to sit on hold for six hours with this stupid desk phone in her hand?

Then she remembered something. Something Warren once said.

They bug everything. Emails, texts, phone calls, messages… it's all monitored 24 hours a day. They're always listening.

Again, the music cut out and the voice said, "You are currently 383rd in the queue. To maintain your place in the queue, press 1. To leave press 2 or hang up."

They're always listening, he had said.

She placed her fingers on the telephone hook and ended the call. Slowly she released the hook and heard a dialling tone buzzing from the handset.

Always listening.

Connected to no one and listening to a dialling tone, Purity took a deep breath and started talking.

"My name is Purity St. George and I am ready to make a deal."

The monotonous buzz of the phone line stretched out, unchanging and Purity had a fleeting feeling of absurdity - she was attempting to converse with a dialling tone. She really hoped Warren was...

The tone cut out, replaced with an echoing silence. Purity's breathing sounded heavy in the earpiece.

Then a male voice. Distant, metallic. "We're listening."

"You have my mother, Rosemary St. George. Let her go, drop all her charges and I'll hand myself in. No tricks. No stalling tactics. Just let her go."

The phone line pinged and clicked, the sound of static bouncing through the airwaves and Purity wondered if she had been heard. She was about to repeat herself when the voice finally replied.

"Agreed," it said.

And the line went dead.

51. END OF THE LINE

Purity staggered out of the house leaving the front door wide open behind her, but it didn't matter. Unlike The Terminator, she wouldn't be back.

Whatever happened from here onwards, the house was history. It was no longer her home, no longer anyone's home. And even if no more Monoliths were built, there would be no stopping the demolition now. Sometimes you needed to fight for the past, sometimes you just need to let it go and pick your battles - fight for the past or fight for the future. Right now, the only thing Purity could hope for, was even capable of, was fighting for her mother's future.

At the end of the road, she stopped. Framed by the houses on either side of Festive Road, the Monoliths burned and smouldered -

they couldn't have much longer left.

50,000 people those things would hold, that's what they had said.

No, don't think about that.

The image of her mother would not shift from her head. She had lost too many people in too short a time.

50,000 though? No. Stop it.

She was damned if she was going to lose one more.

Losing one parent is unfortunate, losing two? That's just careless.

Dad's words caught her by surprise and a cry escaped her throat. She had spent so long and made such a good job of locking her grief up, keeping the pain weighted and tied deep inside her, far away from her daily thoughts that when the chains cracked, they shattered instantly and completely. Purity dropped to her knees in the middle of the road, howling like a wounded animal. A thick, guttural sob shook her entire body as she squeezed her arms tight around her chest, rocking.

She lay on the cold, wet tarmac, legs tucked up, wailing.

She was still crying when the unmarked black vehicles arrived.

BOOK 4
Yes Minister

52. LONDON CALLING

"Look at them," said Prime Minister August gazing out of the window. "Sheep… blindly herding from one lost cause to the next. Pathetic."

Thousands of protestors congregated behind the Cabinet Office, filling the vast gravelled parade ground between the Cavalry Museum and Admiralty House. From students to pensioners, all ages were present, a sea of heads and waving arms. Placards and banners demanded NO MORE MONOLITHS. HIGH RISE? LOWLIFES. CUT CORNERS COSTS LIVES.

A small group of youths had banded together and were playing drums and trumpets creating a tribal, melodic accompaniment to the chanting and shouting. The top floor of 10 Downing Street, however, had thickened walls, reflective, bulletproof glass and was completely soundproofed.

From here, the cacophony was very easy to ignore.

August watched as a cluster of three pink balloons tied together by a yellow ribbon drifted out of reach of a three-year-old girl crying on the ground.

Gender stereotyping. That's six months and a £300 fine for your careless parents, he thought.

"You know, they made a balloon of me last week, did you see that? It was all over the feeds, I'd be surprised if you missed it. Big yellow thing in a dress, crazy hair. I think they were trying to be offensive but I actually thought it was rather good. I would have offered to take it off their hands but the bloody police only went and shot the damned thing down."

He chuckled, "You should have seen it. Bloody fools had filled it with hydrogen. It went up like a mini Hiroshima. Everyone hit the ground screaming - thought the terrorists were back. No... they didn't hang around much after that.

"It's a shame they can't put their talents to good use. just imagine what they could achieve if they all applied themselves instead of pissing away their time on this... What *would* you call this, exactly?"

He turned his back to the window and faced the girl in the chair. Purity sat upright with her arms and legs securely clamped to the modified wheelchair. She was dressed in an orange one-piece jumpsuit and wore a black nylon sack over her head, blinding her. Printed across the hood were the words PROPERTY OF HM GOVT.

"Oh, how rude of me," said the Prime Minister with mock surprise. "Miss Sims do take those off her, will you? We're not animals."

"But sir, she's a terrorist with a history of violent..."

"I don't think we have much to fear from a teenage girl, do you? Just do it, please."

Hattie peeled the hood from her head and Purity blinked in the light. A black strap held an orange ball tightly in her mouth forcing her to breath hard and fast through her nostrils, panting like a dog. Hattie twisted the clasp and the straps relaxed.

Purity spat the gag onto the carpet and glared at August, "Where's my fucking mother?"

The Prime Minister raised an eyebrow.

"My you're a feisty one, aren't you? Did you know she was a feisty one, Hattie?"

"No sir, security did not make that clear."

"I'll have to talk to them about that."

"Where is she!?!" Purity screamed.

He frowned before making a realisation.

"Oh, the woman! Calm down, dear, she's perfectly fine. We were never going to hurt her, she was just the bait. Lovely lady, lovely. Very pretty for her age. Well defined cheekbones. Doesn't say much though, does she?"

He lowered his mouth near Purity's ear. "Between you, me and the gatepost, I think she may be a bit of a vegetable. Such a shame."

Purity violently tugged at the restraints, "You bastard!"

August took a step backwards, startled. "Remind me to listen to your advice more often, Miss Simms. Got quite the potty mouth, this one."

"Appears so, sir."

Hattie unzipped a medical satchel and held up a small white plastic cylinder in a simple trigger housing - a pneumatic injection gun designed to deliver medicines without needles.

"There's no need for that, " said August, placing his hand over the device. "If I wanted to listen to her snoring, I'd play her the Chancellor's last budget speech. I just want a chat."

"I've got nothing to say to you."

He moved to the cabinet at the back of the room and removed a tablet from its vertical dock. He held his thumb over the reader as it passively scanned his face and analysed his voice patterns.

"We had her mother put into a nursing home, didn't we?" he asked.

Hattie nodded. "We had to move her to Richmond. She was scheduled to go to PHC6 until that went... offline."

"Ah yes, the Health Camp fiasco..." His voice trailed off thoughtfully as he paced in front of Purity. "That was another one of yours, wasn't it? You've been a busy girl, Miss St. George. Extremely busy."

He swiped across the glass surface of the tablet.

On the largest wall of the office, a wide screen flickered and a montage of tabloid newspaper front covers scrolled past, headlines screaming from the page. Here, a grainy aerial photo of the Health Camp in flames: PHEW, WHAT A SCORCHER! There, the burned and battered National Elf mask in closeup, floating in the sea: BAD FOR YOUR ELF? Next, a moody black and white shot of the wrought iron camp entrance gates all bent and distorted, a charred and torn medical flag in the foreground: P.H.S.O.S?

"I have to tell you, you've been a thorn in my side for quite some time. You caused quite a bit of damage there, didn't you?"

"I *know* what went on in there," threatened Purity.

Hattie was returning the injector back into the satchel and froze.

I know what went on in there? she thought. *What does that mean?*

August swiped the tablet, the image on the screen replaced with another tabloid front page. Pasted over a picture of the pier silhouetted against burning wind turbines was the headline WISH YOU WEREN'T HERE?

"The Health Camps are one of this government's biggest success stories. People forget so quickly how it used to be. Before we came in, the Health Service was in crisis, decades of mismanagement, hugely inefficient, massive overspending - it was quite, quite unsustainable. With the introduction of the camps, we created safe, secure environments where people can receive world class, cutting edge treatment. Where the PHS can continue to deliver on its core values - the three 'R's. Rejuvenate. Repair. Recycle."

"I was there, remember," growled Purity. "I saw what they did, I saw the bodies. Your spin won't work on me."

Hattie paled. *Bodies?*

She had heard the rumours, of course, everyone had. But those were a campaign of scaremongering by the opposition or so she had been told - August had always been so dismissive of their baseless accusations. She looked closer at the newsfeed photos, the identikit chalets and faceless brick buildings - what exactly *was* going on behind those walls?

The Prime Minister lowered his head to Purity's level, so they were face to face and spoke softly, as if explaining to a child. "That's just one aspect of the camps. You've got to bear in mind some people just *can't* be rehabilitated or fixed. We're giving them a chance, giving *everybody* a chance to contribute to society."

Purity winced at his warm, sour breath on her skin. "So, people are worth more dead than alive?"

August sighed. "You're taking a very narrow view," he said, and straightened up.

"It's a sad, sad fact that there are whole swathes of society that exist just to drain resources from the rest of us. We're giving them the chance - the *opportunity* - to give something back. I think that's only fair."

"Whether they like it or not?"

August shook his head. "You're a dramatic one, aren't you?"

"The people won't stand for this. When they find out..."

"They won't find out," he interrupted, "and so what if they do? We'll just flood the feeds with another celebrity sex tape or announce a royal wedding. The sheep do love a royal wedding."

He placed his palm on the glass surface and brushed the content away. The image on the main screen was replaced by shaky camera footage of the burning Battersea animal clinic surrounded by fire engines.

Purity's gaze dropped to the carpet. "We were told it was an animal testing lab. We thought they were conducting experiments."

"Except they weren't, were they?"

Purity closed her eyes in silence.

"You burned it down with no thought for that poor man inside. Are animals lives more important now?"

"It wasn't like that," she stammered.

"You left him for dead."

A passport photo of the guard appeared onscreen. Grey hair, big moustache and a name badge on his lapel. MACKAY.

"Is he... is he okay?"

August tapped the tablet and the screen went black.

"He had a heart attack a few hours later," said August, solemnly. "I'm afraid he's dead."

"No! No, he can't be..."

August laughed. "You're right, he's fine. I was just joking with you - he's living in Basildon with his dog."

"Bastard! What is wrong with you?!"

"It was all getting a bit heavy, just trying to lighten the tone a bit. Not too much, mind... there is the small matter of this."

The screen lit up again and a new montage of newspaper headlines scrolled past. Photos of the Monoliths from every imaginable angle, emergency services, personal effects in rubble - every possible variation on the same theme accompanied by lurid, sensationalist headlines. PM ON SHAKY FOUNDATIONS. HIGH CRIMES. THE BIGGER THEY ARE THE HARDER THEY FALL. THE HEIGHT OF STUPIDITY.

He paused the screen on a tabloid story. The photo was of the surviving pensioners gathered by an ambulance, they were wrapped in thermal foils and clutched mugs of tea. They all smiled and held thumbs up to the camera. The picture was entitled THE MONOLITH NINE.

"The Monolith Nine, can you believe that? They've got a name already - they're celebrities. And for what... surviving? Is that all it takes, these days? Still, nine survivors out of 27 thousand"

"27?" Asked Purity?

"Equivalent to the population of, oh... Stratford-upon-Avon."

"27 *thousand*?"

"Could have been a lot worse."

"Worse? 27 thousand people are dead!"

"I know, I know and it's terribly sad, but Monolith One at full capacity holds about 50 thousand. It wasn't even half full. Could have been a lot worse, hell of a lot worse.

"The papers are trying to pin some blame on me, somehow," said August. "Can you believe that? Did I know they'd saved money on the foundations? Of course I did. But it's not like I planted a bomb in there, is it? No, they'll not pin this one on me. It was your lot."

"No. It wasn't meant to happen like that. It was only going to be..."

Be what? thought Purity. *Property damage? A statement? A warning?*

No, it was becoming more and more clear that Delphi had been planning for this to happen since day one.

"You know these people?" he asked as five portrait photos slid onto the screen in a row. Purity recognised them instantly. Delphi, Gabriel, Ariel, Warren and Samson. All bar one, dead.

"Your face tells me all I need to know, Miss St. George. We know this is your cell: Delphi, birth name Peggy Delmont. Studied Philosophy and Hate Studies at Wilberforce Humphries University. *Hate Studies...* is that even a thing?

"Gabriel, birth name Walter Henry. Dead. Served four years at Her Majesty's Pleasure in HMP Stanley Fletcher for illegal substances and offence crimes before going missing twelve months ago on day release.

"Samson. Birth name, Samuel Spencer. Dead. Also studied at Wilberforce Humphries before dropping out to start her own diet plan: FantabuLoss. Wait, I remember that; that was her? Became a millionaire aged 19 and look at this... gave it all away a year later to the homeless. What a pointless waste.

"Ariel. Birth name Sarah Windsor. Dead. No criminal record.

"Warren Wingford. Missing, presumed dead. Also, no criminal record.

"That's quite a ragtag team of fugitives

and activists you pulled together. Tell me, how did you recruit them?"

"How did I... what?"

"This team you built. You knew exactly where to hurt this government. Where did you get your information from? Who gave you your orders?"

Purity chuckled, a small laugh that grew and grew. "You think I was in charge? Me? You really don't know anything, do you? Delphi was the leader, she took the orders. We never even saw who she was talking to."

August rubbed his forehead. He was convinced this Purity girl was behind all this, but her response rang true. How could he have got it so wrong?

"Now that is.... annoying," he said.

Choosing to ignore her amusement, he carried on. "Look at the problems you've caused me. This economy can't survive on the Russian and North Korean trade deals. We need Americana on board. Your explosive shenanigans at The Health Camp have not only seriously jeopardised our hopes of a new trade agreement with the Colonies, but also set back our homeless reduction program by years.

"You think you've struck some kind of moral blow for freedom? Give it six months and the streets will be clogged with vagrants, you'll see what the public really think then. Moral outrage never wins when confronted by mild inconvenience.

"And now this - our glorious solution to the housing crisis, the shining jewel in our plan to fix this country, gone, dashed away in an instant, vanished in a puff of smoke. All your doing, all this was you. The people need to see that justice has been done, you understand, the will of the people cannot be ignored. We need a very public example."

Purity sank into her chair, shoulders slumped, head bowed. Deflated. Beaten.

Finally, she whispered, "So that's it then. You're going to execute me."

"Execute you?"

August carefully placed the tablet back into the dock and waited for the charging icon to display. It always took longer than he expected.

"No, Miss St. George, I'm offering you a job."

53. EVEN BETTER THAN THE REAL THING

Hattie opened the heavy oak door. Waiters wearing white jackets and black gloves wheeled in three trolleys and parked them end-to-end in the middle of the room. The trolleys were silver and covered with intricate white lace tablecloths, piled high with food and drink. Ornate hand painted bowls and plates contained cooked meats and cheeses, fish, burgers, crisps and cake - a mini banquet on wheels. In a silence broken only by the clinking and rattling of plates and bowls, the serving staff removed lids from steaming pots of stews and soups, laid out a selection of cutlery and left the room.

    Breakfast cereals she hadn't seen for years

were arranged in a neat display: SugaBix, Money Puffs (featuring that anarchic Money Monster), Sgt Saccharine - *Put some Bang in your Bowl!* Morning Glory - *What a Way to Start the Day!* Irritable Bowl Syndrome, ReadyBrexit. Scattered on a silk cloth were banned candy bars such as Bloateasers, Kurdish Delight and Scrunchy Bars.

The Prime Minister lifted the fragile silver lid on the teapot and inhaled the aroma of the hot leaves inside.

Purity just stared at the spread before her - she couldn't recall ever seeing anything so lavish. Suddenly the buffet at her father's wake seemed even more pathetic. The combination of smells made her stomach rumble.

"You sound hungry," said the Prime Minister, "Try something.

"I don't think so," Purity said, the defiance strong in her voice.

August plucked a burger from a gleaming platter and laid it on a folded, monogrammed Number 10 serviette in front of her. The surface of the patty gleamed and shone with oil, and musky, barbecued tones radiated from the toasted sesame seed brioche. It looked like the incredible, sumptuous photographs you would see in food adverts, not the pale, dry, limp thing you really received.

It was like no burger she had ever seen.

"Oh, go on. I think you'll like it."

Her mouth was watering, *actually* physically watering, and curiosity seized the moment. She hesitantly raised it to her mouth and took a tiny bite. She chewed slowly, the flavours releasing in bursts. Woody notes with a rich, savoury, smoky tang and a zesty kick that lingered on her tongue. Not only did it look unlike any burger she had ever seen, it tasted unlike anything she had ever tasted.

"What *is* that?" she asked between chews.

"Since the Animal Equality Act, the only meat you've ever known has been grown from plant extract," August chuckled. "This is the real thing."

Fifteen years earlier after long and bitter campaigning, the Equality Act was expanded to include the animal kingdom. The same basic rights enjoyed by the country's citizens now applied to pets and livestock, in fact *any* living creature. While this was a landmark moment for animal rights, it brought with it a huge unforeseen problem: an animal could only be killed for food if it had given its explicit consent.

Cattle and sheep, essentially granted their freedom, roamed free in their thousands. Wales was hit particularly hard with stories of feral sheep packs descending from the Valleys killing hundreds in Merthyr Tydfil and Pontypridd. The meat industry collapsed overnight. In the frantic months that followed, meat substitutes flooded the market while scientists worked on plant-based alternatives. The Meat Riots lasted for weeks. Ordinary people pushed to the edge - Edgetarians - would smuggle livestock across county lines under the cover of darkness in a desperate attempt to fuel the black market.

"This... this is banned," realised Purity. "These are *all* banned."

August nodded and waved towards the window at the mass of people in the square. "To them, yes. Their tastes aren't... *sophisticated* enough. They'd just gorge on them until they were sick, then demand some more," he shrugged. "And that would only put us back into the mess we were in before."

Purity returned the burger to the table and wiped her fingers on her jumpsuit. They left a greasy smear on the orange fabric. "One rule for you, and another for them?"

"What's your point?" asked August.

"You act like you're better than them, than us. You're not, we're all equal."

The Prime Minister crossed his hands behind his back, facing the gathered masses outside and sighed. "Maybe some of us are just a little bit more equal than others."

Purity froze, recognising the phrase immediately. Words from her past, a simpler time. #MOREEQUALTHANOTHERS.

"I never asked you... what do you think of Downing Street?" he asked. "The black brickwork is very striking don't you think?"

She didn't answer, his previous words still rattled around her head.

"After World War ll," he continued, "London had taken a bit of a kicking, and this old place was in desperate need for renovation as you could imagine. Anyway, when they came to it, they discovered the bricks were actually yellow! Can you believe that? Centuries of smog and pollution had stained the bricks from the colour of sunflowers to that of coal."

He lifted the silver teapot and poured the hot liquid into a fragile china cup.

"But...but... and this is the thing, everyone was so used to seeing it like that, they ended up painting black over the bricks. Hiding its true colours, so to speak."

Purity shook her head. "All this time and the most famous front door in the world is a lie."

"I'm sure there's a message there," chuckled August. "Damned if I know what it is though."

He poured a drop of full fat milk from a glazed porcelain jug into his cup.

"I only mention this because as part of the job we'll throw in a complimentary flat in Mayfair. Similar architecture to this, it's very grand. I saw your old house, so I expect it's more than you're used to - you can live like a queen, or a king... whatever you're into. It's so hard to keep up these days."

He shrugged, "You'd have a generous retainer. You'd be set up for life, can't imagine you'd have to work ever again."

"I don't understand. Why me?"

"Why you... why you," he repeated, tipping a spoonful of sugar into the hot drink and stirring. The metal chimed melodically against the porcelain.

"Because the problem with this place - it's full of talkers. They all love to hold an enquiry, run a summit or emergency meeting - talk a subject into the ground rather than actually deal with the problem themselves."

He paused with the china cup against his lips.

"And because one teenage girl with a phone has accomplished more in three months than our entire media agency has in the last ten years. You have millions of followers, you're an inspirational leader and most importantly, you get things done. I could, quite frankly, do with a slice of that pie."

"Why do you care? I thought you hated the people? Sheep, wasn't it?"

"Oh you say that is if it's a bad thing. Sheep are docile and easily led - as long as they're fed and watered the herd will keep it's head down and carry on."

"These sheep voted you in!"

"You realise most people don't vote, don't you? Sixteen years ago, when we first came to power, barely 50% of the population bothered."

"The turnout was 52.4%," Hattie corrected.

"Think about that. There's a very vocal minority that like to shout and moan a lot, but half the people in this green and pleasant land don't care. They really don't."

"Like sheep," suggested Hattie.

August nodded. "It was obvious early on that we needed to harness that somehow - weaponise their indifference."

He clapped his hands. "*Weaponise their indifference*. Isn't that a terrific phrase? I got that from President Crass, he's got some great material. We really need to get some of his writers on board. Look into that, Miss Simms."

Hattie opened a new mail on her tablet and started typing, though her mind was elsewhere. She was more aware than most that the Prime Minister was a monster but the earlier comments on the health camps had really shaken her.

"So, the first thing we did when we came into power was to quietly change the rules behind the scenes," continued August. "On the surface, the voting system is essentially the same: one person, one vote, tick a box on a screen or in a booth, whatever. We just gave it a little nudge to make use of that 50% who don't bother. Now a no-vote presumes you're happy with the status quo, so that vote automatically goes to the standing government. We could have an election tomorrow and win just through the weight of apathy."

The Prime Minister chuckled to himself. "Never underestimate the power of sheep."

Purity thought about his offer. "What's the catch?"

"There is no catch. Every now and again we might ask you to post one of our messages, but you get to carry on doing whatever it is you do and get paid handsomely for it. All I ask is you give us a heads up before you post anything too... inflammatory?"

"And if I say no?"

"Why on earth would you turn it down? It's an incredible offer."

"And if I say no?"

August finished his tea and returned the delicate cup to its saucer. "Noosenight falls on the same day as the Purity Day celebrations tomorrow. - the people will be expecting *something* special."

It would be easy to say 'yes', so easy.

She could say 'yes' and game August, play the system, work on the inside to bring him down. He'd be expecting that of course, but still, who wouldn't want to live in opulence like this? The money, the big house, the ability to do what she liked, when she liked and for what? The odd post here and there on something she might not agree with?

Was that really such a big deal?

She caught herself. Yes... yes it was.

Samson had been crushed saving her and the lives of complete strangers. Gabriel, riddled with bullets had allowed her to escape. Delphi and Arial, standing up for something they believed in had both been torn apart. Tom was almost dissected alive for a lie.

And there was Dad.

They had all fought for their beliefs in their own ways and paid the price for it. She was shocked that turning her back on their sacrifices for the sake a few shiny toys and an easy life had even crossed her mind. Shocked and disappointed with herself.

The banquet of rare and illegal foodstuffs glared at her, an embarrassment of culinary riches looking less and less a desirable commodity and more an obscene display of wealth and privilege. There was no disguising it for the bribe it was.

Rancid bones to a starving dog.

Sirens to sailors.

And Purity was acutely aware how well it ended for those ancient seafarers.

Follow your dreams and don't settle for second best, her dad had said. *It's your world. If you don't like it, change it. Never give up.*

"No," whispered Purity.

"I'm sorry?" said August, surprised.

"I said 'no'. Find yourself another puppet."

August glared at her, eyes bulging, his mouth a narrow scar. He had tried to reason with her, cajole her, persuade her and even bribe her. He had played good cop, bad cop and every-thing-in-between cop but the lady wasn't for turning.

No one could say he hadn't tried.

"Take her away," he said quietly.

54. WELCOME TO THE BLACK PARADE

"It's a bit much, don't you think?" said the Archbishop. The giant Queen's head led the parade down The Mall on eight spindly silver legs. Blind, glowing eyes rotated mechanically, projecting lasers into the sky. From her wide-open mouth, nestled amongst huge jewelled teeth, the Puritan Under Tens Genderless Choir sang "God Save The Queen" while children dressed as angels swung from her golden beard playing trumpets.

August shook his head and gestured at the crowd. "Oh, look at them... the plebs love it. Though you'd think they'd come off their bloody phones and actually enjoy the experience, wouldn't you?"

About a thousand citizens had been fortunate enough to get a prime position outside Buckingham Palace; a mass of heads surrounding the Victoria Memorial. The vast majority of commoners, however, swamped St. James' Park and The Mall, watching the ceremony on giant screens dotted between the trees. Red and white streamers and bunting was strung between lamp posts, clusters of balloons bobbing and floating in the warm, evening air. Some half a million people were present wearing coloured bowler hats, faces painted in the red and white of the George Cross. They cheered and sang, waved flags and glowstick, all the time recording the whole event on their phones.

"It's exactly what the people need," explained August.

"A joyous celebration?" asked Runcible.

"No," sneered the Prime Minister. "A distraction."

Around the Memorial, a circular stage had been built for the musical performances later that night. Large screens dominated the back of the stage and pulsing red and white lasers fanned into the sky, inscribing patterns in the clouds. From an elevated balcony behind the stage, August and Runcible could watch the whole show privately.

The Household Cavalry followed in close formation behind the Royal Spider. Another casualty of the Animal Equality Act meant that after over 300 years of horse riding, the regiment had to swap to another kind of horsepower, the soldiers now riding motorcycles instead.

"Still, it's very impressive," said the Archbishop.

"A celebration of all things British," nodded August, as the soldiers revved their North Korean Panghyon KJ350 bikes enthusiastically.

A dozen men and women danced into view, dressed in white dungarees with red sashes criss crossing their chests and lilies stuck out of their back pockets. They all wore identical PHS standard issue spectacles and antique wired hearing aids. Bell pads fastened to their shins jangled rhythmically as they moved. A tall wooden pole mounted on a wheeled trailer towered over them with red and blue ribbons trailing from it which they held as they danced around it. The crowd clapped in time with the drums, cheering the Morrissey Dancers on.

August squinted. Floats and performers sailed through the sea of faces and flags along The Mall, stretching all the way back to the Edwardian gateway of Admiralty Arch.

"You know, this could be the biggest Purity Day ever."

Fake, overzealous screams cut through the music and a gaggle of children in hospital gowns ran past in a smoothly choreographed chaos. The crowd booed in good cheer as a tall, skinny animatronic figure suspended by a mobile crane shambled into view, peering over treetops and pumping noxious smoke from a huge fake cigar. It wore cherry-red flared trousers and a gold sequined vest, its craggy yellow-toothed grin dwarfed by rose tinted shades and an unruly mop of blonde hair. Long, golden chains trailed from its neck and shoulders like Marley's ghost, rattling on the causeway. A gleaming medallion read:

I'LL FIX YA!

"I don't get this avant-garde stuff," said August.

The brass band receded, replaced by a modern pre-recorded dance track. A wide float trundled forward where a cheeky Geordie duo were introducing a bemused four-piece pop group from a multi coloured flashing dance floor. 'Lettuce, Gammon, Bacon & Tomato' were the latest winners from talent show, 'The P Factor' and they mimed their Christmas number one 'Return To Gender' perfunctorily to the uninterested crowds, demonstrating their equal right to be just as bad as each other.

Another mobile stage, towed on a separate trailer featured the winners of 'Britannica's Got Talent'. Last year's elderly tap dance troupe 'Brunel's Old Boilers' were consigned to history, replaced by nubile pansexual Koreans in lycra dancing and writhing in electrified metal enclosures, their expressions both seductive yet terrified.

'Faraday's Cage Dancers' were hypnotic to say the least.

After a short delay, a dozen people in grey boiler suits and Terrence August rubber masks marched ahead of a depressing grey float, noticeably smaller than all that had gone before it - the token protest float. On the wheeled platform, a badly modelled head the size of a car lay on its side while a vast hobnailed boot on a hydraulic lift stamped down on it repeatedly. Running the length of the float, a banner read:

1984 WAS NOT A BLUEPRINT

"Never was a big fan of history," August shrugged.

Arranged in a ten by ten grid, one hundred scantily clad models sat stationery in one hundred wheelchairs as they trundled forward in perfect formation. The crowd whooped and cheered as the dancers stared silently in the distance to the dance music.

'Hawking's Honeys' were always a family favourite.

A giant inflatable football bounced into the crowd and was punched back eagerly. The Three Lions ran in and out of the citizens, dazzling with their sporting prowess and skill. Earlier processions had included three *actual* lions, but unfortunate fatalities and newfound animal rights had put an end to that. Now the three players in the parade were men who *identified* as lions. One was early in the process but the other two had already began surgical augmentation - by next year it should be a wholly different show.

The last float trundled into view on sturdy caterpillar tracks - a conical red and white striped tower that took up the entire width of the road. At the height of two houses, with a wooden slide spiralling down its circumference to the base, Transgression Tower was an impressive sight. At the peak, on a round stage under a red domed roof stood a grotesque, yet familiar figure.

The National Elf.

55. PARTY FEARS TWO

"What's this?" Purity stared at the cupcake in front of her. She sat cross legged on a hard rubber mattress, the low, iron bed creaking in time with the motion of the room which rocked slowly. The cell, if it could be called that, seemed ancient; the rough, dirty, uneven wooden panels suggesting the interior of a pirate ship from some children's book. The crescent shaped room had curved timber walls and above - high above - oak beams supported an ageing ceiling where a yellowed - and barred - window offered views of a tiny slice of grey cloud. A grubby, muddy light filtered into the room and the air was humid and claustrophobic.

Hattie placed the cake on the end of the bed - a fist sized chocolate muffin topped with a generous spiral of butterscotch cream, sprinkled with fudge pieces. Planted on top - not *quite* vertically - burned a lonely red candle.

"It's your birthday, isn't it?" offered Hattie. "Your records say you were born on Purity Day?"

Her birthday. She had completely forgotten all about it. How old was she now? Seventeen?

She felt older. Much, much older.

The candle flickered on the condemned woman's last supper, taunting her to make a wish, but her belief in miracles had long gone. Purity reached forward - her arms strapped together in restraints - and pinched the flame out between her fingers, a thin trickle of smoke escaping in a hiss.

"Happy Birthday to me," she muttered, gazing up at the limited view of freedom.

Through the narrow window, the roar of a crowd filtered through. High above them on the roof of Transgression Tower, the Elf played to his audience - the cheering and shouting punctuated with whistles and horns while a hypnotic rhythm of drums provided a backing track. Purity knew there was always a big turnout for the live Noosenights, she had seen it often enough on TV, but this sounded bigger than usual. A lot bigger.

She turned away from the sight of dark thunder clouds and noticed Hattie hadn't moved. She was still stood facing her by the cell door, but she looked different. Deflated. Her shoulders drooped, her head bowed and she picked at her fingernails nervously. Her eyes darted skittishly around the floor.

This was not the same woman she had met before.

"What... what you said," Hattie mumbled, "about the Health Camps. Is it true?"

Purity frowned. Why would she make something like up?

"Of course, it's true," she answered. "You actually believe their lies?"

Hattie anxiously scratched the back of her arms, ugly red streaks appearing on her skin.

"Oh God, you do," realised Purity. "I can see it in your face. You've believed every single word they've fed you. You stupid, stupid..."

"I have to!" erupted Hattie, bloodshot eyes glaring, her face etched with torment. "My sister is in there!"

She fell back against the wooden beams, head in her hands, shrinking even more. Small sobs escaped her lips. "I have to."

For the longest time, Hattie just stared at the ground, shaking. Finally, she wiped her nose with the back of her hand and sniffed loudly.

"She... She had... a dog. When I say 'had', *he* adopted *her* - this cute little rescue bulldog called Rigsby. And every time he heard music he'd stand up on his back legs and beg for a biscuit with a paw. You should have seen it, it was the funniest thing. Something his previous owners had taught him, I guess. Except this one time they were at some big event - the Queen's Birthday Parade, I think. Anyway, just as the Queen goes past, the brass band starts playing. Rigsby stands up doing his party trick and someone shouts 'That dog's doing a Nazi salute!'

"She was arrested on the spot - hate speech, obscenity, animal kidnapping. Her employers found out, she lost her job. She couldn't keep up payments on her house, she lost that.

"I gave her some money but what else could I do? She couldn't stay with me, I live in a pod! She spent a few nights living rough up on the Embankment. I told her to hand herself in, declare herself homeless. August told me, *convinced* me, the Health Camps would help her, would save her. So I pulled a few strings, got her fast tracked."

Hattie rubbed her eyes, they were pink and raw. "Don't you see? I told her to hand herself in. I sent her to that awful place. It was my fault. All my fault."

"I'm so sorry," Purity whispered. "But the camps... everything I said was true. People go in, they don't come out. The sick, the elderly, criminals, dispossessed... anyone who doesn't fit in. They're picked up and quietly taken away. There's no medical intervention, no rehabilitation. It's a farm, nothing more, nothing less.

A government sanctioned organ farm on a national scale."

Purity lowered her head. "You were lied to. We all were."

Hattie pulled her phone from inside her jacket. The display flared up automatically showing a photo of a girl not much older than Purity. She had long brown hair tied back into a ponytail and hugged a scruffy looking dog tightly.

"This is her... this is Francis. Did you... did you see her, while you were in there?"

The camp held thousands, there was no way Purity would have remembered her.

"I'm sorry. There were a lot of people and..."

Acknowledging the futility of the question, Hattie hastily stuffed the phone back into her pocket with embarrassment. "No, it's okay," she stammered. "It's fine, it's fine."

Abruptly, the drums stopped and the crowd cheered.

The locking mechanism unlocked loudly and the cell door swung inwards. A single pimple-faced guard, not much older than Purity, stood on the threshold brandishing a shokstick and a small medical satchel. Draped over his arm was a golden hood embellished with silver lightning trim.

Years of Noosenights meant there was no

mistaking this gaudy headwear.

The guard raised the stick at Purity and it crackled angrily.

"Time to go," he barked.

Purity slid off the bed and stood up eyeing the humming device cautiously.

"There's no need for that, Private," said Hattie. "I'll take it from here."

She held her hand out.

The guard hesitated momentarily but he knew full well who she was, and more importantly who she reported to. "Yes ma'am."

He loosened his grip on the shokstick and it sprang back to its handheld state. Hattie clipped the weapon to her belt and hung the satchel over her shoulder. She presented her outstretched arm and he solemnly folded the ceremonial hood neatly over it. The guard stood upright and saluted, sharply snapping his heels together, before climbing through a small wooden hatch back to the driver's cockpit.

Two other cells filled the circular space. One was empty, but from the second a shrill voice shrieked, "Told you, you couldn't run forever."

Behind the bars, a woman sat on the corner of the low bed in darkness, arms clamped together at the wrists. She wore the familiar orange jumpsuit and white sneakers of all convicts.

Purity's brow creased. She seemed familiar, but out of place.

"Got what you deserved, bitch," smirked Roni Lister.

This was the woman who had hounded her from her home and pursued her across Paddington and the Monoliths, and now here she was incarcerated.

Awaiting execution.

As if reading her mind Roni shrugged. "What can I say? The PM needed a scapegoat."

The short corridor ended at a set of rusted iron elevator doors. Next to that, a small, square wooden table was affixed to the wall. Hattie pushed the call button. She opened the satchel and retrieved a gag - the same gag that was used earlier - which she laid flat on the table alongside the ornate hood. She unzipped the inner compartment and lifted out the injection gun and a glass vial containing a clear liquid.

"What's that?" asked Purity, concerned.

Hattie inserted the vial into the instrument and screwed it tightly into place.

"Something we give to all the prisoners before they go out. It's a lethal sedative; numbs the brain's nerve centre, encourages a docile state of mild euphoria. Reduces the chances of the prisoner panicking or creating a scene. Makes it... easier."

She pointed the gun upwards and tested the trigger. It barked a pneumatic hiss and a feint cloud of moisture rapidly dispersed from the nozzle. "We're not barbarians, you know."

Outside, the drumming had started again, this time slow, relentless. The crowd became louder, the cheering becoming a chant. A bell rang and the brown doors rattled open revealing a small, empty, cramped elevator.

A one-way trip with a single stop.

This was it.

The end of the line.

56. HIT ME WITH YOUR RHYTHM STICK

"The National Elf!" yelled August, clapping maniacally. "I love this guy! Big fan!"

The Elf wore the classic harlequin patchwork outfit, curly toed boots and tasselled hat, though not in its traditional colours. The red and gold patches had been replaced with black and silver, projecting a far more sombre version of the character. In both hands he gripped a long, silver stick - not unlike a baseball bat inscribed with ornate latin text *Quam ego disrumpebantur*.

The tickling stick.

The Elf danced and pranced around the cage, cackling and whooping, swinging the stick back and forth. Occasionally he would leap up and bat the dome hard in time with the music. A loud ring echoed through the sky and the crowd cheered and clapped.

Expectation was in the air, and the people didn't have to wait long.

He bowed to the masses on both sides of The Mall then stood aloof, his arms outstretched, chest puffed out.

"That's the way to do it!" he shrieked and the audience erupted in a frenzied applause.

The floats and performers turned right at the Palace onto Constitution Hill, departing noisily. The last float slowed by the memorial as Queen Victoria's statue looked on disapprovingly, coming to a stop by the main stage. The Elf marched around the perimeter of the tower's platform facing the masses who greeted him with euphoric cheers. He whipped his arms in the air again and again. Louder. Louder. The chants became hollers, the hollers, screams. He threw his head back basking in adulation as the cacophony washed over him.

"Look at them, they really love him," said the Archbishop, unable to fully understand what he was seeing.

August nodded sincerely. "Money well spent, my friend. Money well spent."

The Elf grabbed the safety railings and propelled himself onto the spiral slide, waving to the people as he descended. As he reached the bottom, he bounced onto the stage, arms in the air. He span around, facing back down The Mall at the tens of thousands of faces and bowed.

"it's meeeeeeeeee! The National Elf!" he cried. "At your service!"

As if scoring the winning goal in the last second of the last minute of the World Cup, the crowd erupted. On cue, a sonic boom shattered overhead and everyone look up as five Russian Mikoyan Mig-29 stunt aircraft roared over the palace trailing parallel plumes of red and white smoke.

The *Red* Arrows.

August dabbed the corner of his eye with his handkerchief. "Makes you proud to be British, doesn't it?"

As the people cheered and chanted, the music faded down and the lights onstage dimmed. In August's earpiece the show's producer spoke flatly.

"You're on Mr. Prime Minister."

57. BLACK CELEBRATION

"Friends. Puritans. Countrymen… and women. Lend me your ears!" Prime Minister August stood alone under a single spotlight, the stage in darkness. Before him, half a million citizens faced him in the dark, half a million phones held up watching. And that was just the live audience. Tonight, he had the full attention of the nation.

And he loved it.

"Tonight should have been a party, a celebration, a joyous declaration of all things British. All things that make this nation great. But a shadow has been cast over us. And it is a long, dark shadow indeed. What happened in the early hours of last Thursday was one of the most unimaginable tragedies our country has ever seen. Nearly 30,000 good men, women and children lost their lives in a terrible act. A terrible act of unspeakable terrorism.

"I stand before you to say: This should never have happened."

August raised his head, taking in the audience. They were transfixed, almost hypnotised, hanging on his every word. Right there, right then, he knew he had them.

"So tonight, let our celebrations be a tribute. A tribute to all the brave men and women who lost their lives in this obscene tragedy. Let us remember them and celebrate their lives.

"Allow me to introduce some very special ladies and gentlemen. People who I've got to know very well over the past few days. People who I have come to regard as 'friends'.

"I give you… The Monolith Nine!"

To the right of the stage, a stand lit up. The surviving members of the disaster waved and bowed, unsure of their newfound celebrity.

"These good people," he continued sincerely. "These strong people, I promise you, they will want for nothing!"

A respectful applause rippled through the crowd.

"As I look out, I see proud faces, strong faces. I do not see a nation cowed in fear. I see bravery. I see hope. I see courage."

August shifted his stance and slowly

paced across the stage, the spotlight following him as he walked.

"Seventeen years ago, you, the British people were blinded by promises of previous governments, you had lost touch with honour and freedom, you had lost everything. Before that day, God had withheld his blessing from our people. Dissension and hatred had descended upon us. With profound distress, millions of the best people of Britannica, men and women from all walks of life had seen the unity of the nation vanishing away, dissolving in a confusion of political and personal opinions, economic interests, and ideological differences."

He hung his head, shamed. "The misery of our people was horrible to behold. Just horrible."

"Millions of workers were unemployed and starving; the working classes impoverished. Decades of austerity nearly destroyed Britannica - the richest and fairest corners of this nation turned into a smoking heap of ruins.

"But it was in those hours when our hearts were troubled, when we struggled with the future of our great nation, that a new party was born! The Puritan Party!

The crowd applauded again, louder this time.

August allowed himself the tiniest of smiles - the old German speech he had found on the feeds was actually working.

"The inheritance which fell to us was indeed, a terrible one. The task with which we were faced was the hardest which had fallen to any government in living memory. But we were filled with unbounded confidence, for we believed in the people. We believed in *the will* of the people!

"The Puritan Government regarded its first and foremost duty was to revive in the nation the spirit of unity and cooperation. We preserved and defended those basic principles on which our nation was built. We regard Christianity as the foundation of our national morality, and the family as the basis of national life. Anarchy was replaced by a Puritan discipline as the guiding principle of our national life. The Puritan Government did, with iron determination and unshakable steadfastness of purpose, rescue the people from the quagmire into which they had fallen, overcoming unemployment and provide the conditions necessary for a revival in trade and commerce.

"May God Almighty give our work blessing, strengthen our purpose, and endow us with wisdom and the trust of our people, for we are fighting not for ourselves but for Britannica!!"

The crowd cheered and August grinned, soaking up the adulation.

Who needs a speechwriter? He thought. *This is easy.*

"If Britannica is to maintain this political

and economic revival, one decisive step is absolutely necessary: Overcoming the menace of Christian extremism in Britannica. We of this Government feel responsible for the restoration of orderly life in the nation and for the final elimination of extremism in any form. We recognize no extremist, we see only the British people, millions of good, honest people who will either overcome together the difficulties of these times or be overcome by them.

"As with any evil regime, take out its leader and the system unravels. Terror cells fragment, lose direction. They wither and die. You kill the root, the whole tree rots away."

He walked to the centre of the stage in thought. "Which is why I'm pleased to make this announcement - we have a very special guest here tonight, very special indeed. I promised you the centenary celebrations would be special, and what could be more special than the execution of the leader of the Christian Extremists!"

Arms wide open, he grinned.

"Ladies, gentlemen and everyone in between, I give you... Purity St. George!"

58. THE SUN ALWAYS SHINES ON TV

"**M**iss St. George, you're live to the nation. Please do not swear!" said August to the camera. On the screen, Hattie had taken the golden hood from its ceremonial cushion and pulled it over Purity's hair. Her face filled the giant screen, edge to edge.

She squinted down the lens. "Fuck you."

The crowd gasped in collective shock and the transmission was disconnected instantly. The sound could have been censored automatically of course, but August was counting on Purity getting in one last act of defiance and she hadn't disappointed. The crowd booed.

Never underestimate the public's capacity to

be offended, he thought.

"My, my... I can only apologise for the language used there. Guests are given strict instructions on how to behave - this broadcast *is* going out live to every television and feed in the country right now, after all. She is incapable of following *any* rules or regulations, it seems."

In the VIP gallery, Maud Slocombe peered over the top of her horn-rimmed spectacles and squinted at the image on the screen. The girl's hair was different, but there was a familiarity about the eyes. She tugged the sleeve of Mr Humphries in the chair next to her.

"Is that...?"

"The girl," he replied. "It's the girl who saved us."

59. EVERYTHING CHANGES

Hattie held the hood above Purity's eyes and they stood face to face in an uncomfortably intimate moment.

"At this point, they usually ask the convict if they have any last words," said Hattie quietly. "But I only want to know one thing. Why did you do it, Purity?"

"Do what?"

"All of it."

Purity blinked in the eerie twilight of the tower. She had travelled so far in such little time for nothing and she was tired. So very, very tired.

"I just wanted to make a difference," she said, tipping her head back and closing her eyes.

"My dad told me you can't change the world on your own," she remembered, smiling. "But if you can make a person think, you can change their mind. If you can change a mind, you can change a belief. If you can change a belief, you can change a culture. And if you can change a culture… well then, maybe, just maybe, you *can* save the world."

Purity opened her eyes and looked directly at her captor, serene, at peace with the world.

"If I've made anyone think, if I've changed even *one* mind, it was worth it."

Hattie turned the lethal medical instrument over in her hands, lost in thought. It suddenly felt very heavy in her palm.

If I've changed even one mind, it was worth it.

She pulled the golden hood down concealing Purity's face and gently placed the gun against her bare neck.

"See you on the other side, bitch!" cried Lister, leering against her cell bars.

Hattie squeezed the trigger.

60. THE FINAL COUNTDOWN

"And if you've only just tuned in, where have you been?!?"

On the giant mobile screens arranged around Hyde Park, the people watched the live broadcast. Not only on the giant monitors, but on their phones, tablets, watches, laptops... indeed everywhere. The episode of Noosenight was simultaneously transmitted live across every tv channel, radio channel and every feed - anyone using any device would have no choice but to watch it. 60 minutes of compulsory entertainment, force-fed to the nation every week while a faceless, regionally nonspecific male voice commentated over excitedly.

"You've joined us at a very important time. We're only a few moments away, when the doors of Transgression Tower finally open and that dastardly recidivist will be revealed, "he said, rolling his r's like a machine gun.

The camera swung across the crowds gathered outside Buckingham Palace and focused on the last float of the procession - the candy-striped fairground slide parked by the main stage.

"Found guilty of terrorism and the largest multiple murder in Britannica's history, can you believe that? She has been sentenced to over 32,000 consecutive life sentences with no chance of parole. Now that's going to drag, let me tell you - by my reckoning she should be out sometime in the year 34,000AD."

The view zoomed in on the Elf who pranced and danced before the crowd.

"As is tradition, she will be greeted from the tower by the nation's favourite, the National Elf, who will lead her through the Choir Invisibule."

The broadcast switched views to two dozen figures dressed in white hooded robes. They stood in lines on either side of the walkway, palms pressed together in prayer, heads bowed.

"Today, I'm told - and this is very exciting - they will be performing a moving tribute specially chosen for the occasion, so that's something to watch out for."

The camera tracked slowly past the motionless, ghostly figures stood in silence.

"Then she will reach the end of the stage, and the end of her sorry journey where she will finally pay the price for her crimes. The ultimate price."

At the back of the stage, an unusual configuration of bars, struts and pulleys squatted in the shadows like some surreal mechanical spider.

"And don't forget, after the main show tonight you can tune in to PBC2 and catch up on all the backstage gossip with those Noose Women. Now, I know Noosenight's Sunday hangings have become a regular fixture in the schedules, I don't know about you but I always make sure I'm near a screen with a cup of tea after Songs Of Praise finishes. But, no, this year, they thought, as it falls on Purity Day they'd do something a little bit different. A little bit bigger."

The contraption creaked and shuddered forward into the light.

"Obviously they are bound by broadcasting regulations, so we can't show any blood or indeed their faces. And it can't be too gruesome, we do have to remember our younger viewers after all. It seems only right then, on the anniversary of the Purity party, that we look back, that we celebrate the old ways. That we pay our respect to the past that has shaped who we are today."

Chains clanked and rattled as the machine

trundled into view.

"Well, they had promised surprises this year, they had promised something new... and there it is. Would you just look at that!"

A stocky mobile base on giant spoked wheels carried two long wooden arms hinged with a counterweight at the back. The arms extended forward and a simple wooden chair dangled from the end.

"Handcrafted in Newcastle in oak and cast iron, using a combination of traditional and modern techniques, the stool recreates the machinery as favoured by James VI in 1597. The 'cucking' or 'ducking' stool, as it was known, was the most popular form of punishment at that time. Now if, like me, you thought these were just used to detect witches, then you'd be wrong!

"No, they were more commonly used as punishment. Smaller crimes might only involve two or three 'dunkings', more serious infractions, well, the sky's the limit! The Iron Lady, they're calling it. A solid, ruthless, uncompromising machine.

"I'm sure this is... oh, wait... we have movement! Yes, we have movement. The doors are opening on Transgression Tower!"

The image blurred sideways, switching to a closer fuzzy view of the striped fairground slide. It snapped into focus on the Elf pulling the ornate doors at its base open. Inside, a figure waited.

"And there she is, the star of tonight Purity Day celebrations. Convicted murderer, anarchist and terrorist leader... Purity. St. George!"

The camera found the orange jump suited figure in the doorway, arms bound together and zoomed in on the silver hood pulled tight to protect viewers sensibilities. The caption overlaying the broadcast simply read:

PURITY ST. GEORGE - TERRORIST

Warren 'Wingnut' Wingford tapped the tablet screen, pausing the display. He spoke quietly into the microphone on his headset.

"Target sighted, I have eyes on the prize. We are good to go."

61. REBEL REBEL

"Purity is moving south, I repeat south along Spur Road."

High above the main stage in a narrow platform behind the main screen, Warren sat cross legged on a metal gantry surrounded by technology. He cradled a tablet in one arm and typed one fingered on a laptop balanced on a splinted knee. Half a dozen smartphones of differing shapes and sizes lay in a straight line by his feet, cables running between them. He pinched the glass surface of the tablet, zooming in on the orange suited girl in the golden hood embossed with silver.

"Oh P," Warren whispered, "what have they done to you?"

The event music died away, replaced now by a single, monotonous drum beat. Slow, funereal, accompanied by an eerie melodic chanting.

If it was a song, Warren didn't recognise it.

The National Elf slow-danced and slow-pranced in time with the canticle, leading the blind prisoner on a long chain through the crowd like a wounded pet. The people booed and spat, throwing cartons and rubbish at her. Some had come prepared for the event and threw rotting fruit or vegetables. In the olden days she may have been pelted with eggs, but these days even eggs were afforded exactly the same rights as animals, so popup stalls all over the event now sold easily throwable biodegradable merchandise. The crowd, red faced and angry pushed against the barriers on either side of the road, bawling and shouting.

"Hangin's too good fer yer!" yelled a taxi driver from Dagenham hurling a browning lettuce, the vegetable glancing off the golden hood leaving a greasy mark.

"Yeah, go back to where you came from!"

"Murderer!"

"Traitor!"

The chanting grew louder, picking up pace - a grim death march promising no good at the end of it. The Elf yanked the chain, pulling his pet away from the mob, steering her towards the stage. After the previous years' disaster with the sacrifice falling and breaking their neck before they had even reached the noose, a ramp had now been set up in place of steps.

"Purity is on the ramp," muttered Warren,

peering down through a narrow gap in the lighting array. "You should have eyes on her any second."

From his crow's nest he could see the heads of the Choir far below arranged in perfect lines, and among them, the top of the Elf's black hat and Purity's golden hood sparkling under the stage light. The Elf and his offering paused. Lined up on either side of them were the men, women and otherwise of the Church's prestigious most holy musical ensemble - The Choir Invisibule, clapping and swaying in harmony.

Handpicked and highly trained, the choristers spent years living a reclusive, ascetic lifestyle, fully devoting their lives and voices to God. They wore pale, full length robes with wide, elaborate hoods casting dark shadows over the faces - the Choir were a force to be heard, not seen. The lament - a thoughtful introspection on reaching The End of The Road - reached its crescendo, the Choir waving their arms high in holy praise. Lowering their heads, they filed off the stage in an awkward protracted silence and a subdued, respectful applause rippled through the audience, punctuated by the odd, out-of-place whistle.

Boyz ll Men would have been proud.

The lights dimmed and all the spotlights merged into one, highlighting the gargantuan ducking contraption at the end of the stage.

Warren tapped a function key on the laptop and pulled up the itinerary.

"Final approach," he said into the microphone.

"The Iron Lady."

62. A KIND OF MAGIC

In silence, the National Elf secured his prisoner in the handcrafted wooden chair, locking the bulky wooden clamps over both her arms and fastening the buckles across the chest of the orange jumpsuit. He rattled them dramatically, demonstrating their security to the audience as if he were a magician in a performance.

Which, in truth, he was.

He bent over, pretending to tighten a strap, his comically oversized crooked beak of a nose brushing intimately close to the golden hood.

"Two sweeteners, Expresso?" whispered the Elf.

63. SONGS FROM THE BIG CHAIR

"Finally," sighed August, as the screens flared into life. "I thought they'd never get on with it."

"It *is* quite a build-up," replied Archbishop Runcible.

The chair and its precious cargo lifted off the podium, raising and turning on a complex system of gears and pulleys. On the main screen, and replicated on the others across the Park, a pre-recorded montage began to play - news and feed clips set to music chronicling Purity's rise to fame. Or infamy.

"Purity St. George was born and raised in this, our greatest city, only minutes from the Monoliths," began the generic voiceover. "From an early age, like many teenagers she demonstrated rebellious tendencies..."

In grainy black and white, Purity turned in her school corridor and stuck her tongue out, two fingers raised to the camera.

"But unlike many teenagers she chose to channel this destructively.... indulging in hate crime..."

A closeup of the 'defaced' #ALLLIVESMATTER poster filled the screens.

"Constantly in trouble with the constabulary, damaging public property..."

Now shouldercam footage of her being pursued over garden fences.

"Until coercing other like-minded fanatics into joining her terror cell. Responsible for a wave of violence and terror on this fair nation and the plotting of vile atrocities against our duly elected government."

A lamppost CCTV view showed Purity and Samson kneeling over the body of a security guard by the road which faded into shaky phone captures of Purity pleading with Ariel in the middle of panicking protesters.

The giant arm of the Iron Lady rotated, extending hydraulically and the chair swung over the cheering masses lit by a fit-inducing strobe of phone camera flashes.

"She escaped incarceration, crippling an already weakened Health Service..."

A digital machine scan of her palm and the numbers 29 imprinted there zoomed in followed by the results of her profiling test, the words blown up in giant type.

I WILL BE BURNING DOWN PARLIAMENT KILLING EVERYONE INSIDE.

Blurred, high contrast nightcam video of the Health Camp explosions burst across the screens, intermingled with CCTV ground level recordings from the camp.

"..and went into hiding where she plotted her greatest and final atrocity - the ultimate revenge on this beautiful city and its law abiding citizens."

Helmet cam recordings from Team Rod, Jane and Freddy flashed past. Gabriel rapidly firing a pistol, soldiers trapped in a lift, a drone exploding.

"Why did she choose this? What drove her? Maybe she just didn't like the people enjoying their freedoms. Maybe she envied the dream of a home for everyone, the dream the Monoliths represented. Maybe, just maybe it was living so close to the dream that pushed her over the edge."

In the VIP area, Maud stood up and pointed at the screen shouting as loud as she could, "No! That's not what happened!"

Seeing her distress, the audience nearby strained to hear her, but her voice, tiny and frail, was trampled under the volume of the presentation. She tapped at her lapel microphone and wiggled the wire. "Is this on? Is this thing on?

Hello?"

Creaking and juddering, the dunking chair crossed Spur Road and came to a stop above the St. James Park Lake. The montage ended on a selfie of two teenagers: Purity and Warren smiling at the camera with Monolith One lit by the sunset behind them.

A memory of simpler, more innocent times.

"Maybe we will never know. What we do know, is this: Purity St. George has been found guilty of high treason."

The image faded to black.

"The sentence is death."

The National Elf pushed a long wooden lever and the chair plunged into the black, icy waters of the lake, instantly vanishing beneath the surface.

"Yes!" cried August, fist-pumping the air.

64. PANIC

"Come on, Wingnut. What's taking you?" crackled Tom's voice.

Warren pulled the connector from one of the smartphones and plugged it into the next, hammering the virtual buttons on his tablet. A complex tangle of wires hung from the devices and fed into an exposed electrical panel on the gantry.

"I know... going as fast as I can."

Being of such importance to the government, Noosenight - the weekly hour of compulsory propaganda - was protected by the highest security protocols available. Certainly, every previous attempt to hijack the signal had ended in failure. There was simply no way for anyone to stop, redirect or change the broadcast - it was literally unstoppable.

Warren snatched a cable from the back of

the laptop and piggybacked the smartphone to another, then swapped a connector on the wall.

Speaking from inside the Elf's giant head, Tom spoke into his headset, "Purity's under the water, we're running out of time!"

"I know," Warren hissed.

"She's already been down there for…"

"I KNOW!"

Tom tightened his hand on the ornate lever. This wasn't what was supposed to happen, this wasn't the plan.

How long *had* she been under?

He looked at the jeering crowd then up at the long oak arm stretching over the lake and made a decision. He pulled the lever back hard. Pulleys and gears clattered and rattled as the engine responded instantly, winding the chain back in and lifting the dunking chair up out of the lake. The crowd cheered as the chair and its occupant swung wildly, dripping water on the people closest to the shore.

August blinked, confusion in his eyes. "What? What's going on!?! That's not supposed to happen already!"

He pointed at the Elf. "You there! Put her back! Put her back in!"

But the Elf wasn't listening - he was too busy bowing to the audience.

August looked up at Purity still strapped into the chair, choking and spluttering, straining against her restraints to break free. This also did not go unnoticed by the crowd. Seeing the hangings on tv, on a screen was easy, distancing, but witnessing this distress, this slow and painful torture first hand, that was something else entirely. The cheering died down. In the front row some children started crying and some isolated booing started.

With an air of panic, the Prime Minister scrambled down the aluminium steps and onto the stage.

"Get her back in!" he growled, sprinting as fast as his stubby legs would carry him, across the platform towards the Elf. "Now!"

The Prime Minister struck the Elf mid bow, his full weight behind his shoulder. Caught unaware, Tom toppled onto his side, his head striking the aluminium scaffolding with a crack. Eyes bulging like a madman, August flung himself around the lever and pushed it forward to it's full extent. The Iron Lady hissed as pneumatic brakes released and the chains ratcheted noisily, dropping the chair sharply back into the lake in a torrent of water.

"You!" he panted, pointing at the Elf, "You are *never* working here again!"

August hugged the lever as tight as a 70s celebrity clutching an alibi and watched as the ripples in the lake subsided. Bubbles popped on the surface around the chain, first in a busy mass but soon tapering out in sparse clusters. There was no cheering from the crowd this time - other than the odd wailing of a child, the people were silent.

August closed his eyes and sighed - maybe next time they should go back to simple hangings. But give it time, the people would understand, the people would get it.

Everything was back on track. No more drama. No more surprises.

The Iron Lady had sung.

The main screen flickered and he was suddenly looking at himself.

"The people?" sneered the face on the colossal display.

"Fuck the people."

65. PEOPLE ARE PEOPLE

A fuzzy, bleached shot of the Health Camp came into focus on the giant screen, the old, wrought iron gate sharp in the foreground. REPAIR. REJUVENATE. RECYCLE. The image shook, focusing on a huge tower belching smoke into the sky as lost and broken souls in dressing gowns shambled aimlessly like zombies across harshly lit streets.

August's eyes grew wider and wider, almost bursting from his ruddy face.

"Where... Where is this coming from?" he panicked, spittle flying from his lips. "Make it stop! Make it stop!!!"

The view faded to containers overflowing with bloody gowns. Then dozens of skulls and femurs burning deep within a furnace and rows of bloody rusting saws and tools glistening in the firelight.

The unrest in the crowd became more tangible as parents covered their children's eyes and the booing became less isolated.

In the control booth, the wall of monitors all showed the same footage while technicians and operators pushed buttons and toggled levers ineffectually.

"It's not us, sir!" cried the producer over his earpiece. "We don't know where it's coming from."

The images kept coming. A nurse cowering in fear with blind eyes and a sewed mouth. A homeless man in an operating theatre, the Elf hunched over with a scalpel in one hand and power drill in the other.

"Just bloody well turn them *all* off then!"

"We... we can't," said the operator, flustered. "The screens are locked to broadcast for the full hour. It's... it's a security feature."

August watched a closeup of a corpse, pale and waxy. Where eyes once gazed gaping black sockets remained, its mouth messily sewn shut, thick wiry thread twisting through the cracked lips like barbed wire.

"Security feature? Security feature!?!"

Refrigerated containers full of bodily organs - livers, brains, kidneys. Canisters of blood. Canvasses of stretched skin. Teeth. Hair. Gaunt patients wandering dazed through smoke filled ruins. Guards surrounding inmates, beating them with sticks.

On the lighting gantry high above the stage, Warren lowered his head, exhausted while Purity's AOJI 9, hot in his hand, fed a steady stream of video directly onto the screens.

There was no way of stopping the public broadcast, he knew that.

And in the end, he hadn't even tried.

All the tv cameras, everyone's tablets, everyone's phones, they would all be pointed at the stage and the testimony unfolding on the giant screens. One message uploaded to the feed would be lost in the churn, ignored. But half a million messages broadcasting simultaneously to the entire country? Every man, woman, lesbian, gay, bisexual, transgender, transsexual, queer, questioning, intersex, asexual, ally, pansexual, child and animal would see it.

The people would witness it, the people would record it and the people would upload it. It would be the people that broadcast the message for him. It would be the people that bore witness and the people that spread the message.

A testimony for the people, by the people.

The crowd surged forward against the barriers, the metal groaning under their weight. They yelled and shouted, now brandishing their flags like weapons. August whimpered and hunkered down further still on the lever. A lettuce flew over the crowd, exploding messily against the Iron Lady.

Sensing the shift in public mood, constables quickly moved in, forming a formidable line between the barriers and the stage. The show of force; however, only seemed to incense the people even more. Cartons and cans sailed overhead, ricocheting off constable's helmets.

Hurled high, a bottle of Sunny D-Spair smashed into a spotlight, bursting in a shower of synthetic orange juice, sparks and hot glass beside Warren. He flinched, instinctively shielding his face and the laptop tipped from his knee. A tiny yelp escaped his lips as he flailed to grab it, but it was already out of reach. In a blink, the cables pulled taut and snapped, killing the video feed and leaving the hardware tumbling towards the stage.

August blinked in the sudden unexpected darkness - the shame of his government's vilest secrets still raw, seared into the retinas of the nation. Even by his own standards, this was shaping up to be one of the monumentally worst days ever.

Maybe that was the end of it. No more surp...

The laptop exploded into expensive shrapnel at his feet and bounced off the stage floor into the barriers, mangled and bent. He squinted up at the banks of lighting and walkways above the stage.

"There! Up there!" screamed August, seeing a shocked, fiery-haired face staring back.

"Get that ginger!"

66. I PREDICT A RIOT

"Wingnut, you complete and utter bungle," murmured Warren to himself. He limped along the narrow metal gantry behind the main screen, the splint clanging loudly on the mesh flooring as he dragged his leg behind him. To one side of him the now dead big screen, on the other, a framework of lighting banks and a very long drop. He reached the end of the walkway and afforded a quick glance backwards.

A constable was rapidly climbing up the access ladder onto the scaffolding, even from here he could see the shokstick and taser dangling from her belt - he was pretty sure she wasn't after a polite conversation. Beyond the officer, he could see - and hear - the frenzied audience shaking and rocking the barriers, the line of constables looking more and more agitated. Down was clearly not an option.

Warren grabbed the railing and climbed.

Tom picked himself up, dazed - the comical Elf mask had taken the brunt of the impact but his forehead now bleeding, throbbed insistently. The apparatus in the headpiece smoked and whined and he twisted the giant head free, throwing it to the ground. He gulped the fresh air down, so much better than the rank, recycled breath inside the mask and saw the chain still sank into the lake.

How long had he been out of it? How long had Purity been down there?

At the opposite end of the stage, Maud Slocombe left the relative safety of the VIP area and tiptoed through the debris of broken glass and greasy unfinished Novichok Noodle cartons. The Prime Minister, so fixated on the angry mob, only realised she was behind him when her handbag started beating his head.

"Stop that!" she whined. "She's just a girl!"

He yelped and fell back off the lever, covering his head as she got her second wind, raining down blow after blow on his bald patch.

"You horrible little man!" she scolded.

Seeing the Prime Minister under attack, a constable broke the line, drawing his taser. "Armed police!" he yelled, pulling the trigger. The electrified dart struck the pensioner square in the chest, charging 1200 volts directly into her frail 94-year-old heart. She inhaled sharply, her mouth desperately trying to form a sentence but instead collapsed to the stage.

Dead.

The Monolith Nine were now the Monolith Eight.

"Murderers!" shouted voices from the crowd.

The mob surged again.

The barriers tipped.

And fell.

Oblivious to the chaos unfolding beneath them, the constable aimed her weapon at Warren on the gantry above her. The electrified needle crackled past his ear and glanced off the handrail, spinning over the side.

Warren moaned, running as fast as his good leg would let him, but the hard fact was the constable was closing on him. He was only one floor away and it was obvious he could not outrun her.

The constable reloaded a cartridge into the taser and pointed it along the empty gantry.

"Nowhere to run, ginger. Might as well give yourself up now!" she shouted, glancing over the side. She was very near the top of the screen now - there was no denying it was a long way down to the stage.

Treading slowly, she reached the end of

the walkway, but he had already gone.

She frowned - for a man suffering with a ginger disability, he was fast.

The crowd attacked the police line in a spontaneous, chaotic wall of noise, limbs and makeshift weapons. Grandmothers and children fought alongside nurses and investment bankers. Young and old, poor and the rich, white and black, gay and straight... all brought together under a common goal no-one could have predicted. But even before the first blow had landed, the constables had their shoksticks drawn and ready. With a crackling hum they brought the charged batons down on the attacking horde. Harsh blue flashes cast strobing shadows as civilian after civilian fell, people scrambling and screaming to get away.

Tom cupped a hand to his earpiece. "Now, damn it. Now!"

From the sides of the stage, the pale, cloaked figures of the Choir Invisibule emerged ghostlike, leaping onto the police line from behind. There was no singing now, merely the sound of fists raining down on the constables, breaking ribs and snapping arms. Tom unsheathed the ceremonial Tickling Stick - a gleaming silver baseball bat - and proceeded to tickle the coppers most violently, sharing its joy and love equally among them. There were no favourites - the Tickling Stick had time for everyone. Skulls cracked and limbs shattered. Shoksticks and tasers were ripped from the constable's hands and tossed aside as the Acapella Singing Troupe of Purity Health Camp 06 wreaked Old Testament justice on the law folk.

And as quickly as it started, it was over. The skirmish, as bloody as it was, only actually lasted mere seconds; the street coppers no match for Tom's well-trained team.

The homeless had been practising more than just singing during their incarceration, it seemed.

The headless Elf approached the Prime Minister, shoving him aside as the annoyance he was and August fell, sprawling comically over the bodies of his protectors. Tom gripped the lever and heaved it back to its starting position. The chains clanked and rattled as the chair lifted out of the water once again. As it reached its full height, there was a loud grinding as gears shifted and the arm began retracting, swinging the wooden chair back round to the stage. The dunking stool hovered over the podium and landed with a bump, lake water dripping from the contraption and pooling on the boards.

Calmer now, the mob watched in silence, phones recording respectfully.

Tom looked at the limp, motionless body in the chair. He saw no movement, she must have been under for 6 or 7 minutes, at least.

No-one could have survived that.

Heart pounding, Warren watched the soles of the constable's feet through the corrugated floor as she moved away. Only when he saw her start climbing to the next level did he dare a slow, controlled exhale. Sandwiched under the gantry in a tight crawl space, Warren shuffled back towards the comms panel on this level. He dug his fingernails into the panel lid and it popped off easily exposing a familiar mess of cables. Contorting, he squeezed his arm into his jacket pocket and retrieved the last smartphone, still attached to a mass of wiring.

The battery was nearly dead but at least this time he knew what he was doing.

Tom stepped cautiously towards the hooded human sacrifice on the centre stage.

"Expresso?" he said softly, almost a whisper.

But there was no movement. Nothing. He took another step closer when the loudest gasp erupted from the golden hood. A thick, fluid heave mixed with a coarse, rasping cough.

"Expresso!" cried Tom in alarm.

"Oh, for God's sake!" cried August, wielding a taser - a taser he had liberated from his fallen guard. "Why won't she just die!?!"

He fired the dart at Tom, striking his neck and he toppled over in surprise, twitching erratically. August threw the pistol, instead lifting the Elf's bloodied ceremonial Tickling Stick from the floorboards.

Above him, the main screen suddenly lit up but he paid it no attention. In a fluid move, he swung the bat as hard as he could, striking the golden hood.

The crack of the skull was loud and shocking.

Grainy footage of the smirking face of Prime Minister Terrence August glared down, over his shoulder the cordoned off ruins of a bombed out KostlyKoffee in the rain. He leaned into the camera uncomfortably close to a woman reporter, raindrops running down his nose in high definition. He spoke through gritted teeth.

Warren had spent hours enhancing the audio and scrubbing out the background noise, but in the end he would be the first to admit it was worth it.

"You don't get it, do you?" echoed August's voice from the speakers, enhanced, crystal and clear. "I could commit murder on the steps of Buckingham Palace, and still be in power tomorrow!"

The video looped.

"...commit murder on the steps of Buckingham Palace, and still be in power..."

On stage, August swung the bat, a sickening red trickle bloomed in the fabric.

"...commit murder on the steps of Buckingham Palace..."

The stick landed again, the maroon trickle becoming a flood.

"...commit murder..."

The head under the hood deformed, lost its shape.

"...murder..."

He swung again, shattering collar bones.

"...murder..."

August stepped back, panting heavily, letting the Tickling Stick drop from his fingers. He coughed, wiping the spatter of blood from his eyes and turned to face the nation.

His nation.

In a silence, crushing, almost tangible, thousands upon thousands of faces stared back. Shocked and numbed. Horrified and disgusted. An open gallery of faces and phones.

Judging.

Recording.

He staggered backwards and fell against the bloody chair, exhausted.

"*That's* the way to do it," he whispered.

As one, the people mobbed the stage with cries of rage and loss, of anger and righteous revenge. They swamped August, piling on top of him, kicking him, punching him, biting him, hitting him, breaking him. A nation's grief manifested in physical violence. Extreme physical violence. August vanished under the people, but the people kept coming - they came to him until they had taken everything and he had nothing left to give.

And then they took some more.

But he ought to be pleased.

Finally, *genuinely*, he was carrying out the will of the people.

EPILOGUE 1.
LIKE A PRAYER

"How is he?" asked Archbishop Runcible. The Prime Minister had been rushed to St. Rylan's Royal under police convoy and now lay strapped to a hospital bed in a secure wing, unconscious. Multiple drips dangled above him feeding drugs into his battered limbs and torso while a myriad of needles and tubes entered his body. Electrodes fastened to his misshapen head and chest led to a stack of gleaming white medical equipment where screens monitored his vital statistics with a steady, monotonous blip.

By anyone's standards, the beating had been severe. Dislocated fingers hung from shattered hands on fractured arms, jagged bones protruding from blackened, torn skin. One leg bent sickeningly at the knee while the other was twisted at an alarming, impossible angle, the foot nearly pointing backwards. Hair had been torn from his head in ugly welts and his jaw hung slackly under a flattened purple nose. One eye was swollen closed like a bloody watermelon while the other... well, the other was no longer there. Internally, collapsed lungs, a ruptured spleen and punctured bowels held the promise of a lifetime of hospital visits and long and painful days ahead if he survived.

If he survived.

"I think it's safe to say he'll never play the piano again," said Deputy Prime Minister Ramona.

By the time the ambulances had managed to fight through the crowds by the Palace, the angry mob had dispersed, leaving the beaten, disfigured body of Terrence August laying unceremoniously ignored.

On reviewing the official recordings, Police were left trying to identify over a thousand civilians from the epicentre of the beating. An impossible task, and one where they knew they would never realistically find the actual perpetrators - invariably settling on choosing a scapegoat from the footage and prosecuting them very publically for it.

Truth or no truth, justice must be seen to be done, after all.

"On the plus side," said Ramona, "The girl's

dead, at least."

Emergency services had erected privacy screens around the ducking stool and quietly took down Purity's body away from the prying eyes of the public. There was no fuss, no fanfare.

Nothing to see here, move on.

"That's one less problem to worry about," she finished.

"I don't know," countered the Archbishop, "Jesus did some of his best work after his death."

Ramona frowned, not really understanding. She tapped one of the hanging bags of plasma, watching the fluid drip into the airlock.

She sighed. "The paranoid old bastard's left us in a right pickle."

"What do you mean?"

"It's not common knowledge so you're probably not aware of this, but in the last few months August was convinced there were those in the party working against him, vying to have him removed. Can you believe that? He actually thought I was plotting some kind of takeover."

Runcible was more than aware of this state of affairs but said nothing, instead settling for raising a bushy, grey eyebrow quizzically.

"I don't know how or when he did it, but he repealed the ministerial law of succession," she continued. "Now, I, or *any* member of the party for that matter, won't automatically take his place. A Prime Minister can only be *voted* in or out."

August's sheets were starting to stain with blood and the room smelled of meat. Real meat, not that synthetic nonsense the public had to tolerate.

"He looks quite voted out, to me," said Runcible.

The Deputy frowned. Was that a joke?

"No, he needs to be democratically *voted* out," she explained, "*By the people*. Then, and only then can the successor be democratically voted in."

"That doesn't seem unreasonable - It's like a... safety valve, if you will... to protect democracy."

She nodded. "Yes. But the whole process... it could take months."

Deputy Ramona's shoulders slumped in defeat and she rubbed her forehead. "The government's in freefall."

The Archbishop opened the blinds slowly allowing striped morning sunlight to flood into the room, savouring the tingling warmth on his skin. He squinted at the sun rising over the skyline of the great City - commuters rushing to work, double parked vans making deliveries, buses and taxis clogging the streets. Just people living their lives, going about their business on a new day. A new day promising endless possibilities.

A new dawn.

When he finally spoke, it was calm, almost

contemplative.

"It very much sounds to me like you need a third party to step in. Someone just to keep their hands on the wheel, keep the engine ticking over, so to speak. Until you can sort this mess out, at least."

"An interim leader," pondered Ramona. "Yes. Yes, that could work."

"They'd have to be someone impartial, mind. Neutral, Unrelated to either party, yet still trusted by the people."

Ramona shielded her eyes against the Archbishop silhouetted in the sunlight. "Would you... do you think *you* could do it?"

Runcible turned slowly in mock surprise. "My dear girl, I wasn't suggesting..."

"No, wait... it makes perfect sense. There's no-one more impartial - the Church has always sat outside of party politics and you have to be one of the most trusted figures in Britannica."

The Archbishop stuttered. "This is highly irregular. I'd have to..."

"Please?"

The life support machine pinged in the prolonged silence and Runcible squeezed the garish, gold crucifix dangling from his neck.

"This is only until August recovers?" he asked.

"Or he's voted out, yes."

Runcible gently raised the cross to his lips and kissed it.

"Very well, it would be my honour."

He smiled. August would need round the clock medical care for the foreseeable future. Expert care in a private, secure facility far away from the people who despised him - it was only fitting to send him to one of his flagship Health Camps.

And with the sitting Prime Minister out of the way, well, who knew what other laws might need looking at?

Visibly relieved, Ramona asked, "What are you going to do first?"

The Archbishop thought for a moment.

"You know, the nation has suffered long enough. The decent, hard working citizens of Britannica have spent too long on their hands and knees scrabbling around in the dark in misery and despair. The people need to see there is light at the end of the tunnel. You know what this country really needs?"

Ramona raised her eyebrows expectantly, waiting on his answer.

Runcible lowered his voice until it was almost a purr.

"A royal wedding," he said.
"Now get me the Queen."

EPILOGUE 2. SAY HELLO, WAVE GOODBYE

The porter wheeled the body into the temperature-controlled mortuary deep under St. Rylan's Royal Hospital. This far underground, the quiet was broken only by the hum of refrigeration units and the rattle of trolley wheels on the black and white tiled floor. A dozen square stainless-steel doors lined the wall, each housing a retractable, airtight chamber.

This was where they stored the dead.

The porter parked the gurney under an empty compartment and lowered the side bars. He didn't really do politics, but he knew exactly who the body was before him - he had seen the chaos of the live broadcast the night before.

Everyone had, it was still dominating the feeds this morning and would for some time to come.

The manacles and chains had been cut free, but she still wore the one-piece jumpsuit and hood - the body remaining untouched for the autopsy later. The shoulders of the outfit were stained a deep, dark red and the hood, once golden, was now a sickening patchwork of bloody black.

Working down here he had seen some sights, but what they had done to that poor girl made him shudder - you wouldn't do that to an animal.

A small, bronze ID tag hung from a band around her bruised wrist and he turned it over in the neon strip light.

MS. PURITY DAVID ST. GEORGE - DECEASED

"Sorry, love," he apologised as he pulled open the metal door. It hissed smoothly on pneumatic hinges and fine tendrils of cold mist trickled out. He unlocked the trolley bed and pushed. It was designed to slide into the compartments with the minimum of effort and it clattered easily along it's rails. Mid clatter, he paused with a frown on his brow. The ID tag swung back and forth, glinting in the artificial light - something about it bothered him.

No, not the tag.

The hand.

He slid the gurney back slightly and took

hold of Purity's pale, stiff fingers. He had seen it on the video last night, and on the breakfast feed this morning - that montage of everything Purity had done, all the crimes she had committed. The numbers branded in the middle of her right palm.

    Red 29.
    Slowly, he turned her hand over.
    It was blank.

EPILOGUE 3. THERE IS A LIGHT THAT NEVER GOES OUT

The barista had a smile like a coffee cup - full and inviting.

"I'm terribly sorry, but it appears your payment has been declined," he said softly, somehow managing to combine warmth and concern in equal spoonfuls.

Hattie Simms blinked at the contactless terminal, puzzled. There should be more than enough money on her account for a Strawberry Latte and Espresso Grande, but there it was in black and white.

PAYMENT DECLINED

The silver haired barista waved the payment machine under Hattie's nose like a hi-tech donation tray, respectfully taking donations from customers' accounts. He was older than typical KostlyKoffee staff but was keen, sensitive with kind eyes.

"Would you like to try again?" he asked gently.

In the weeks following Purity Day, Hattie had kept a low profile.

If official sources were to be believed - and she, more than anyone knew they rarely could - August was in a coma. The Monolith Eight and relatives of those killed in the disaster had banded together, raising a multibillion pound class action lawsuit against a dozen ministers, the Mayor and specifically the Prime Minister. It was clear he would never hold office again, indeed the closest he would probably get to politics would be on the receiving end of a Noosenight special.

Archbishop Runcible's first act in power was to scrap the Monolith Program. The towers were scheduled for complete demolition; the land returned to greenfields and a shrine of remembrance built at its heart.

Secondly, he demanded a full and frank inquiry into the Health Camps.

Of course.

Lastly, in a landmark speech designed to win hearts and minds, he warned terrorists their days were numbered, their acts of war on Britannica's soil would not be countenanced. Ministers were already drawing up new security measures, new plans, new ways to track down and defeat those who would do harm against this mighty nation.

If there was to be war, Runcible had said, it would be on his terms.

And it would be Holy.

Purity Day had left a mark, that much was sure - the feed seeming to unearth fresh footage of the nights atrocities on a daily basis. And every time Hattie saw the procession from new and exciting camera angles, she was reminded of her last conversation with Purity St. George.

Every single time.

"I just wanted to make a difference," Purity had said inside the mobile, candy striped tower. "My dad told me you can't change the world on your own, but if you can make a person think, you can change their mind. If you can change a mind, you can change a belief. If you can change a belief, you can change a culture. And if you can change a culture... well then, maybe, just maybe, you *can* save the world. If I've made anyone think, if I've changed even *one* mind, it was worth it."

Hattie pulled the golden hood down over Purity's face and gently placed the drug injection gun against her bare neck.

Lister, her face squeezed against the cell bars leered, "See you on the other side, bitch!"

Hattie squeezed the trigger and swung the gun around between the bars, planting it firmly on Lister's throat. The weapon barked a pneumatic hiss as the lethal sedative flooded her system.

Lister gurgled and gasped hoarsely trying to clutch at her neck and fell back onto the bed. Her body twitched briefly, then relaxed, her breathing shallow and steady, eyes staring vacantly.

"What are you doing? What's going on?" stammered Purity.

"Something I should have done a long time ago," replied Hattie peeling off the golden hood and unlocking her restraints.

Purity rubbed the circulation back into her wrists. "I don't understand."

Hattie pried open the wooden floor hatch revealing the road trundling past below. Rungs led down to a mechanic's service space nestled in darkness behind the huge caterpillar tracks.

"Go on! Go!" she urged, bundling Purity onto the ladder. "You'll be safe down there. After the float leaves the stage it'll travel up Constitution Hill back to the depot. You'll be long gone before anyone finds out."

"Why are you doing this?" she asked. "You don't know me. You don't owe me anything."

If I've changed even one mind, it was worth it.

Hattie looked at the teenager who had single handedly shut down every vile plan and scheme the government had raised, and smiled.

"You changed a mind."

Officer Roni Lister, as slight as she was, was only a vague match for Purity's size and shape, but it was close enough - the public expected an orange suit and a golden hood and that's what the public got. Lister was not a good person by any stretch of the imagination, but the sedative ensured she would have felt very little at the end.

At least that's what Hattie told herself.

We're not barbarians.

Words she still clung to.

In the days that followed, new groups appeared on the feed. At first only one or two, but within weeks there were hundreds. Followers of Purity's life story, they had chronicled and archived every post, photo, video or comment she had ever made, preserving them for future generations. Living by her moral code, advocates of her work.

They called themselves Purists.

Hattie had thought long and hard about reaching out to them but in the end, she didn't need to. Three days ago, an email arrived in her inbox. That in itself was unusual, who used email anymore? There was no message, just a photo attachment of a high street receipt for a Strawberry Latte and an Espresso Grande.

And two sweeteners.

Which was why now, exactly one hundred days after the fateful events of Purity Day, Hattie Simms found herself on New Islington high street in the extensively renovated branch of KostlyKoffee.

The silver haired barista offered her the payment device again.

"Would you like to try again?" he asked gently.

Hattie held her smartphone over the device again.

Again, the warning buzzer buzzed.

The Silver Barista slotted the reader back in its holder and located a pristine laminated card pinned to the till. He studied it thoughtfully before returning it to its spot.

He lowered his voice, "Can I ask you to come through to the office?"

Hattie glanced around the coffee shop. Everyone was going about their business, working on laptops, playing on phones.

She was invisible.

Nervously, she nodded and he raised open the counter on hinges to allow her through. He ushered her down a narrow, unremarkable corridor to an unremarkable metal door. He pushed his thumb against a single lit button on the wall and the door slid aside revealing a cramped elevator.

Silver Barista held the doors open, "Ladies first."

She smiled at his old school disregard for gender neutrality or equality and stepped inside. It was only as she had entered the cabin she noticed the mark on his hand - a small grey number tattooed in the centre of his palm.

She opened her mouth to speak but the door was already moving behind her.

"Hey!" yelled Hattie, but the door closed on his sympathetic smile, the lurch in her stomach telling her the room was descending.

The journey was short and Hattie emerged in a dimly lit, musty subterranean tunnel. A string of flickering yellow lamps hung from the wall, running the length of the corridor and ended at a large round iron door. The door was ajar and light poured through the gap together with voices, conversation and laughter.

Hattie approached cautiously, straining to hear and rested her hand on the cold, rusted metal.

"Hattie!" shouted a voice, "Come in. Come in!"

The chamber was large and circular,

capped with an elaborate domed ceiling. A giant marble crucifix dominated the main wall and a bank of monitors showed live feeds continuously.

Hattie, however, noticed none of these things.

All she saw was the people.

Dozens of people filled the room. People of every age, ethnicity, gender and haircut sat on ledges and balconies, filled alcoves and arches. Thomas Blodwyn Jones, the homeless man in the Elf costume, looked up from the maps strewn across the large round table and smiled.

It wasn't toothless.

On crutches, Warren 'Wingnut' Wingford lowered his tablet and nodded at Hattie.

The last figure, a girl, teenage but wise beyond her years, turned around and grinned.

"We've been expecting you," said Purity.

A small black bulldog broke through the group and scampered towards her yapping, it's claws skidding on the shiny floor. It planted its bottom at her feet, panting with its pink tongue hanging out. The dog raised itself up on its hind legs and saluted.

A Nazi salute.

Laughter erupted through the audience and a teenage girl, head shaved, clinical gown stepped forward. Hattie's sister.

Thank you, Hattie mouthed.

"It was the least I could do," said Purity.

The art of being invisible, hiding in plain sight, that's what Tom had called it. The ability to come and go as you please. They were never going to change the world with August breathing down their necks but now, with the world thinking she was dead maybe, just maybe, she might have a chance.

Hattie looked at the devoted gathering, all hanging off Purity's every word. This girl had brought them all together, made people think. She had given them a belief.

It was a movement.

A following.

If I've changed even one mind, it was worth it, Purity had once said to her.

It was worth it.

Preview Of Britstopia Book 2

A GREEN UNPLEASANT LAND

John Kinderton

When a plane carrying the royal couple crashes three days before the wedding of the century, Purity St.George must mount a daring rescue across the border wall into the radioactive no mans land that is Wales.

In a race against time with American troops and the Archbishop's holy warriors, she faces frakquakes, mutant sheep and... a dragon?

A GREEN UNPLEASANT LAND is book 2 in the bestselling BRITSTOPIA series.

A GREEN UNPLEASANT LAND

"Leaves," said Liberty Lincoln. "Tastes like wet leaves."

The american wrinkled her nose at the bitter, citrus steam rising from her tea. Prince Henry smiled and raised his delicate china cup in a mock toast. "Tea leaves picked by orphaned children for a bowl of rice on the hills of Ceylon - It's a classic british institution, sweetheart."

Libby eyed the beverage with suspicion.

"I don't know how you can drink this crap."

"Now you're marrying into the royal family, you'll have to learn to embrace these things."

Gingerly, she placed the cup back onto its fragile, overpatterned, overpriced saucer and turned her attention back to her diamond encrusted smartphone.

"Give me a KostlyKoffee every time," she muttered.

The RAF QE3 banked south over Liverpool, descending through britannic airspace on its secure air corridor back to London. After a week of wedding planning with her parents in Washington, the royal couple were finally returning home for the big day. Externally, the Korean PyongSan looked like every other air force plane, inside however told a different, heavily modified story. The endless cramped rows of cattle class seats had been removed entirely - the interior space partitioned off into a series of offices and meeting rooms. A large, carpeted, open plan lounge occupied the central section decorated in smoked glass and walnut trim while lush, maroon silk curtains embossed with gold trim draped the tiny windows.

"Pygmies," said Libby.

Prince Henry paused, the teacup barely touching his lips. "Pygmies?"

"Diana's wedding dress was 25 feet long, I want a 50 foot dress," she continued. "Carried by pygmies. A hundred of them dressed up in waistcoats, trailing behind me down the aisle. They can carry it in their mouths."

Henry regarded his wife-to-be across the

aisle of the aircraft, not quite sure what he was hearing. Maybe it was the engine noise.

"One hundred pygmies?" he asked carefully.

It was not a phrase he had ever expected to hear come from his mouth.

Libby scrolled through the photos on her feed - wedding dress after wedding dress in ivories and creams, each more elaborate, expensive and exclusive than the last.

"Yes!"

"Are you sure you mean pygmies, sweetheart?"

The princess-in-waiting finally broke her gaze from her phone.

"Tiny, smelly things," she explained, exasperated. "Always getting under your feet, begging."

She shook her head. "Your grandma's got hundreds of them?"

Henry sighed with relief, the penny finally dropping.

"Oh," he corrected, gently. "You mean corgis."

Libby waved a perfectly manicured hand dismissively. "Pygmies. Corgis. Whatever."

International incident averted, the prince settled back into the soft leather.

"We can ask about the dogs, of course," he said, "though I'd rather not draw the attention of Animal Rights extremists."

In the 13 months since Archbishop Runcible had taken over the running of the country, incidents of christian terrorism, unsurprisingly, had plummeted. Other oppressed groups, however - flat earthers, creationists, the vegans - wasted no time filling the vacuum left behind.

Libby flicked her screen over to the guestlist. "I want this to be the biggest wedding ever, I want every royal in the country there."

Henry raised his eyebrows. "What, even my brother's wife?"

Libby scowled. "Especially her. I'm not having her looking down at me, I'll show her how you do a proper wedding. This is going to be the wedding of the century, it's going to be talked about for decades."

Her large brown eyes glazed over as she pictured the big day - the guests, the crowds, the attention. "The Queen's favourite grandson and Americana's Sweetheart."

"The prince and the pauper," Henry chided.

"'Pauper?'" said Libby, indignant. She tossed her head back and ran a hand through her lustrous, black hair. "I'm the star of the biggest tv show on the planet. You think I'm marrying you for money?"

The prince chuckled. "Of course not, dear. Everyone knows it's because of my sparkling wit, rugged charm and the size of my estate. I expect the royal title never crossed your mind."

A soft chime rang through the speakers. "This is your captain speaking, I hope you're enjoying your flight. We have entered Britannica airspace where the local time is 10:31am and the weather a brisk 16 degrees with light showers and the promise of sunshine later. Air traffic control at RAF McPartlin-Donelly tell me there's quite a crowd waiting for your arrival, so I suggest you make the most of the current peace and quiet."

The overhead seatbelt lights blinked on with a soft chime.

"As we begin our final approach to McPartlin-Donelly can I ask that you stow away any loose items and return your seats to their upright…"

Her voice trailed off.

Then softly, "What?"

A dull thump reverberated through the hull and the cabin shook. Henry's cup leapt from the table and shattered against the window, warm tea covering his white Armani shirt.

"Bugger!" he said looking at the brown streaks running down the glass. But it was the sight beyond the glass that held his attention.

The starboard engine, or what was left of it, bled thick black trails of smoke into the sky, flames licking through the tangled metal seeking purchase against the rest of the wing. The PyongSan lurched to one side, the port turbines screeching as they worked to do the job of both engines.

In the cockpit, Captain Salwah James eased back on the throttle, reducing power to the dead engine. Multiple buzzers and alarms filled the cabin and she flicked them off one by one.

"Engine two out. Losing height!"

"Flaps unresponsive," panicked her co-pilot, Carolgees. "We're drifting!"

As the wipers battled against a barrage of raindrops, the second in command squeezed his face against the windscreen and craned his neck to get better sight of the wing. It quickly became apparent why the flaps were unresponsive.

They had gone.

The aircraft fell into a shallow dive through grey clouds. Mountains and forests filled the view and beyond that, a wide expanse of water. James strained against the wheel.

"Aim for the sea!"

Carolgees threw a shocked glance sidewards at his superior - he knew as well as any pilot that a hard landing was always safer than water. "Are you mad? If the impact doesn't kill us, we'll drown."

The comms panel exploded in a shower of white sparks but Captain James remained focused on the horizon. She tipped her head at the navigational array. "Look where we are."

The co-pilot rested his fingers on the

centre console and spread them against the vibrating glass surface of the touchscreen. The map zoomed in on the blinking icon of the aircraft, revealing details of rivers and mountains beneath. Text markers scrolled past, villages and towns in unpronounceable combinations of letters he hadn't seen for years.

The Independent Province of Cambria.

Wales.

Carolgees paled. All things considered, they would be better off ditching in the ocean.

"I'll aim for the sea."

In the cabin, the tea-streaked window shattered, filling the confines with a fury of smoke and noise. Liberty screamed.

"Hold on, sweetheart," yelled Henry, clutching his seat belt. "Grab something."

The QE3 rolled hard and where the sky should be, Henry saw nothing but an expanse of green, rain soaked vegetation.

Leaves.

Wet leaves.

Continued in A GREEN UNPLEASANT LAND.

OTHER BOOKS BY JOHN KINDERTON

A Green Unpleasant Land

BRITSTOPIA BOOK 2

THREE DAYS before the wedding of the century, the plane carrying Prince Henry and his American bride-to-be suffers a horrific crash.

TWO DAYS before, Purity St. George leads a rag tag team across the barrier wall into the radioactive hellhole that is Cambria in a desperate rescue attempt.

ONE DAY before. Fighting hostile military forces, mutated beasts and Archbishop Runcible's fanatical Disciples, Purity must race against time to locate the couple before the big day and the wedding that will unite the two great nations.

From the underground prayer dens of London to the grim northern wastes and the border wall to Wales, A GREEN UNPLEASANT LAND is the direct sequel to BRITSTOPIA - a particularly British dystopia.

instagram/britstopia

OTHER BOOKS BY JOHN KINDERTON

Puritannica

BRITSTOPIA BOOK 3

"Please do not adjust your set. The problem is not with your screen. The problem is with your government."

Gripped in the iron rule of an absolute monarchy, the citizens of Britannica live in fear and apathy on an endless diet of Chlorinated Fried Chicken and back-to-back episodes of I Love Libby.
In the void left behind by Purity St. George and her followers, rebellion takes many faces, but none more unexpected and terrifying then the once treasured National Elf. A face promising anarchy and change.
No matter what the cost.

"In this we are unwavering.
In this we are unconditional.
In this we are... Unanimous."

PURITANNICA is the third book in the BRITSTOPIA series - a particularly British dystopia.

instagram/britstopia

OTHER BOOKS BY JOHN KINDERTON

Ghost Town

A BRITSTOPIA SHORT STORY

In a pandemic ridden Britannica, Joseph St. George embarks on a hazardous journey across Puritan ruled London in pursuit of his own holy grail.

In the decade before BRITSTOPIA, GHOST TOWN explores a world of curfews, censorship and banned substances.
Oh, and toilet rolls.

instagram/britstopia

Printed in Great Britain
by Amazon